LONG SHADOWS

A totally gripping crime mystery

DEREK THOMPSON

JOFFE BOOKS

First published 2020
Joffe Books, London
www.joffebooks.com

ISBN 978-1-78931-430-4

"No good can come from a waning moon." — Anon

PROLOGUE

A blue sheen covered the land, illuminating creatures of the night — predators, prey and scavengers in the dance of life and death. But there was nothing natural about the gunshot that split the silence, before the body fell and blood seeped into the soil like the sacrifices of old. Only, this time, someone else was watching.

CHAPTER 1

Detective Sergeant Craig Wild stared forlornly through the windscreen at the cattle blocking the road. Lazy wipers cut across his view like the world rhythmically flipping him the finger with both hands. This had to be someone's idea of a bad joke. First he'd overslept and now this. 2016 was definitely not his year. He closed the window against the stench while the herd streamed around his car. A farmer trudging behind raised a stick like a half-hearted apology, although he'd forgotten to tell his face.

Wild followed the cows' progress in his wing mirror, drumming the fingers of one hand against the window to play them out. "Any time today." Two weeks on duty since transferring from London and the Wiltshire countryside still gave him palpitations. When there was barely a cow in sight he turned the ignition and moved off swiftly in case any changed their mind.

DI Marsh's Caledonian tones crackled through the radio. "Craig, where are you?"

He swore under his breath and held the handset several inches from his face. "Nearly there, boss. Sorry . . . ma'am. I got lost and missed the turn-off for the lane."

"Well, get a bloody move on."

He swung wide around a puddle he could have swum in and checked a pencil drawing in his lap. No reliable phone signal for a map of course. Come back, London — all is forgiven. Well, nearly all.

Three field gates and a derelict cottage later, he found the track. He clocked a uniformed officer a little way up, a sentinel at the mercy of the elements. She nodded as he passed and he thought he might have seen her before at the police station — maybe on his welcome tour — only he wasn't the greatest at putting names to faces. He clung to the steering wheel with one hand as his Ford Focus bounced along the ruts, his other hand grasping for a lone pill in a cup holder. Mud and water sprayed liberally up the car — he'd have to take it to a carwash when the weather lifted.

Further up the field a familiar forensic tent awaited him. A small gathering of vehicles had already arrived. Even the private ambulance was there — he'd be last to the party. He parked alongside the others and changed into wellies stowed in the boot. No point ruining a decent pair of shoes for a dead man. Everyone stopped working as he approached. He'd got used to being the main attraction: the transfer from the Met, or — for those who had done their research — the DS who'd got sick after an armed robbery went tits up. What would it be this time — loaded questions or a loaded silence? He wasn't sure which he preferred.

Rain spattered over his hood, making it hard to hear. He eased it back as he entered the tent and waved some ID needlessly. "DS Wild." He pulled out a packet of nitrile gloves from a box in his coat pocket. "What's the situation?"

A uniformed sergeant nudged a younger man in an umber suit that was trying too hard. Given the circumstances, Wild took him to be a detective constable and not a twenty-something on work experience.

The DC lifted the plastic sheeting. "Victim is an elderly male, deceased. Cause of death appears to be a shotgun wound." He said it without irony and glanced to the sergeant, who nodded encouragement. "Dr Bell has done a preliminary examination."

Wild skipped the pleasantries and bent down to the corpse. Judging by the damage, a single barrel had been unloaded in the mouth. Effective but messy.

The doctor handed him a sheet of notes and a body outline marked up. "I'd say it happened late last night or very early this morning."

Wild glanced over the paperwork before passing it back. "Who owns the field? We'll question them first."

The young DC sniggered. "Might be difficult, Skip — he's the one lying here with half his head missing!"

The uniformed sergeant cleared his throat. "This is DC Ben Galloway and he still has a lot to learn. I'm his uncle, Sergeant Galloway." He extended a hand.

Wild sniffed the air. "Well, he can start by bagging the victim's hands for residue. Should have done that right away."

The sergeant stiffened. "We were expecting to find you on site when we got here. I was only dropping off Ben and the PC. In your absence we've been busy trying to preserve the scene and make up for lost time."

Wild conceded the point with a nod. "Okay. What's the victim's name and how did he get here?" His stomach groaned — he could murder a bacon roll.

Sergeant Galloway read from his notes. "Alexander Porter, sixty-eight. No recent history with the police and no convictions. There's a historic attendance for a domestic, but that's over fifteen years ago."

Wild glanced to the men and then down at the farmland track, where the lone copper still waited like a scarecrow. He already knew there were no other cars on what passed for a road because he'd driven up and down it twice. Only one track in and out, and he'd arrived too late to secure the site so everyone and his mother had already driven through. The DI would have a field day. However . . . sixty-eight wasn't *eighty-eight.* The late Mr Porter might have walked across the field.

"How far does — *did* — the victim live from here?"

DC Galloway deferred to his uncle.

"I'd say three or four miles."

Wild blinked slowly, conscious that these were now his colleagues and nothing would be gained by losing his temper. A second examination of the victim's hands made his heart sink. The calluses on the right hand told their own story.

"Has anything been moved — beyond the weapon you've bagged, I mean?"

DC Galloway's voice cracked. "Bagged . . . ?"

Sergeant Galloway drew himself to his full height, all five foot nine of it. "We didn't find any shotgun when we arrived. We conducted a thorough search," he waved an arm in a loose arc, "but came up with nothing. I thought it best to discuss it with you before reporting it — probably some ghoulish trophy hunter. Could be whoever phoned this in? Not to worry — we'll ask around."

Wild felt his jaw slacken. *Perfect, just perfect.* No one spoke. Instead, they all looked at him, eager to hear what came out of his mouth.

He pointed to the victim's right hand. "And where's his walking stick?"

No one answered so he stepped outside to swear in private. After a few paces he heard someone running behind him and then a heavy hand landed on his shoulder.

"Wait up, DS Wild. As one sergeant to another, we need to stick together on this. It's not as bad as it seems. I'm sure the shotgun will turn up — I can think of a few people . . . well, let's just say I'll be making some targeted enquiries!" Sergeant Galloway laughed and slapped Wild hard on the back. "It's only a suicide, after all."

Wild slipped free from his hand. "You're sure of that, are you?"

In the absence of a better plan, he followed the sergeant back to the tent and let them finish their work. He watched the scene dispassionately, as an outsider: the sergeant, nurturing and authoritative towards the DC, the pathologist, focused and businesslike. The DC, trying not to balls it up. Not so different from London, Wild told himself. And then nostalgia sank into his guts like a punch.

He stood to attention and clasped his hands when the body bag went out, an old habit instilled in him during his first days on the force. The private ambulance left first, closely followed by Dr Bell's Toyota saloon. Sergeant Galloway and his nephew went off in the van together. Not good for objective record keeping, but Wild didn't want to cast aspersions. Even if he had been warned about rural, close-knit communities and their *Wicca Man* tendencies at his leaving do, back in Camden. The do that very few people attended.

Once the affable sergeant and the DC had quit the site, Wild stepped outside again and tuned into his surroundings. It helped take his mind off the potentially career-limiting report waiting for him back at the station. Rain spat lazily against his coat, heavy and indifferent. There was farmland as far as the eye could see and sheep in the distance, probably. Beyond the fatality field, rising up to the ridge were two other fields — one beside it, about the same size, and another, smaller field that nestled between the two further up. From his vantage point the middle field looked unfarmed. Above it all, high on the ridge and half-shrouded by trees, the ruins of Montford Abbey cut a jagged outline against the sky.

Birds chirruped from hedgerows that enclosed the middle field, probably as pissed off at the weather as he was. Wild turned slowly, taking it all in, and an unexpected smile crept up his face. At least he had an investigation to get his teeth into. No more missing tractors or holiday home break-ins. Alexander Porter's death demanded top billing. A man who habitually used a stick did not travel miles without it just to off himself in his own field. Well, not unless he hitched a lift for the big occasion.

Wild stared at the lone copper. Poor sod. He didn't miss being in uniform.

"Right, can't stay here all day," he said aloud to an empty field. Steph used to say he liked the sound of his own voice. Then again, Steph said a lot of things that turned out to be questionable. He changed back into shoes and then radioed his boss with an update.

If DI Marsh sounded impressed, it was only because she'd set the bar low. DS Wild had not come highly recommended. More of a necessity after his predecessor moved on at short notice. Wild never asked about it — he didn't care. The DI hadn't flowered it up at their first meeting: 'We need a replacement DS and beggars can't be choosers.'

He started rehearsing his review as he drove down to the lane, until the lone police officer flagged him down from behind the fencing.

"DS Wild?" She wiped the rain from her face. "I was first on the scene this morning. They told me to prevent any unauthorised vehicles going up the track. Sorry, I couldn't take any tyre impressions — they dropped me off without the kit. But I did take photographs, on my own initiative, before anyone went through. Is that alright?"

He nodded. "Well done. Can I borrow your camera?"

Her face tightened. "It's my work mobile — I can email or text you the pictures."

"What's your name?"

"Marnie Olsen." She waited to see *that* look. "Mum watched a lot of Sean Connery films. It could have been worse. I might have ended up as a Bond Girl — Honey Ryder or Plenty O'Toole." She paused, watching his face redden.

Wild stalled, trying to forget Pussy Galore from *Goldfinger*. He dug out a business card with the mobile number scratched out and another scrawled above it. "Send me the pics and I'll buy you a pint."

Olsen made a futile dab at her forehead. "Coffee in the canteen will be fine."

Wild nodded. "Fair enough. Can you secure the gate after me and then head up to the field for half an hour or so? Take a look around and stay visible — in case anyone gets curious. Keep an eye on the ruins — that's a good vantage point."

She struggled to stifle her excitement. "Absolutely. What am I looking for?"

"Aside from a missing shotgun, we're looking for the victim's walking stick. It's a suspicious death at this point, so tread carefully." He saw the way her eyes sparkled and wondered when he'd last felt like that about the job. A long time ago. He tapped the accelerator, drawing the conversation to a close. "Come and find me when you get back to the station. It's Craig, by the way — Detective Sergeant Craig Wild." He couldn't be sure she'd heard him and he didn't stick around to find out.

CHAPTER 2

Wild made it to Mayberry police station in under an hour. He enjoyed the transition from countryside to semi-urban sprawl — vagrants huddled by bus shelters, roundabouts, and litter-strewn fast-food outlets all offering a little slice of home.

When he switched off the engine in the car park he could practically hear the blinds rattling. Here's the Big City Boy, come to ring the changes. So wide of the mark it was tragic. Thirty-seven, soon to be divorced, and all he wanted to do was keep his head down and concentrate on work. No plans for the future — unlike Steph, who even now had DCI on her doorplate and an eye on the next rung of the ladder.

He wandered back to his desk and checked his emails. Well done, Marnie Olsen, he thought as he clicked on her name — and most of the pictures were in focus. She'd go far, only probably not at this nick. He stared at the screen, trying to make sense of the track marks that weren't waterlogged. Now, who could he ask about a database of farm vehicles for elimination purposes? As he glanced away from the screen he caught DI Marsh watching him from her ivory box. She raised an index finger and pointed at her desk. He took the hint. He was a detective, after all.

She blinked through her glasses, resting one hand on a Rennie Mackintosh paperweight. He'd asked about it on his first day, trying to ingratiate himself with the new boss. It hadn't worked. Or maybe Glaswegians had a different notion of charm.

"How did you get on, Craig — anything to tell me?"

He pondered how best to answer, mindful that Sergeant Galloway might have already delivered his version. DI Marsh folded her hands in her lap. He took that as a good sign.

"Well, ma'am, there are some anomalies . . ."

She nodded. "Uh huh. Why don't you talk me through them?"

He smiled. Like being back on probation. He kept it to facts and gaps until his summing up. "In my judgement, it's still a suspicious death."

"Is that right?" Her accent was pure Glasgow, somewhere between authoritative and menacing. "In that case I look forward to reading your report. On ye go then. Unless there's anything else?"

He made as if to get out of his chair. "Actually, there was one other thing. DC Galloway is a bit too cosy with his uncle in my opinion."

Marsh smiled slowly. "And you think a lot of your opinions? You've not met Ben Galloway before, have you? He's been away on a course." She picked up a pen and clicked it twice. "Your observation is noted, although we're not exactly awash with staff."

"How about Constable Olsen? She seems keen. I could use someone local to do the legwork . . ."

"Someone without relatives here at Mayberry, you mean? I'll think it over."

* * *

Marnie Olsen walked over to Wild's canteen table and took a seat opposite him. "You owe me a coffee."

He studied her deadpan face and only saw the joke when she cracked a smile. "No problem. Play your cards right and you might even get a biscuit."

When he returned, she was going through her notebook.

He slid a coffee and a miniscule packet of shortbreads across the laminate. "I'm a man of my word." He sat back down while her eyes tracked from her mini shortbread to his full-sized chocolate bar.

"What? I haven't had breakfast. How did you know I'd be here, anyway?"

She cupped her coffee. "When I got back here to change . . ." she left the accusation for him to work out for himself — the last time he'd seen her she'd looked like a drowned rat, ". . . my sergeant passed on a request from DI Marsh. She said to check for you and if you weren't here she'd get someone to run me out to the victim's house."

Wild smiled. A suspicious death and an assistant. Things were looking up.

CHAPTER 3

Wild noted the state of Porter's car beside the house — rust, scratched bodywork and faded stickers that likely belonged to the previous owners. A car that screamed spendthrift to the discerning eye, or tight bastard to everyone else. The key sat in the ignition, waiting forlornly for an owner that would never come.

Olsen approached the vehicle cautiously, conscious that working with Wild could be a golden opportunity. She stalled, spotting what Wild already had. "It's unlocked." She took a glove from her pocket to lift the passenger door handle, but Wild intervened.

"Don't bother." He gestured towards the house and checked the wheelie bin — empty — carefully positioning it up against the side door. If someone were still in the house he wasn't chancing a one-on-one encounter. Heroics were for idiots. They'd go in together through the front door with Mr Wheelie as the element of surprise.

The door had been forced — a muddy scuff mark suggesting it had been kicked in. Wild eased the door inward with a pencil, letting it run its full ratchet-squeal arc. He blinked in recognition at the yellowed floral wallpaper, like something one of his aunties would have had. A faint smell of stale milk and too many cigarettes gave the air a tang of despair.

Losing patience, Olsen peered through one of the downstairs windows. Grimy net curtains filtered the view, an unintended kindness. "It doesn't look like he's had many visitors in a long while."

Wild growled. "Well, he had one anyway. Come on. Let's go in." They were welcomed by creaking floorboards and the slow ticking of a clock. Wild called out to the near silence, "It's the police." No takers. He shrugged and pointed down the hall, stepping past a mound of old newspapers.

Someone had given the place a superficial going over. Kids would have taken the car, even if it was a shit heap, so Wild dismissed that possibility. A grudge then, or a decoy for whatever someone had *actually* been looking for. He considered that as he started the tour.

The front room chaos hadn't touched a whisky bottle standing sentinel on a coffee table. A glass tumbler beside it held the remnants of a dram. Wild looked up to attract Olsen's attention, but she had already seen it.

She nodded. "One for forensics."

They shared a half-smile. As if a burglar might have got thirsty, midway through ransacking Porter's hovel. Olsen crossed the room and Wild covered the other half. He saw nothing except neglect. Books thick with dust, one worn slipper upended on the carpet, and a ceramic figurine with the legend 'Skegness' adrift on a windowsill. Strange to think that someone's happy memory had been abandoned to a thick film of grime. Wild wasn't even sure where Skegness was, but the little statue wasn't much of an advert anyhow.

The other downstairs rooms comprised a Sunday Best parlour — undisturbed and immaculate, apart from cobwebs and copious dead flies — and the kitchen. This seemed to be where Alexander Porter had done most of his living, when he still had that option. A thick woollen blanket slumped over a fireside chair suggested Porter might have slept there too. More newspapers and a spread of envelopes, mostly unopened, mostly brown and windowed, completed the picture. On one wall, marooned against the same floral wallpaper from long ago, a schoolboy looked out from a colour photograph — the face no longer quite a child's and hinting at the man he would become. Wild put the boy's age at thirteen, maybe fourteen, estimating a current age range from the late Mr Porter's final tally. A second photograph on the mantelpiece showed Porter leaning on a stick, a small dog at his feet. Wild took pictures of both and added them to his mental list for bagging up on the way out. Another wall sported a black metal cross, stark and unforgiving.

Wild struck gold at the back of one of the open drawers — two shotgun cartridges. He turned to Olsen. "There must be a cabinet for a shooter upstairs." He saw the look on her face and instantly regretted his words, aware that he'd reduced himself to a caricature London copper.

She led the way upstairs and Wild tried not to notice her backside. More debris at the top of the landing gave him a welcome distraction. She paused outside a bedroom door and glanced back. He waved a hand: ladies first. She extended her baton, yelled, "Police — I'm coming in!" and turned the handle.

Wild followed, a step behind. The first thing that caught his eye was the ruptured firearms cabinet in one of the alcoves. Judging by the damage to the locks, someone had used tools to prise it open. The cabinet was bare. He reached for his notebook. "One thing's for certain, Porter didn't break into his own gun cabinet."

Olsen nodded tentatively. "And he didn't break into his own house either." She thought for a moment. "How do we know whether this was done before Porter died or afterwards?"

Wild nodded. "Good question — we don't. And without the weapon we can't assume that Alexander Porter's shotgun was the one that killed him."

CHAPTER 4

In London they used to say, short of a mass murder, there were always parking spaces at the mortuary. In this case, out in the sticks, that amounted to precisely three spaces — with two occupied. Wild parked and walked the length of the car, drawn to a dull line along the rear panel. It looked like someone had keyed it. He thought back, came up with nothing, and entered the mortuary with what his mother used to call 'a face like a smacked arse.'

The door swung behind him with a satisfying thud. Loud enough to wake the dead. He grinned momentarily. It'd make collecting evidence a bloody sight easier. Another door creaked open along the hall and a disembodied voice called, "Is that you, Sergeant Wild?"

He popped a cough sweet in his mouth. "Yeah." As he resumed walking, a neon light flickered above him.

The late Mr Porter lay on stainless steel, a plastic sheet draped tastefully over what remained of his head. Dr Bell stood back to admire his handiwork. "I had hoped to be finished by now, but I've still got the head to examine." One look from Wild told him there was no need to rush on account of visitors. "Just the preliminaries, then."

An assistant entered from another door, her shiny green scrubs a sharp contrast to the greying cadaver. Dr Bell glanced over his shoulder. "Ah, Belinda, let me introduce Detective Sergeant Wild — he's joined the local constabulary from London."

She looked distinctly unimpressed. Wild didn't react — he'd seen a lot of that in the past few weeks. Belinda extended a hand and he noticed the coral nail varnish.

"Belinda Scott, Anatomical Pathology Technologist."

Wild figured that she looked young and spent a lot of time and effort justifying her position. Or maybe social skills weren't part of her training. He took the handshake and then circled back to Dr Bell.

"Anything useful, Doctor?"

"Cause of death, I think you've already ascertained — massive head trauma, caused by a firearm. In addition, the late Mr Porter had advanced cirrhosis of the liver, and a dodgy ticker as well. Not exactly a picture of health."

Wild gazed at the array of surgical instruments laid out for the feast.

Dr Bell pointed to the cadaver. "I take it you noticed the bruising to the ribs."

"Yeah, and suicides don't usually beat themselves up first."

"Quite. You may be interested to learn that his last supper was rabbit pie washed down with best bitter. Not a bad choice. Either he ate in a rush or he was intoxicated enough not to notice, because I also recovered lead shot from the stomach."

Wild conjured with the information. Judging by the state of Porter's home, he'd not cooked a meal there for some time. *Rabbit pie? Who was this guy, Elmer J. Fudd?* His phone rang and he headed for the door. "Excuse me a moment."

"Hi, it's Marnie, Marnie Olsen?"

He cringed. Statements as questions. So last year.

"I'm following up on family and next of kin, like you asked. There is a son, Nathan Porter, living in Kilmarnock. I thought you might want to ring him yourself, or get the local police there to notify him? Also, I was wondering about . . ."

He cut across her. "Any idea where someone could get a rabbit pie, maybe as a takeaway?"

"Not very likely. What about in a pub meal?" She paused, evidently answering her own question. "I'll get on it and ask around, if that's okay?"

"Sure." He tried not to sound needy. Local knowledge would take a long while to acquire, once the locals had thawed.

After the call he let DI Marsh know that he'd asked Marnie Olsen to follow up on some enquiries. He took pains to explain it was only routine stuff to free up his time. "Once I find my feet with the local community . . ." He left the conversation hanging.

DI Marsh picked up the silence. "I'll square it for today. And then you'll have to buddy up with Ben."

As Wild ventured back inside, he stopped at the inner door. The surgical saw was already humming away merrily. He eased the door open a few inches and spoke up. "I'll be in my car. Come and get me when you're done." He'd seen three post-mortems in his career. Once as a bet, once as a favour, and once out of guilt. It was always the face that got to him. Well, that and the skull. He finished his cough sweet and sucked on another, inhaling menthol as he gazed up at the sky and wondered what the point was of weighing half a brain.

As he'd expected, Belinda got the job of hostess, tapping on his car window to summon him. He put his notebook away and followed her.

"Nasty scratch." She pointed to his car's side panel.

"Yeah, tell me about it."

She led him back into the mortuary without further comment. He'd often wondered what kind of person chose a job like that, or what it did to them. As he entered the room he glanced over at the cadaver, relieved to see it was covered from head to toe.

Dr Bell nudged a tap with his elbow and water stopped gushing into a stainless-steel sink. He turned to one side, water dripping off his hands. "You've already had the highlights and I'll get the full report over to you some time tomorrow. Please give my best wishes to DI Marsh — what do you make of her?"

"I get the impression she doesn't take any prisoners."

Belinda's face twitched and Wild closed his mouth, recognising an ambush.

"That's a fair assessment." Dr Bell chuckled to himself. "Sorry, couldn't resist. We're a tightly knit professional community and we always like to test the incomers."

"I'll bear that in mind."

Belinda cast Dr Bell a withering look and walked past him to a table on the far side of the room, lifting off a report and checking it against the one beneath it. Satisfied, she carried it over to Wild.

Dr Bell finished drying his hands. "Thank you, Belinda. Well, DS Wild, no doubt we'll be seeing you again in the future — vertically, of course."

Wild fashioned a smile and started walking. He got the impression that Belinda would have liked a private word, although his impressions weren't always reliable. Back in the car he texted Marnie Olsen: *Contact me if you find anything out — my phone is always on.*

He smiled at the screen. Because, hey, what else was there to do with his time?

CHAPTER 5

Wild's shopping marked him out as a singleton — a curry for one that he'd probably split over a couple of days, a four-pack of lager to last the week, a TV mag to avoid flicking through the channels (but he would, anyway), some frozen chips, a large bar of chocolate and some healthy yoghurts to offset everything else. No need for veg as there was still some left in the freezer and something green lurking at the back of the fridge. The lad on the checkout for ten items or less judged him silently, moving the goods past the scanner with all the care and dedication of someone who thought the world owed him a better living than the one he'd attained. Wild unfolded his bag-for-life, carefully packed everything up and then paid the boy, indifferent to the people behind him who shuffled from foot to foot like a static conga.

As soon as he got inside the front door he set the shopping down in the middle of the kitchen and switched Radio Four on — less about intellectual stimulation and more about the sound of human voices. Old habits died hard and he still hadn't got used to an empty house. After putting the shopping away he took off his shoes and left them in the hall, changing into the slippers he'd brought back from Morocco. Steph had ribbed him for weeks about how they smelt of goat. He sometimes pictured her now, holding court in New Scotland Yard. A rising star, so the press said, and no rising star needs dead weight attached. Maybe she'd always seen it coming, which explained why she'd kept her own name after marriage. Clever Steph, always the better detective.

Time check: six thirty. Thirty minutes to go. He'd eat afterwards and make do with a cup of tea in the meantime. No word yet from Marnie Olsen, which disappointed him. He had hoped she'd be able to cut corners and save him some time. Oh well, never trust a plod to do a detective's job. First thing tomorrow, he'd regroup and get stuck in with Ben Galloway in tow. Solving Porter's murder could get him onside with DI Marsh. It never hurt to try and impress a senior officer . . . well, unless you were married to her at the time.

Radio Four called him back to the kitchen, two antagonists picking apart a political scandal like carrion crows. Wild filled in the blanks — he was good at that, deciphering the unsaid. A junior minister caught on camera making promises to a potential backer, the player being played. The two pundits chewed the carcass over until it was tenderised enough for public consumption.

He boiled a kettle while the computer booted up and glanced in the full-length mirror, the one he still hadn't fixed in the hall.

Not bad. He sucked in his cheeks and straightened up to five foot eleven. Maybe it was time to start using the weights again. He angled his head to see where his hair was thinning at the back and blew out a breath.

Now came the familiar tension. Would she be there? He took the tea over and logged in, automatically moving the mouse over the Skype icon. Two minutes to go. He blew on his tea and took a sip, running through a mental checklist — personal phone switched off and out of reach, no distractions. Last time, he'd got a sales text during the call and Jackie had been so upset that she didn't show up the following week.

Time. He clicked through and held his breath for the three-tone-squelch and swoosh. A black screen faced him.

He heard her breathing softly, somewhere off-camera, and waited for her to speak first.

"Craig, are you there?"

He knew she could probably see him, but he also knew this exchange reassured her.

"I'm here, Jackie. How have you been?"

She took a sharp in-breath and moved out of the gloom, stopping when half her face was exposed. "I'm . . . okay." The redness on her face suggested otherwise.

"Why don't you tell me about your week?"

"Alright then." Her voice brightened.

He listened, barely moving, only smiling a little when he thought it was warranted. She spoke in generalities, keeping him at bay. Trips to the shops and some terrible television programme she'd mentioned before — he wished he'd checked his notes before the call.

Top right of his screen, a clock marked the minutes. "Has Tony been in touch?"

Her face tightened and she brushed at a hair he couldn't see. "Not directly. Friends of *friends* . . ." She made the second friends into a parody of itself. "I was thinking of getting away for a couple of days . . ."

The sentence lingered and he knew exactly when to catch it. "I can let you have a hundred, if you need it?"

She sighed. "I feel terrible taking money from you like this."

"It's fine, honestly. I'll send it over by PayPal tonight."

"What would I do without you?'

"There are people who can help you. I may not be in London now but I still have contacts."

"I'm fine as we are, as I am, I mean. What's it like in your new digs — gonna show me?"

"Nah. Nothing much to see." He glanced at the boxes still taking up space at the side of the room.

"What you need is a woman's touch!"

She laughed, and he laughed too.

"I think the new beard really suits you."

He stroked the three days of growth for effect and unconsciously tightened his stomach muscles.

"Gives you character." She edged into the light, stopping abruptly as his work mobile rang.

"Two secs." He cringed a little because he knew she'd throw a fit. Too late now. He glanced over his shoulder and held the phone close. "DS Wild."

"It's Marnie Olsen?" She didn't sound certain herself. "Listen, do you fancy a quick drink and some pub food? Maybe some *rabbit* pie?"

He grinned. "You're kidding? Well done! Where do you want to meet?"

"I'll be outside the George — do you know it? About two miles from Porter's field — I'll text you the details."

"I'm leaving now and I'll be there as soon as I can." He cut the call, stifled his glee and moved back into shot. "I'm sorry, Jackie, something's come up from work — I really have to go." He closed Skype down, quickly, trying not to catch the last glimpse of her face, open-mouthed and furious.

Olsen's text arrived, enabling him to look up the location online. Perfect. He changed back into work shoes, grabbed his wallet, warrant card and keys, and headed for the door. Behind him in the kitchen, Radio Four was still putting the world to rights.

CHAPTER 6

Wild felt a frisson of excitement as he threaded a final B-road to reach the George. It wasn't exactly on the tourist trail. An imposing building, sitting at one end of a village. Wild judged it to be a coaching inn in its former life, back when the road had led to somewhere other than beyond the fields. The paintwork confirmed his suspicions that its glory days were long gone, even though the car park boasted several cars and a tractor.

He rang Olsen's mobile and heard a bar room serenade, including an accordion struggling for airplay amongst raucous voices.

"I'll come out to you."

She looked different out of hours, her biker jacket and jeans seeming exotic compared to the eager, studious copper he'd been working with. Now she was the one in the know.

"Are you hungry, Skip?"

"Craig, or Wild," he corrected her. He couldn't tell if she was making fun of him so he fell back on certainties. "Yeah, I'm famished. My treat."

They went inside. The décor made it a proper pub, the sort of place rarely seen in London any more. Not unless it was a designer's fantasy of what a real pub ought to look like.

A pair of antlers jutted out from a wooden beam, as if they'd been an afterthought, and a scythe adorned one of the walls, out of reach to tiny hands but accessible to everyone else — a health and safety nightmare.

A few steps in Wild noticed the temperature had dropped. As they walked through to the back bar someone wolf whistled. Olsen killed that with a glance. Wild closed the door behind them, muffling most of the noise. The back bar was completely deserted. Wild called out, "Shop!" and they heard footsteps.

The landlady appeared behind the bar. "What can I get you? Another cider is it, Miss, now your, er, friend is here?"

Olsen nudged Wild towards the chalked-up menu, where three items were on offer: Country Pie, Fruit Crumble, and Mixed Ice Cream. This was a pub that kept things simple.

Wild took his cue. "Country pie sounds good. Is it homemade?" He caught Olsen's smirk.

The landlady blossomed with pride. "All local produce, made locally exclusively for us. 'Ere, you're not one o' them vegetarians, are you?"

Wild raised a hand. "Nah. The only thing I won't eat is octopus. I'll give anything else a go."

"Well, you won't find no octopus in our pies. A bit of rabbit maybe, and some pheasant."

He nodded. *Maybe*. Bloody hell. They didn't believe in committing themselves. He ordered a cider for Olsen and picked something local, mostly to curry favour with the landlady, and took the drinks over to the table.

Olsen raised her glass. "Cheers, Craig." She took a gulp. "I have a confession to make — I looked you up. The whole station has. No one can quite work out what you're doing here. So don't be surprised if people start asking about DCI Hutcheson."

He sat back and considered his options. In the end, the police was one big family and people talked. What was the point in letting people get it wrong? "Alright, Marnie, three questions *each* while we wait for dinner."

She cut straight in. "Are you still married?" She stalled and raised a hand to her mouth. "Oh God, I'm not . . . you know . . . I'm not *interested* in you. No offence."

He settled back to enjoy her discomfort. "Still married but rest assured, a civilised divorce is being worked out as we speak. No doubt with a non-disclosure clause attached. And what about you?"

Olsen forced a smile. "There's plenty of time for that when my career's on track."

He didn't believe her, but now wasn't the time. "University?"

"Computer Science and Psychology. You?"

"School of hard knocks, graduating in the university of life." The look on her face told Wild she'd come up against this attitude before, so he backtracked. "What made you pick those subjects?"

Her frustration was palpable. "Because I want to get on. Modern policing is all about information and people, see?"

"And you reckon you'll get on staying around here?" The words rolled around his mouth like gravel.

She looked crestfallen, as though he'd just told her that her career prospects were screwed. He got it now. No further questions, your honour.

A door swung behind the bar and the landlady reappeared, carrying two plates in tea towels. "Here are your country pies. I'll leave you to it." She smiled at Wild, as if to tell him he was punching well above his weight. He decided not to disenchant her.

"What do you think?" Olsen thrust her knife into piecrust, squeezing the filling out the sides.

"I'm wondering why Porter came here and who he met."

Olsen swallowed a mouthful of food. "Ask the landlady."

Wild took another bite. She had a point.

"Seems to me that Alexander Porter had a reason for being here, unless it was his usual haunt. Only he hadn't taken his car." She considered her own words. "Oh, hang on." She wielded her fork over her plate, stabbing a boiled potato. "What if Porter *did* come by car and the killer took his car home afterwards and that's when they broke into his gun cabinet?"

Wild let her talk on, adding a word or two while she spouted outlandish theories and some entirely plausible assumptions. He got the distinct impression she didn't often get the chance to display her intelligence.

"Craig, could we DNA test his car key, steering wheel and the door?"

He could almost hear Marsh's voice uttering a one-word answer: budget. The more enthusiastic Marnie Olsen became, the faster she ate. Wild realised he'd been so engrossed that he'd only eaten half his dinner. He decided against taking a pie sample for analysis when he thought about the ridicule he might have to endure. He'd probably live out the rest of his days at the station as Bunny. Besides, what did rabbit in a pie prove?

His teeth jarred. "Bloody hell." He skipped politeness and fished about in his mouth with his fingers, extracting a dark object that clattered to the plate. "A piece of shot. Do you think they might have been lamping rabbits over the fields that night?"

Olsen fought the urge to laugh. "What, and he tripped? For one thing, you wouldn't use a shotgun at night — you'd scare everything away. And for another, you don't need the cover of night for rabbiting if you know where to find them. I mean, you could use a shotgun but a ferret and a net is a cleaner way of doing it."

Wild wrapped the piece of shot in a serviette and placed it in his inside pocket.

". . . And so I was wondering if you'd put in a good word for me with Detective Inspector Marsh."

Wild blinked at her and realised his attention had wandered. He pieced together her last sentence and delivered the bad news. "I think today was a one-off, sorry. I will mention you, though, if an opportunity arises."

She cast him a look that would make angels weep. Poor soul. He understood. He remembered the hard graft to make DC — Steph had already made DS before then, naturally.

They ran out of things to say and spent a few minutes in silence, interrupted by the occasional raucous cheer from next door as the accordion stopped. When the door swung behind the bar and the landlady emerged, they both breathed a sigh of relief.

"Alright, my dears? Everything to your satisfaction?" She smiled to the unhappy couple, who did their best to show willing. "Anything else I can get you?"

Lost for an answer, Wild flashed his warrant card and did the introductions. "Actually, there is."

The landlady crossed her arms. "It's all above board here, officers."

Olsen gestured to a nearby seat. Wild figured this was psychology in action and let her get on with it.

"We're investigating the death of one Alexander Porter."

"You mean the old fella in the field. Dreadful accident." As she made the statement her eyes searched both their faces.

Olsen leapt straight in. "How often did he drink here?"

"Here?" the landlady flustered, wringing a tea towel in her hands. "Oh, I couldn't really say. He comes in from time to time. Never says much — not to me, anyway."

Wild didn't bother correcting her use of the present tense. He left Olsen to take details and went off to find the gents. The singing continued in the main bar but a sea of eyes watched him wander through. After he'd peed, he stepped outside to the car park, turning slowly to see a face at the window, silhouetted against the orange light inside. He strolled past the cars, wondering whether to take down every number plate, and arrived at the tractor. He took out his mobile phone and took a flash picture of the tyre tread, just because it was there. He had no plan.

Re-entering the bar, he swung the door in too hard and it collided with a metal umbrella stand. Looking closer he saw it was trench art — fashioned from an artillery shell and engraved with a cross and the year 1916. A collection of walking sticks poked above the rim.

One of the younger customers got up, straightened his sweatshirt and twisted his lip. "Something I can help you with?"

Wild sized him up and thought better of it. Firstly because he was still settling in. And secondly because he was shit at scrapping. Making an arrest, no problem. But a straight-out pub fight? No, he wasn't the brawling kind. He flashed his warrant card again, like a get-out-of-fight-free card.

"Maybe you can." He raised his voice. "I'd like to speak with anyone who remembers seeing Alexander Porter here or speaking to him on the day he died."

A wall of silence confronted him. He picked up the umbrella stand, contents and all, and started across the room to a chorus of disapproval.

"I'll bring them back tomorrow."

He put his head through to the other bar. "Time to knock it on the head." Then he realised he hadn't paid for the meal, and lugged the umbrella stand to the bar. "Potential evidence," he said for Olsen's benefit, as the landlady scurried away for the bill.

He unlocked his car and turned to see several faces at the window. "Marnie, do you need a lift?"

She jangled her motorbike keys. "No thanks. What's your plan with tonight's bounty?"

"I'm gonna take the sticks home and check them against that photograph we found on Porter's wall. Just in case."

"But why take the stand?"

He furrowed his brow. "Easier and quicker, I s'pose." He stashed the goods and opened his driver's side door.

Olsen took a deep breath. "Can I come too?"

"You really are keen. You'd better follow me back, then."

CHAPTER 7

Wild kept to a steady speed, checking periodically for Olsen's headlamp. Farmland became villages, and then the outskirts of town, where a small terraced street had become home. London could have swallowed his neighbourhood whole in one of its postal districts. Then again, London had spat him out.

Olsen was only seconds behind him. She parked up and locked her bike helmet away while he heaved the umbrella stand and its contents out of his car boot. He faltered in the porch, wondering what she'd make of his slippers routine.

Her first words through the doorway reassured him. "Boots off?"

"If you wouldn't mind."

She paused for a moment at the sound of voices, and then cottoned on that it was the radio.

"Come through." He lugged the umbrella stand to the living room, placing it beside the sofa. "I'll put the kettle on, shall I?" He didn't wait for an answer.

Olsen turned about the room slowly, taking in clues about his life. Plenty of books grouped by author, although not alphabetically, thank God. She picked out Tolkien's works in the bookcase — no surprises there — and then her eyes drifted to ground level where a Dorothy Parker biography looked like it had seen better days. Her curiosity piqued, she was about to take it out and see if, as she'd surmised, it had been a gift from someone else, when he called out that tea was on its way.

The other large piece of furniture was a wall cabinet almost equal to the bookcase, housing a collection of DVDs that would have seen out a nuclear winter. Strange tastes, she concluded, spotting sci-fi and football best-ofs sitting cheek by jowl with French cinema and war films. Lots of war films.

She heard a spoon rattling against a cup behind her. "Do you take sugar?"

"No thanks. I'll take a biscuit though, if you have any going."

He passed her the mug of tea and then reached to his pocket, where a chocolate bar protruded like a cowboy's six-shooter.

"Oh, hang on a second."

She figured he had dashed off in search of coasters — he seemed the type — but he soon returned with a bed sheet. She raised an eyebrow as he gestured for her to stand clear while he spread it out on the carpet. Next, he laid the umbrella stand down in the centre before collecting his own tea from the kitchen.

He knelt down beside the artillery shell. "Right, we're good to go."

She joined him on the floor as he searched through his phone, swiping pictures until he found the one he wanted. Taking the fact that his hands were full as a hint, Olsen carefully tilted the umbrella stand to slide out the walking sticks, along with old cigarette butts, beetle carcasses and a couple of empty crisp packets.

"So we're looking for a match to the photo?" She held out her hand for a refresher.

"Oh yeah, sorry." He passed the phone over.

There were nearly a dozen sticks, some coated in enough grime and fluff to suggest they'd been discarded a long time ago. One likely contender fitted the bill, its bony handle a fair match for the one in the poorly lit phone image.

Olsen asked for the phone again. "Not sure about the stick though. See that ridge in the wood there?"

"Yeah, he could've had it repaired though. You know, if it was of sentimental value."

She reached to one side and took a sip of tea. "Am I missing something here, Craig? We could have checked the sticks at the pub. Why bother taking them away?"

He stirred his tea. "Honestly? I wanted to piss them off. Someone saw Porter there — guaranteed. A little cooperation wouldn't have gone amiss."

"Well, you won't get any now." She sipped tea to break eye contact.

He frowned — fair point. "What about CCTV, inside or out?"

Olsen laughed and snorkelled her tea. "At the George? I don't think so." She went to break off some chocolate, noticed the panic in his eyes, and only took a modest amount. "Did you notice the tractor in the car park?"

"Hard to miss. I photographed the tread — you never know, we might get lucky." Except he knew no one was that lucky. It occurred to him that she was the first visitor to set foot in the house since he'd moved in. And to his surprise he was enjoying the experience. "I'll bag up Porter's stick and get it forensically examined."

"In what?"

He thought for a moment. "I dunno, a bin bag?"

Olsen laughed. "Is that what they do in London?" She took more chocolate, mainly to watch his reaction, and then carefully got to her feet. "Well, thanks for the tea and including me in your investigation."

He set his cup down. "I couldn't have done this without you — I'll be sure to tell DI Marsh."

She was still smiling at the door.

Wild replaced the other sticks in the umbrella stand and then manoeuvred the sheet so he could tip all the crap back in as well. In an ideal world he'd get a DNA swab from every stick but he couldn't see Marsh wearing that, especially with the high probability of cross-contamination. Still, a pub meal with another human being and some evidence gathering wasn't a bad evening at all.

Once he'd cleared everything away he stared at the screensaver on his computer, pondering his next move. He hit the return button and accessed Skype, so sure Jackie wouldn't be online now that he didn't even bother sitting down. A voice message waited for him.

"If you've got more important things to do than listen to me, maybe I shouldn't be helping you. I'm taking a big risk with Tony — you know that." Her voice slowed. "I'll let you know when I'm ready to talk again. I don't want to hear from you till then."

"No," Wild said to the screen as he closed Skype and opened PayPal. "But you're quite happy to take my money."

* * *

Wild woke early with the dawn chorus and what sounded like seagulls. He felt excited, aglow, like Christmas for coppers come early. A suspicious death, a growing collection of evidence, and maybe — maybe — a colleague he could depend upon. A bit of a looker too, in a funny sort of way. Not that he'd go foraging in that direction. He scratched absentmindedly at his bare wedding finger. Never again.

He made it to the George around eight o'clock, the milk delivery already stacked by the side door. Mist rose from the surrounding fields. It could have been the setting for a low-budget horror film, and he knew just the locals to put in it. He rapped on the door a second time and reflected on the previous evening. Were they all scared to talk to him or indifferent? Or maybe Porter had enemies?

A light shone through the glass and came closer until the landlady's face pressed against it. "You again." She unlocked and then unbolted the door. "What do you want?"

He hoisted the umbrella stand in the air. "One set of walking sticks returned. Hopefully everyone got home safely."

"No thanks to you if they did."

CHAPTER 8

Wild pushed the swing door to the open-plan office and the detective team turned in unison towards him. DI Marsh leaned forward from the edge of the desk she'd perched on. "Detective Sergeant Wild. Good of you to join us." Laughter echoed round the space.

He considered his options and went with, "I was unavoidably detained, ma'am. Collecting evidence that I've just delivered to the forensics team." He felt the divide in the room, that collective intake because he'd marked himself out by choosing explanation over apology. He sat across the room from DI Marsh deliberately and copied her stance on the edge of a desk. "Could somebody recap for me?" He blinked slowly. That *somebody* being the DI herself.

DI Marsh approached the whiteboard where photographs and conjecture mixed company with facts.

"Okay." She rapped a knuckle against the board. "Alexander Porter, aged sixty-eight. Body was found on his land — two fields are rented out for farming and the third one . . ." She looked over at DC Galloway.

"Known locally as Fortune's Field. Cause of death: shooting. No weapon found at the scene."

She glared at DC Galloway, who turned a whiter shade of trauma. Then her gaze found Wild again. "Perhaps you'd like to update us all with *your* progress?"

Wild did the eye-contact thing with everyone in the room. It wasn't difficult because they were already staring at him. Then he crossed the no-man's land of worn-out carpet and stood beside the whiteboard, consciously claiming the space. A quick glance behind him, so he didn't mention anything they already knew, and off he went.

"PC Olsen and I attended Porter's home address. His keys were in the vehicle, which was parked outside his house and unlocked." He listened to himself adopt his 'court' voice, the one he used for giving evidence. It seemed apt because right then he felt like the one on trial. "The front door had been forced and the gun cabinet upstairs had been broken into. No firearm was found at the scene. We recovered two photographs," he turned and tapped the A4 blow-ups on the board, "one of which shows a distinctive walking stick. That stick was not present at the murder scene or in Porter's home." He noticed how the word *murder* punctuated his speech and hung in the air like a bad smell. Emboldened, he moved about a little and clapped his hands together to try and rouse his audience. "The post-mortem revealed that Porter had eaten rabbit on the day he died."

DC Galloway piped up. "That's not a crime, is it?"

The room shared the joke, although Marsh only seemed to tolerate it. She tilted her head towards Wild, silently urging him to get on with it.

"No, not a crime, but potentially evidence of where Porter ate his final meal." He saw Galloway take a deep breath, and cut him off. "Porter hadn't cooked anything at home for some time, judging by the mess there."

Galloway closed his mouth.

Wild continued. "PC Olsen checked the local pubs and found only one that sold pies containing rabbit meat — the George. We concluded Porter must have eaten there before he died."

"Couldn't have done it afterwards." Ben Galloway played the crowd.

Wild thought about playing football with Galloway's testicles while he waited for the team to settle. "As I was saying, Constable Olsen checked the menus of all the pubs and the landlady at the George confirmed their pies contain rabbit meat. The pub is also a relatively short distance from where the body was found. We visited the George together last night," he paused for the inevitable comments, "and the pies did indeed contain rabbit, and I recovered a piece of shot that seemed to match the one found in Porter's stomach."

Marsh shattered his train of thought with a single word. "Circumstantial."

He locked eyes with her. Fair enough, he'd play. "True. However, we also retrieved a walking stick with a head that appears to match the one in Porter's photograph. I'm awaiting a forensics report to confirm it."

Marsh was clearly a woman of few words. "Very good. And full marks to PC Olsen. Please pass on my thanks when you next speak to her."

It felt like a loaded comment, and he couldn't tell whether she was complimenting their tag-team, or putting him in his place. Judging by the silence in the room, neither could anyone else.

Galloway had a face on him that could have soured milk. He cleared his throat with all the subtlety of a heckle. "I, er . . ." His eyes darted from the DI to Wild, as if unsure who to try most to impress. "I've contacted the solicitor closest to Porter's home and I collated the details of the farming families who work the surrounding fields."

Wild estimated that all took an hour, tops. Still, full marks to Galloway for doing what he was paid for.

"Good work, Ben." DI Marsh threw him a verbal biscuit. "Okay, let's break this down around the team. DC Galloway, I'll put you with . . ."

Wild knew what was coming and tried to smile graciously at the unwanted and unreturnable gift.

". . . DS Wild. Focus on the solicitor." She tapped her fingers together. "Actually, before you do that, give the house another going over. There must be an address book somewhere."

Yeah, Wild thought to himself, unless someone took it when they stole the shotgun. He tuned out as Marsh assigned families for colleagues to check out. He couldn't help wondering if she had decided to deliberately keep the incomer at arm's length from the locals.

After the briefing, Galloway sauntered over, notes in hand. "Ready when you are, Skip." It sounded like an insult.

Wild rattled his keys. "Come on then. Walkies."

CHAPTER 9

Wild let DC Galloway use up oxygen on their drive over to Porter's house.

"So, I reckon if I do bide my time there'll be a DS post at the station eventually, which would suit me down to the ground."

Wild concealed a smile. "You don't fancy spreading your wings and trying somewhere else in the meantime?"

Galloway looked affronted. "What, like London?"

Wild shrugged. "Like . . . anywhere. A new area, even a new station will give you more experience. That way when you're ready to take your Sergeant's exam . . ."

Galloway nodded enthusiastically. "Right, right. I see what you mean."

Wild glanced over again. They really were getting younger.

Porter's car was still there, in the drive.

Galloway was halfway out of the car before Wild had turned off the ignition. "Do you want upstairs or downstairs?"

Wild deliberately rolled the car forward a little, causing Galloway to stumble. "We'll work room to room, together. Follow my lead." He tried the front door key. A good repair, overall. He wondered who'd be paying for it.

"Kitchen first, I think." An easy win, if by easy he meant nothing achieved. Dusting powder was still in evidence on the doors and drawer handles. Despite wearing gloves, he touched as few surfaces as possible. He set Galloway to work at the opposite side of the room, glancing over occasionally to watch him in action. "No, take the drawer out fully, in case there's something taped underneath."

Galloway followed instructions okay but seemed to lack initiative. Wild remembered how Marnie Olsen just got on with it. Shame she wasn't there instead.

After the kitchen came the mausoleum front parlour — untouched by human hand. Nothing doing there. They fared no better upstairs, moving from room to room like unwelcome guests, working methodically and coming up empty-handed. On impulse, Wild checked the cistern in the bathroom, Galloway peering over his shoulder like an apprentice toilet inspector. A half-brick lay at the bottom. Wild lifted it clear to reveal a key.

"Nice one, Skip!" Galloway sounded impressed. That, or he thought kissing arse was a great way to build bridges.

Wild tried the key in what remained of the firearms cabinet lock — a perfect fit. "Interesting." He waited for Galloway to offer up an opinion and gave up waiting.

The bedroom was sparse. Unloved might have been a better word. Devoid of the chaos downstairs, the gun cabinet notwithstanding, it stood as a hollow monument to a life unmourned. Wild picked through each drawer slowly, as if he might accidentally disturb a memory. Galloway watched him from the doorway, saying nothing, betraying his concentration in his breathing.

Wild stopped abruptly without turning. "What do you notice about this room?"

Galloway cleared his throat. "There's not much in it."

"True. More fundamentally," Wild closed another drawer, "Porter didn't sleep in the master bedroom. It's like he drew a line under his former life. What do we know about the wife?"

"Erm, deceased, I think. I can check."

Wild let it pass and moved on to the wardrobe, assailed by the odour of mothballs as he opened the door. Three jackets hung there and he checked every pocket, as well as the linings. Either Porter wasn't big on sending Christmas cards or someone else had got to his address book first.

Galloway advanced a couple of steps into the room. "What about the son — or is it a nephew?"

Wild felt under the mattress and along the sheets on a fool's errand, coming up with bugger all. "We'll request the call logs. I don't suppose you spotted a mobile phone charger anywhere?"

Downstairs, Wild lifted the phone free from Porter's junk mail and set it on top of the pile. Greasy fingerprints, freshly powered, were still visible on the handset. Wild picked it up and knew from the dialling tone that a message had been left. He took out his mobile, hit the record app and held it close to the phone before he dialled 1571 to retrieve any messages.

"Hi Dad, it's Nathan. Look, I'm sorry, okay? I thought I could sort it out. I'll be in touch when things have died down. Just give me a little more time. Bye."

With no other messages Wild stopped recording and played it back on his mobile phone. Having mentally digested the call, he tapped in the code for the last caller's number, jotting down the digits on an unopened envelope before transferring them to his notebook. As Steph used to say, 'Like a real detective.'

"This is recent." He did his thinking aloud. "Otherwise the forensics team would have picked it up."

Though tempted to keep the lead for himself, he rang the DI to share the good news. If he thought it would deflect criticism from their inability to find an address book, he was disappointed. By the time they'd searched every reasonable and unreasonable place, lunchtime was knocking on the door of his stomach.

"Fancy a pub lunch, Ben? I'm buying."

Galloway's enthusiasm lasted until he realised there was only one pub on Wild's mind: the George.

Wild smiled as they pulled into the car park. It was like taking a dog to the vet's. He recognised one or two stalwart members of the local community from his previous visit, and from the looks on their faces they hadn't forgotten him either. He ordered sandwiches for two and chose a table in the main bar. He raised a glass to his fellow patrons, taking perverse pleasure from Galloway's discomfort. "Cheers, all."

CHAPTER 10

Wild left the George to the same loaded silence that had greeted him. Galloway had nipped outside already and was busy checking his mobile. He looked up nonchalantly as Wild approached. "Okay, Skip?"

Wild was in two minds about reminding him of his name, but let it drop. At least it was a step up from *Sarge*. He walked to his car. "While we're here, have a look at these scratches — what do you think?" He watched Ben Galloway half paying attention.

"Dunno, Skip. Did you drive against any bushes — brambles, maybe?"

Wild twirled his key on his index finger. "Yeah, maybe that's it." Maybe, only not on both sides of the car.

Next stop, Clarence Hollings, solicitor. With its large carved wooden sign and polished brass plates, the timbered building embodied respectability. Wild read the names before he crossed the threshold — Hollings and Gresham. He put a hand on the great oak door, throwing a line behind him. "Let me do the talking."

Judging by the architecture, the offices had once been a sizeable family home, the sort where servants came as standard. Wild clocked the CCTV peering at them on his way to the open door marked Reception, where a secretary's hands flew almost silently across a keyboard, her gaze fixed in rapt concentration. It felt religious. Wild coughed to get her attention.

"DS Wild." He flicked out his warrant card for show. "And this is—"

"Why, hallo, Ben. Are your parents keeping well?"

Galloway reverted to an eight-year-old. "Yes, thank you, Mrs Henderson."

Mrs Henderson lowered her glasses. "Somebody did ring from the police station — we expected you earlier." She looked to the wall clock for effect.

Wild tried his best smile. "Unavoidably detained on police business."

Although she nodded, her face told a different story. "I'll check if Mr Hollings is free." She lifted the phone, pressed a couple of buttons and spoke so quietly that Wild had to strain to eavesdrop from across the desk. She sighed, satisfied, and replaced the handset before delivering her verdict. "He'll be down to see you shortly. If you'd like to take a seat?"

Wild rummaged through the magazines spread out in a fan on an antique coffee table — a choice between dogs, shooting, livestock and *Reader's Digest*. He plumped for the latter. Galloway had turned his attention to a large pastoral scene on the wall. Wild couldn't decide if Galloway was enthralled by it or trying to avoid eye contact.

"Now then, Ben, is your Becky still engaged to that accountant chap?"

Galloway was blushing as he turned around. "Far as I know, Mrs Henderson. We don't see much of her these days, working shifts at the hospital. Especially now they've bought a flat . . ." He stopped talking.

Wild caught the envy in Galloway's eyes. So, sister Becky had an independent life, which suggested Galloway was still in the bosom of his family. Or his mother. A buzzer clicked outside and Mr Hollings appeared in the doorway. Tall, thin and blessed with an aquiline nose to hold up his round glasses, Wild judged him a good stand-in for an undertaker.

Mr Hollings collected them, entered a key code and then stooped to get to the stairs. Wild admired the colours streaming in from a large stained-glass window at the top of the staircase. The heraldic crest bore a Latin motto that Wild neither understood nor cared to know.

Hollings stalled, one hand on the banister. "It's beautiful, isn't it? One of the building's many original features."

Wild read that as business was good — cattle, property and land conveyance, probate . . . Hollings moved off solemnly up the stairs, his soft shoes making hardly a sound as he led the procession. Galloway drew level with Wild, his hands pressed together. Wild imagined him as a choirboy. What else would there have been to do around here?

Hollings opened the door and held it open. Aside from his computer, parked in one corner of the room, the office was a complete throwback. Box files crowded the shelves, along with ribboned folders. A thoroughbred racehorse hung over the fireplace, in need of a clean. The solicitor retreated to his side of the desk. "Please sit down, gentlemen." He waited for them. "We drew up a will for Mr Alexander Porter quite some time ago." He leafed through some notes on his desk. "Four years ago, in fact."

Wild noticed Galloway leaning forward and instinctively eased back, as if to counterbalance his enthusiasm. Galloway glanced to Wild and took out his notebook.

"And who's the beneficiary?"

The door opened abruptly and a younger woman entered the room, bearing a tray with one cup of tea — best china — and a small plate of biscuits. She gasped at the sight of the guests.

"I'm so sorry, Mr Hollings. There wasn't an entry in your calendar."

Hollings offered up a bemused smile in exchange for his afternoon tea. "Not to worry, Pauline. These gentlemen are from the police. If you, er, wouldn't mind . . ."

Pauline paled. "Absolutely, Mr Hollings." She backed out like a servant, and pulled the door to quietly.

Wild wondered if she was still behind the door.

Hollings pursed his lips, momentarily embarrassed. "Pauline Henderson handles all our electronic communications and supports Verity downstairs."

Wild noted the shared surname, put two and two together, and muttered "Jesus" under his breath.

Hollings took a sip of his tea — surely Earl Grey — and then opened a drawer. He lifted a bundle free, turning the pages as if for the first time. "The, er, main asset is Fortune's Field and the surrounding two fields — all left to one Gordon Elleth."

Wild let Galloway play secretary. "And what about the house?"

Hollings raised his head and straightened his spine, the shock of white hair reminding Wild of a bird's nest on a pole.

"The house was remortgaged about two years before I drew up the will."

Wild shifted in his chair as Galloway scribbled away. "Is that normal — to risk your home and not use the land as collateral for a loan? It's not as if he farmed it himself. Surely the rental income for a couple of fields can't be that great?"

Hollings threw him a withering look. "DS Wild, you're clearly not from a rural community. Land is like blood, passed down through the generations."

Wild quickly tired of homespun wisdom. "So, why isn't the land left to the son?"

Hollings stared implacably — the sort of stare that protects a lie. Wild nodded to Galloway, who went through a perfunctory list of questions — thorough but unimaginative. Wild let him get on with it and studied Hollings as he responded.

Information extracted, the good solicitor replaced the folder in his drawer, locked it and put the key in his waistcoat. Pure theatre. Hollings sipped more tea and broke off a piece of biscuit. "Please contact me if I can be of further assistance." Their time was up.

Wild got to his feet. "Count on it." He proffered a hand, the personification of community policing.

Downstairs, Galloway popped back to see Mrs Henderson. Wild used the space to check in with his DI. "It's Wild. Porter left the land to a Gordon Elleth."

Marsh practically cackled. "Really? One of the farmers? Interesting. When did he make the will?"

Wild gave her the date and the line went so quiet he thought they'd been cut off. "Well, DS Wild, I took a call from another firm of solicitors — Santers. They heard on the grapevine about Porter and wanted to make us aware . . ."

He waited for the punchline.

". . . Another will. Dated two years after the one held at Hollings and Gresham. Uh huh. I'm heading over there now. If you'd care to join me — alone."

Wild heard Galloway's voice behind him. "Sure," he said into the phone. "Let me get rid of Junior. Send me the details."

Galloway seemed happy enough to make his own way back to the station to write up his notes. Wild dropped him at the edge of town and looped back to head north.

CHAPTER 11

Santers the solicitors sat on the edge of a trading estate, big on parking and low on character. When Wild arrived, Marsh was already waiting in the car park, a bottle of mineral water in her hand. At least, it looked to him like water — she was Scottish after all.

DI Marsh led the charge, striding confidently through the double-glazed doors. A sharp suit met them, teeth and tan on display like a party hostess. Wild took an instant dislike to him. The DI stuck to her water so Wild accepted a coffee.

The suit introduced himself as Corey. "We recently audited our case files and Mr Porter's was one of them, so when his name came up—"

Wild glared. "And how exactly did that happen?"

"I'd rather not say, unless that's pertinent to your investigation. Surely what matters is that I contacted the police?"

Wild felt like pinning a medal to Corey's forehead.

DI Marsh reined Wild in with a gesture. "It would help us to view the contents of Mr Porter's will."

The suit flipped a page over with a flourish. "Any profit from the sale of the house, after monies outstanding on the property, to go to the son, Nathan Porter — there'd been some equity release, so I understand. The three fields — two arable and one not actively farmed—"

"Fortune's Field." Wild chipped in to try and join the conversation.

"If you say so. Anyway, all three fields are bequeathed to a Mr Edwin Causly, who rents one of them for arable farming."

"Isn't that a little unusual?" Wild pushed the point home. "I understand land has emotional attachment as well as monetary value."

Corey's eyebrows danced. "Perhaps it's not such a surprise if Mr Porter and Mr Causly go back a number of years. Plus, Mr Porter's son moved away to Scotland, I believe, so he'd be unlikely to come back and till the soil."

Marsh's antenna twitched. "Where did you come by that information?"

"Oh, you know." Corey oozed discomfort through his suit. "People talk."

"Do they, indeed?" Marsh twisted her bottle top like it was a chicken's neck.

Wild heard two narratives, the one spewing from the solicitor and the one in his own head. Porter must have had cause to migrate his generosity from Mr Elleth to Mr Causly. And maybe generosity didn't come into it at all. He nodded to himself and scribbled a couple of notes.

Corey finished his speech and sat back, arms open, inviting questions. Wild kept schtum and enjoyed the show, taking notes like a good DS.

Marsh stopped wrestling with her water. "Did you know Mr Porter well?"

"Nope, not at all. We do radio campaigns from time to time — we did one a couple of weeks ago, actually. Mr Porter said he contacted us after hearing one of our ads."

Marsh chewed it over. "Not your usual client, I would have thought."

The solicitor flashed his perfect veneered smile. "We're here to serve anyone who needs us."

Wild entered an X in his scorebook. Points deducted for not answering the question. He liked how Marsh operated, noting the way she put the solicitor through the wringer without raising her voice. A masterclass. Mr Marsh, if there was one, must surely know his place.

Afterwards, they sat in Marsh's car, recapping. "Any thoughts, Craig?"

This would be his chance to impress, *would* being the operative word. "It's odd that the bulk of Porter's estate isn't left to his son — surviving heir and all that." He tapped the dashboard. "No, that's not it. The odd thing is that no one else finds it odd. And switching loyalties between farmers — does that suggest a possible motive?"

Marsh sipped her water. "Money's always a strong motivation. Check how the field rents are paid and whether both farmers are up to date."

He started to get out of the car and then thought better of it. "Ma'am, can I ask you something? Is there a reason you're leading this investigation from the passenger seat?" He cringed at how badly that had come out.

Marsh smiled faintly. "Is that what you think? I'm disappointed in you, Craig. I took you to be smarter than that. Porter's death is fortunate — not for him of course. It's a golden opportunity for you to prove yourself. I need a sergeant I can rely on, and you need a fresh start." She reached into the door pocket. "So get the job done and don't fuck it up. Peppermint cream?"

He waved away the bag. "I'll see you back at the station, ma'am." As he opened the car door and glanced up, he saw Corey peering at them through the window.

* * *

Back on the road, Wild pondered which firm of solicitors would be best to handle his divorce. Steph had long since moved out of their flat in Enfield to 'make space,' as she'd put it. Make distance, more like. So when the divorce papers had come from her solicitors — the ones he had to use whenever he wanted to contact her — he wasn't entirely surprised, more a case of *disappointed*. 'Unreasonable behaviour' had seemed like a disproportionate slight on his character when he'd first read it, but getting shit-faced at a police do — an event he hadn't been invited to — well, that had played right into her hands. You couldn't save a sinking ship, she'd said. And that night he'd scuttled it in spectacular fashion.

He tried not to think about the fallout from the raid the following day either. Maybe it was fortunate he only had fragmented memories. Three arrests, one discharged firearm — in his direction — and a scumbag who escaped justice. No one blamed him to his face though, which was probably the only up-side of a breakdown.

Wind forward a few months of sick leave and therapy, followed by closed-door discussions — mostly *about* him rather than with him — and then a Police Federation rep stepping in to suggest mediation to agree the terms of his and Steph's permanent separation. Terms and conditions, more like. No contact, except through Steph's solicitor, no interviews, obviously, and no comments on their (failed) relationship. She hadn't needed their marital home, but buying him out ensured he had no base left in London. Sure, he got to keep his job and rank, but the price of that was being exiled to the shires. Not exactly a brave new world.

His brain shifted back into focus at the first roundabout for the police station. For all its downsides, police work was the perfect antidote to introspection. Other people's problems, the chase, the authority to penetrate their lives and examine their secrets, and — when things played out the right way — job satisfaction like no other. It was a wonder more people didn't join the force!

Ben Galloway met him before he'd made it through the double doors upstairs. "Fancy a coffee, Skip, and I can update you on my progress."

Who was he to deny his subordinate? The canteen was sparse, tables shining and abandoned. He bought hot drinks and chose a table by a window. As he sat down he noticed a couple of uniforms in the car park, standing closer to his car than he liked. He needed to be casual. He opened his trusty notebook with a blank expression.

"Who are those two? Marsh says I need to learn names and build *relationships* in the station. Unfortunately, I'm crap at that." He tapped a pen against his notebook and noticed Galloway nodding in agreement.

"Right, well, the tall one's Glen Ebury and the other one is Simon Rush. Top blokes, both of them." The way he said it reeked of the playground and the false respect given to the tougher boys.

Ebury and Rush pointed at the car as they stood together. Not exactly subtle. He'd let it go for now, but he'd come back to it. He always did.

Galloway's progress report sounded like a bad play rehearsal, a monotone rendition of names, places, and dates of birth — altogether a pub quiz of an investigation.

Wild lowered his tea mug. "What do you make of Edwin Causly?"

Galloway frowned, as if he hadn't fully understood the question. "Oh, there's been Causlys in that area for generations."

Wild smiled at what sounded like a character reference.

Galloway hadn't finished. "They've farmed Porter's big field since the thirties. Even longer, probably. Mr Porter's father bought the land from the previous owner at the end of the war."

"Why didn't they buy it themselves then?"

Galloway rubbed imaginary cash through his fingers. Wild nodded and thought back to Porter's house. How the mighty had fallen.

"Tell me more about the family — beyond their pedigree, I mean." He could see Galloway was struggling. "Who are they related to?" He held back from adding, 'Everybody else, I imagine'.

Galloway relaxed a little. "Old Mr Causly's son, Peter, died during the war. The son's widow moved in with them.

Good people. Go to church regularly, you know. Not much else to say."

This was starting to feel like an *Archers* omnibus. "And the widow's family?"

"She was an Elleth — died a few years back. Her brother's still alive and farms the other field — with help of course. Neither of them are getting any younger." That was it. Done and dusted.

"And what's the score with the middle field?"

Galloway drank his coffee. "Fortune's Field — nothing's farmed there. Never has been. It's a medieval burial ground."

CHAPTER 12

Wild liked to do his thinking away from the office. In London, that would have been the pub or a greasy spoon, but here it only took a few syllables to raise eyebrows. 'Not local, then?' was the frequent refrain, sometimes in more colourful language. His solution was the tourist spots — those designer cafés where everything was organic or gluten-free, even the bacon rolls.

The Labyrinth didn't call itself a café. No, the hand-painted symbol and child-like lettering declared it an eatery and community hub. He'd found it by accident, lured by the scent of decent coffee, like the stuff Steph used to grind by hand at home. For all he knew she probably still did, in her new flat in the city.

He went inside, dimly aware of a piano version oldie playing in the background — the low-key stuff where there's nothing to hum along to. He waited behind a family of four who felt the need to go through the menu aloud, in great detail. As they reached the counter and continued the great debate, he wondered whether to skip lunch in favour of a bag of crisps. A pinafored woman, aged probably late thirties, with a scarf tied at the back of her hair like a soviet factory worker, moved along the counter and beckoned him over to a second till.

"Can I help you?"

He smiled. "You just have." He glanced up at the board again. "Coffee and a piece of walnut cake, please." He held out a tenner, simultaneously hoping he'd get change while remaining doubtful. Mental multitasking.

The ground floor was packed so he advanced upstairs in search of some peace, automatically swerving past one open room at the sound of a screaming brat — the very young variety. There were other doorless rooms along the corridor. In one, a couple sat, cocooned in headphones, their feet touching under the table as they ate a rainbow salad without looking up from their mobiles. They didn't seem to notice, or mind, his sneer at their modern romance. In the third room, the one that was just right, a woman Wild figured to be in her late fifties sat engrossed in a hardback book. It must have been good because she didn't even look up when he walked past her to the window table.

He positioned himself by the window and took a forkful of cake, gazing down at the courtyard. Guitar music filtered up through the gap in the window before the minstrel came into view. His leather waistcoat, cowboy boots and fitted jeans marked him out as an arsehole even before Wild saw the ponytail. His only redeeming feature was his musicianship. The minstrel drifted to a sunlit corner of the courtyard and belted out *Guitar Man* by Bread, with abnormal highs and lows that still managed to sound melodic. And still an arsehole. Wild had him pegged at maybe early thirties — old enough to know better. A girl appeared, presumably from a table outside, and dropped some coins into a top hat. An actual top hat. Her red and white polka-dot dress epitomised summer and youth, and other things that Wild had come to despise. He caught the odd word, something about a party needing live entertainment, and then shared laughter. She sidled up close to the musician, obscuring Wild's vision with that dress and her perfectly tanned limbs, and the sun in her auburn hair. Wild turned his attention briefly back to his cake and coffee, pausing to notice how she practically skipped away. Mr Top Hat slipped a hand inside his jeans pocket for an instant and then struck up a tune. Wild thought back to the buskers outside Camden Town underground station, and the way the dossers lined one of the walls, forcing commuters to run the gauntlet on their way home. This guy, though, judging by his clothes and guitar, he wasn't so desperate.

Wild had started to lose interest, if not disdain, when a familiar face appeared in the courtyard: Pauline Henderson, from Hollings and Gresham. Wild held his coffee cup mid-air, as if moving might give him away. Pauline and the Merry Minstrel locked eyes and she put her hand against his neck and kissed him. He took part, of course he did, but she was the one making the effort. They spoke too quietly for Wild to hear and after a short exchange she left him. Within seconds of her departure, Mr Top Hat was on his mobile phone.

Call it suspicion or metropolitan prejudice but Wild was long enough in the tooth to know when something didn't smell right. He ditched his coffee, wrapped what remained of his cake in a napkin and pushed the table back. By the time he made it downstairs, the musician had packed up his guitar and was putting on his top hat. Sadly, not a prop. Wild passed him and stalled a few paces on, pretending to check his phone for an imaginary text.

As the musician exited the courtyard, one of the staff paused from collecting the crockery, brushed away her fringe and called out, "See you later, Jeb," with a raised inflection so that it sounded like a proposition. Then again, the way she'd smiled, maybe it had been.

Jeb strutted out like he owned every cobblestone, his cowboy boots clipping and creaking as he walked. Wild gave him a decent head start — a top hat would be hard to lose in a crowd anyway — and took an easy stroll after him. Could be something, could be nothing, he told himself as he fetched out the remnants of his cake. He followed Jeb at a safe distance, all the way to the car park where Jeb climbed into a Citroen 2CV, having taken his hat off first. Jeb lifted up the window and dropped a piece of paper as he drove off. Wild kept walking as the car passed and then scrambled to retrieve the litter. It was a car park ticket for an hour, with only forty-five minutes used. Either Jeb packed a lot into his busking performances or he had other reasons for plying his trade there.

Wild considered the ways he could identify Jeb. One: A PNC check on the vehicle. Two: CCTV. Three: Go visit Pauline at work, or wait outside the solicitors and see if anyone comes to pick her up. Four: Actually talk to Pauline. Option four was the easiest, only he wasn't sure why he was so interested in the 'prat in the hat.' As he walked round to his own car he rang DI Marsh to put her in the picture.

"And you're curious about him *why* exactly?"

"He doesn't smell right."

The DI laughed. "I've heard worse! You'd better follow your nose then."

He finished off the cake remnants in his car, napkin held close to his mouth to catch any crumbs. It was only on opening his napkin to empty it outside that he saw a message in blue ink, accompanied by a smiley face: "Do come again." He figured he might, at that.

* * *

The first face he saw, back at the office, was Ben Galloway's — a mixture of earnestness and indolence. It gave Wild an idea.

"I want a private word with you." He took Galloway off to a side room. Galloway sat down and hunched his shoulders defensively. "Ben, how well do you know that secretary we met at Hollings and Gresham?"

Galloway relaxed a little. "She goes to church with my mum. Dad doesn't really bother, unless it's Christmas or—"

"Fine." Wild tried to focus Galloway's mind by willpower alone. "And what about her niece, their IT specialist?"

Galloway blinked a couple of times, as if he were forcing synapses to fire manually. "Pauline? Oh, not so much. I reckon she probably got that job on account of her aunty."

Wild strained his gaze for hidden traces of irony. "Yeah, nepotism is a bastard, eh?"

CHAPTER 13

Wild waited at his desk for the call to come through. Nathan Porter, the victim's son, was attending to make a voluntary statement, fresh in from Kilmarnock. That word still made him smile: voluntary. Like there was any choice in the matter. He flicked through his notes, giving extra attention to the lines ending in a question mark, and took a final sip of lukewarm tea. A phone rang, but it wasn't his. He looked across and saw DI Marsh stir from her chair, pick up the phone and start speaking. She turned abruptly in his direction, clicked her fingers and pointed towards the stairs. Clearly she'd confused the terms sergeant and servant. As he got up to follow her instructions, she left her desk and opened her office door about a foot.

"I'll sit in with you, Craig. I'll be down in a minute."

So much for his plan to give Ben Galloway the wisdom of his experience. He met Galloway on his way down the stairs and broke his heart. Downstairs, Wild was directed to Interview Room Three. He took his seat and breathed in the scent of the empty room, four parts cleaning product to one part body odour, with just a hint of vinyl flooring. He set his notebook and pen on the table and mentally rehearsed what he wanted to say, assuming his DI gave him the option.

As two voices along the corridor broke the silence, he caught DI Marsh doing an impression of casual. The other voice, presumably Alexander Porter's son, spoke with the undertone of conformity that strangers brought along when they first visited a police station. Witnesses or suspects, it didn't seem to matter — no one wanted to be there.

"Now, are you sure I can't get you a drink, Mr Porter?"

Porter followed her in and then paused at the doorway. "Okay, then. A tea would be nice, if it's not too much trouble. Two sugars. And call me Nathan."

DI Marsh looked across at Wild with his feet neatly under the table and let out a sigh. "Please take a seat. DS Wild will keep you company before we start your voluntary interview." As Nathan Porter sat down, Wild looked behind him to see Marsh miming a mouth being zipped before she closed the door.

Nathan smiled awkwardly and nodded. "You must get all sorts in here."

"Yeah, it's a real microcosm of life — saints and sinners."

Wild didn't know why he said it and couldn't think of a follow-up line, so they sat like an old married couple in a restaurant, avoiding eye contact by looking around one another. Each of them turned eagerly to the door when DI Marsh returned.

Marsh took the lead, ousting Wild from his chair so that she could set up the recording equipment. "This is a voluntary interview with Nathan Porter. Also present are Detective Inspector Marsh and Detective Sergeant Wild. Nathan Porter has stated that he does not wish to have a solicitor present. Nathan, I would remind you that you are under caution and that anything you say during this interview may be used as evidence. Also, as you are here voluntarily you are free to leave at any time."

Wild noted the way that Nathan tensed up at the words 'caution' and 'evidence' and cradled his tea in a death grip. DI Marsh leaned back, opened her notes and simultaneously nudged Wild's foot — show time. Wild summarised what he wanted Nathan to know, nothing more. This was a game played in definite stages. They were investigating the death of Mr Porter in suspicious circumstances and there were a number of blanks in his life where they hoped Nathan could provide details. He held back on the curious matter of the two wills because it occurred to him that Nathan might not be the beneficiary of another one, somewhere in the queue. He went on to say that they'd picked up Nathan's phone message on his father's answering machine and that they hadn't been able to make sense of it.

Besides a few murmurs and confirmations, Nathan hadn't said much yet, which struck Wild as odd. Although he'd come in voluntarily he'd actually volunteered very little, which suggested an ulterior motive — probably trying to suss out what the police knew. DI Marsh let Wild's chain extend to the full length she had allotted him and then tapped his foot again to send him back to his kennel.

"So, Nathan, as DS Wild indicated, we recovered a telephone message from your father's phone — and bear with me here as I read your message back from the recording notes: '*Look, I'm sorry, okay? I thought I could sort it out. I'll be in touch when things have died down. Just give me a little more time. Bye.*' Nathan, what precisely did you mean by that?"

Nathan froze for a moment and then he danced to order. "Yeah, of course . . ." He rubbed the back of his neck as if it was aching. "I promised my dad I'd come down and see him because it had been a while. Only it's been manic at work with an unexpected export order for Norway and everyone's expected to put their lives on hold. And when Shannon — that's my boss — came down with flu, well I had to go in . . ."

Wild glanced up at the CCTV camera in the corner of the ceiling and blinked twice. Too much information, so as to bury the lie. Marsh let Nathan's mouth run its course and then politely coughed.

"Well, we certainly appreciate you coming in like this, Nathan, and at such a difficult time. Obviously you'll want to finalise arrangements once we've concluded this aspect of our investigation."

Nathan's eyes narrowed at the word 'investigation'.

Wild got in his next sentence quickly. "Perhaps you could fill in some details about your father's life for background purposes."

Nathan's gaze returned to that far-off place for a little while, as if he were gathering his words — or concocting them. "There's not much to tell really. We come from a long line of farmers, but Dad quickly decided it wasn't for him and rented out the land instead. Mum was a music teacher — taught piano at home when I was growing up — and Dad, well, he liked to try different things."

"Like a businessman?"

Although Nathan laughed, his face told a different story. "You could put it that way, only not a very successful one. Big dreamer was Dad. Never seemed to stick at anything long enough to make a go of it."

"Why didn't he sell the land if he was never going to farm it?"

Nathan looked at him with incredulity. "Sell the land that's been in our family for generations? You're not from the countryside are you, DS Wild? That's not what people out here do."

"What took you to . . . ?" Wild fiddled with his notes for effect, knowing full bloody well where Nathan had relocated.

"Kilmarnock. An engineering job came up a couple of years ago. Seems like longer now." His voice dropped suddenly, like a dodgy connection.

"What did you do before then?" Marsh spoke quietly, her Glaswegian brogue lending the words intensity.

"I worked in moulded plastics locally — at Hardacre's, till they made me redundant." His face suggested pride and regret.

Wild leapt back into the silence. "And what about your dad? Did you see much of him or was it more of a fortnightly catch-up phone call — like me and mine?"

Nathan shifted in his chair a little, making the padded vinyl squeak. "Dad and I didn't always see eye to eye. He could be a difficult man to get on with."

Wild juggled ideas in his head. Marsh hadn't briefed him on what *she* wanted Nathan to know, so he figured he'd follow her lead. When Nathan Porter looked at his watch for a second time, DI Marsh took the hint.

"I think we'll leave it there for now. Thank you for coming in. We will be in touch when we want to speak with you again."

Wild smiled: when, not if. She didn't seem the sort for a slip of the tongue. He showed Nathan to the front desk and signed him out, returning to the interview room where the DI was gazing at her notes. He shut the door and sat opposite her.

"Not exactly the grieving son, ma'am."

"You noticed that, eh? Quite a puffy face, though. Didn't figure him for grief-stricken. We never got a credible answer for the phone message, so what's your theory, Detective?" She ended with a hint of a smile, but he knew he was being tested.

"Well, he's obviously lying or obfuscating." The word felt and sounded heavy on his tongue. "He's apologised for something that has involved Porter — or affected him directly. And at the point of Porter's death, he hadn't sorted it out. And he sure as hell doesn't want *us* to know what it is."

Marsh tidied her paperwork. "See if you can find out about Nathan's work history at Hardacre's — ask around discreetly and also check with the team. What can Nathan have done that impacted on his dad? I can't see Porter lending his son money. Looking at his home he didn't have a pot to piss in."

Wild shook his head. "It has to be money."

Marsh murmured. "Get Ben Galloway to follow up on Porter's bank statements. Maybe there's a money trail. Right, we're done here."

CHAPTER 14

Gordon Elleth's house sat squat on the landscape, like an unwelcome guest. Wild stopped the car in the lane within sight of the farmhouse. He could hear Ben Galloway's breathing and feel the wind outside rocking the car. Wild had already gone through the running order a second time. Galloway didn't seem keen. Or maybe he thought visiting farmsteads was beneath him now he was a DC.

"Okay, any last questions before we go in?"

"No, Skip — you'll lead and I'll keep my mouth shut." He looked happy remembering the drill, like a child who'd managed to count backwards from ten.

Wild threw him a courtesy bone. "And is there anything else I need to know?"

Galloway thought for a moment. "I s'pose you realise Mr Elleth is a church man?"

Wild cocked his ear, waiting for the significance.

"God-fearing, you might say. So no cursing, no coarseness, and no . . ."

"I get the picture." Wild turned the key in the ignition and aimed for the grey slab up ahead.

Gordon Elleth arrived at the five-bar gate and leant over it as if to reaffirm his ownership. He nodded curtly and drew the gate back, the loose diagonal piece moving at its own separate pace with the momentum. He pointed to a level piece of land where they could park. As Wild clambered out of the car, he looked across the nearby fields to the heavy fencing that surrounded Porter's land — so close and yet so far, judging by the change in wills.

Elleth approached without a handshake, standing before them in judgement. "You'd best come in." He shot a cold glance at Galloway that Wild took for abject disappointment.

Two black Labradors emerged as the front door opened, took one look at their master and thought better of it, scuttling back into the house.

"Kitchen," Elleth muttered as he led the way, leaving Galloway at the rear to close the door.

Wild clocked the cooking range, the dogs sitting expectantly in the corner of the room, and a table set out with blue and white china. He might as well have landed on Mars.

"Sit ye down then." Elleth waited and then leaned across his guests to pour the tea.

Wild toyed with, 'You have a lovely house,' but saw no reason to take the piss. Well, not unless it provoked a useful response.

Elleth filled a fourth cup and added milk. "I'll just take this up to Elizabeth — she's reading." The way he said it made it sound like a commitment, or an achievement. Wild couldn't tell which.

He fought the urge to ask if it was Bible studies, and instead played a game in his head of spot the antiques.

Galloway cleared his throat. "What do I do if Mr Elleth engages in conversation?"

"Maybe, I dunno, talk back?"

"But you said . . ."

Wild rolled his eyes. "Use your initiative, Ben. Detect something."

Galloway brightened at that, which irritated Wild all the more. He distracted himself by tracking Elleth's heavy footsteps as they echoed across the ceiling and down the stairs.

One of the dogs braved the space to greet its master and Elleth gave it a single stroke on the head before it returned to its companion.

Elleth took his place at the table. "I've known Alexander Porter a long time, and his father before him. It seems to me that the family lost their way."

Wild let him talk about the old days and farming, and a roll-call of family members long past, waiting for a gap in traffic.

"But it's not for me to judge, Detective Wild. Only God judges," Elleth finished at last.

Wild took his chance and asked, "Mr Elleth, do you ever frequent the George?"

Elleth smiled, his mouth transformed into a sickle blade. "Oh, yes, I visit the George from time to time — wouldn't see my neighbours otherwise!" He laughed to himself and Galloway tried gamely to share the joke.

"What about the night he died?"

Elleth gazed skyward. "I did not see Alexander Porter in the George that night." He lowered his head in Galloway's direction. "Haven't seen you in church these past few weeks, Benjamin."

Galloway reddened. "I've been on courses, Mr Elleth, and then there's follow-up work. Not as much free time since I made Detective Constable."

Elleth nodded slowly. "Well, I suppose we can serve the Almighty in different ways. And what about you, Detective Wild — are you a believer?"

Wild's gaze was drawn behind Elleth to a black cross nailed to the plaster, not dissimilar to the one on Porter's wall. "I try to keep an open mind." He rearranged his face to conform to the lie because there was little sense in antagonising the old goat.

"Well, there is always space at St Matthew's on Sundays. Benjamin can tell you all about it." Elleth collected the empty cups and placed them carefully in the sink. Their time was up. As soon as Wild stood, the dogs went into a frenzy.

Elleth let them get on with it until his patience ran out, commanding them with a grunt.

Galloway seemed sheepish on the walk back to the car.

Wild chose his moment. "Never had you figured for one of the God Squad, Ben."

Galloway looked affronted. "Spare me your mockery. It's about community and people coming together. Don't suppose that's possible in a place as big as London."

Wild unlocked the car. "Oh, you'd be surprised." He smiled to himself. Yeah, there'd been the community of junkies outside the burger bar of a night-time, and the sex workers who plied their trade near Camden Square Park. And not forgetting the community of embittered coppers, for whom Steph had approved his membership. "What's Elizabeth Elleth like?"

"She's a good sort. She helps with the flowers in church."

Wild's nose crinkled at the thought.

CHAPTER 15

Wild found a note on his desk: *My office, as soon as you're in.* DI Marsh's domain had the blinds down, so Wild drew his own conclusions: a bollocking awaited. He figured she'd probably heard him outside. He knocked on the frosted glass.

"Come in."

He wasn't sure how to play it. Last he'd checked he hadn't screwed up anything for at least a couple of hours. Maybe Gordon Elleth had taken offence at his manner. Wouldn't be the first time. He racked his brain and came up with nothing.

The door wrenched open. "Are you planning on joining me any time soon?"

An empty seat looked as inviting as quicksand. She closed the door after him, talking her way back to her desk. "I had a meeting while you were out — with Christine Hardacre, no less."

Wild blinked his ignorance.

"Come on, Craig, you're supposed to be a detective. Christine is a big noise around here. Her family owned Hardacre's, where Nathan Porter worked. It seems he was a little economical with the truth."

Wild looked for a reason for this to fall on his shoulders and failed. Always a good time to ask questions. "Uneconomical, how?"

"You'll recall Nathan telling us he was made redundant? Well, that's not entirely true — he *was* paid off but it was more than a little shady." She swung to and fro in her chair. "I got this off the record so it goes no further, understood?"

He chose to enjoy the flicker of camaraderie while it lasted. "This Hardacre woman is a friend of yours?"

DI Marsh tapped her index fingers together. "More of an acquaintance — in my professional women's network, if you must know. See, Hardacre's had intended to let Nathan go a little while before redundancies were on the table, because of his financial impropriety."

"You mean he had his hand in the till?"

"No, not quite. It seems Nathan had borrowed from his workmates, across the board. It was only when one of them confided in another that they realised he'd shat on a whole bunch of them. Although Christine Hardacre found out about it, she parked a disciplinary because she knew the firm was heading down the river."

"Sorry, ma'am, I'm still missing something."

"Redundancy, remember? Christine Hardacre fixed it so that Nathan received a redundancy payment like all the others — on paper — on condition that she facilitated the transfer of payments to people he owed."

"But, surely, it was her firm's money . . ."

"Aye, well, she alluded to some sort of insurance arrangement, which I don't think merits our attention. The important thing is that he lied. He did have money problems then, so . . ."

"So we bring him in again for a chat."

"Precisely. And this time I won't be my usual friendly self."

Wild wondered what the Glaswegian word was for *schadenfreude*.

Nathan Porter arrived in a police car, and the duty solicitor promised to be there in twenty minutes, although Wild knew it would've felt like an hour. While Nathan was emptying his pockets and getting acquainted with the finer points of processing, Wild nipped up to the canteen — mobile on and volume up, ready for Marsh's call. As he sat by the window, watching another couple of plods looking towards his car, he reflected on the situation. Nathan might still have money problems locally — that could explain why Kilmarnock, wherever that was, seemed an attractive proposition. What it didn't explain was the message on Porter's phone. But . . . but Nathan had rung the police from a mobile, hopefully now downstairs under lock and key, so the location data could eliminate Nathan as a suspect on the night Alexander Porter died. Or at least provide an alibi for his phone.

The two plods drifted closer to Wild's car, not quite looking at it. Where were binoculars when you needed them? A chair scraped back on the other side of the table. Wild looked up to see Marnie Olsen standing before him, tea in hand.

She smiled awkwardly. "Is this seat taken?"

"Be my guest." He shifted his seat to face her.

"How is everything — with the investigation?"

"We've bought Porter's son in — he's downstairs awaiting his brief."

"Everything you need to know will be on his phone."

He raised a tea toast. "Spoken like a true techie." Speaking of which . . . "I don't suppose you've some time free this evening?" He watched her eyes become saucers. "No, nothing like that. I've got an IT problem — something I don't want to talk about here. Only if you're not busy . . . you know . . . jumping out of planes or whatever you do for kicks . . ."

"No, yeah, I can spare you an hour." She lowered her voice, even though the nearby tables were empty. "At your place?"

He nodded. "Ta. Text me whenever's good for you."

She didn't bother checking whether *he* had any other commitments. His mobile broke into song, an escalating ringtone that couldn't fail to annoy. "I gotta go. Let me know, okay? Doesn't matter if it's late. Thanks, Marnie."

By the time he reached the canteen door a table of three coppers had started whistling *London Bridge Is Falling Down*. Wild placed a mocking hand on his heart. Such rapier wit.

Marsh met him on the stairs. He noticed her change of glasses — blue-rimmed, like a mandrill's arse. Nathan's previous bonhomie had evaporated. He sat against the wall, sullen-faced, staring at the table. The solicitor greeted DI Marsh and shook her hand. Another professional acquaintance, Wild surmised. He sat beside Marsh, out on a limb, hands to himself.

The first thing DI Marsh did, after the formalities, was put her mobile on the table in front of them. "I'm expecting information that is pertinent to this investigation," she explained.

Nathan's face paled.

Wild wondered whether Nathan would 'no comment' everything or equally disappoint them with a carefully prepared — and therefore bullshit — statement. He hoped not because he wanted to see the DI in full flow.

"Now, Mr Porter, when we met last time I asked you about a message you left on your father's answering service. Would you like me to refresh your memory with the content of that message?"

Nathan shook his head and his solicitor, taking her cue, piped up, "That won't be necessary."

"So perhaps you would like to reconsider your previous answer and explain your message for me again?"

Nathan moistened his lips. "A while back I had some money problems, nothing major."

Wild and Marsh exchanged a look, and Wild took a congratulatory sigh. "And what was the nature of your money problems?"

"I used to gamble. That's all in the past. I'm on a twelve-step programme now." He read their faces. "I'm serious — you can check my phone. A local group has a WhatsApp community and my key ring—"

DI Marsh glanced at her phone. "Your key ring was noted when you were booked in. We'll get to your phone, don't you worry. And what do you expect we'll find there?"

Nathan pressed his hands on the desk, as if to steady himself. "I'm not saying Dad and me didn't have our difficult moments but we were still family. He acted as guarantor for a loan and, well . . ." He choked on a breath. "I let him down. I fell off the wagon."

Wild wondered if you could have a wagon for gambling but kept his thoughts to himself. "How did your father react?"

"How do you think? He was really pissed off. Sorry, can I say that on tape?"

Marsh nodded. "Nathan, I noticed that your face is still a little swollen. Have you been in an altercation recently?"

He touched his cheek. "Yeah, I got in a bit of a row at a pub. My own fault for shooting my mouth off."

Marsh leaned in. "Any other injuries? Bruises on your abdomen, perhaps. Maybe a medical examination . . . ?"

Nathan started undoing his shirt buttons.

Wild filled in the blanks for the benefit of the recording. "Nathan Porter is voluntarily showing us his upper torso, where bruising is evident."

"Do you need to see a doctor?"

"No, it's fine. It was an argument that got out of hand. Too much drink and too little sense." He laughed at his own joke. No one else did.

Marsh's mobile flashed. "Excuse me, I need to attend to this. Interview suspended at 15.20. At this time Mr Porter will be returned to a cell." She hit the switches. "I'll not be long."

Wild acted as chaperone, arranged tea and biscuits, and then went to meet Marsh in Room T2 — T for Technical. He knocked and went inside. He'd expected the kiosk device to be larger but it sat on the desk and took up about as much space as a tablet, sucking the data out of Nathan Porter's phone. A technician stood beside Marsh, tapping through the inventory for her. Marsh looked pleased.

"Nearly done, ma'am," the technician said. She gave Wild a cursory glance. "Once we're finished we'll transfer it onto a USB, and we'll print anything you need for interview — or court."

Wild got the impression she was putting on a show for the new bloke.

Marsh turned to him. "So, we have corroborative evidence that he has used this phone to call his dad. And we can tell . . . hold on, scroll back a bit . . . he called this other number several times in the week prior to Alexander Porter's death but only once afterwards." She made a note of the number and blithely passed it to Wild. "Get Galloway to check the number and also see if it's on the database."

Wild nodded, eyes still on the technician.

"Now would be good. Then come straight back here."

Wild put on his best impression of *messenger boy* and scurried off.

When he found the DC, Galloway did something strange. Stranger than usual. He looked at the mystery number once, blinked a couple of times, and then dashed away like a scalded cat. Wild was intrigued, but he didn't have the time right then.

When he got back to DI Marsh, she held a collection of printed pages depicting the inner workings of Nathan Porter's life: mobile calls made and received, emails, web history, WhatsApp messages, texts, all laid bare. Wild almost felt sorry for him.

Marsh led from the front when they were all back in the interview room. "Now, Mr Porter, having accessed your mobile phone data, new information has come to light."

Nathan shifted uncomfortably. Wild smiled to himself. He still enjoyed this part — confronting a suspect with irrefutable evidence. Bang to rights, as they used to say back home.

"For the benefit of this recording, the medical officer has examined you at my request and we've recorded your injuries. Do you know who assaulted you?"

"I can't remember. I was drunk."

"See, here's the thing, Nathan. Your late father also showed bruising consistent with an assault, shortly before he died."

Nathan became more alert. "Someone beat up Dad?"

Wild could see the wheels spinning in his head. That was either news to Nathan, or the best act he'd seen in a long time. Time to take advantage of Nathan's distress.

"Have you ever seen your father's shotgun?"

Wild tried to ignore Marsh's sudden out-breath, like she'd taken a punch.

Nathan thought for a moment. "Yeah, Dad kept it upstairs, under lock and key."

Wild and Marsh exchanged a knowing glance. He gestured to her: after you, boss.

"And when did you see it last?"

"I don't know, it must be years ago."

Wild tracked through the folder of paperwork Marsh had collected from Nathan's mobile. "Who's the G-man? There are multiple emails to and from the G-man, mostly discussing payments outstanding."

"He's no one, just a mate who helped me out."

Marsh jabbed at a sheet with a finger. "Some of these texts don't look very friendly to me. 'Bring your account up to date or there will be consequences.' What might they be? Is that why you took a beating?"

Nathan twitched. "No comment." He seemed shocked at his own outburst. His solicitor dropped her pen in surprise.

"Tell you what, Nathan, how about you spend a little more time in your cell while we chase up this G-man. We've got hours yet on the clock — it'll give you time to reflect."

Nathan glowered. "I haven't done anything wrong. I owe some money, that's all." He shared eyebrow semaphore with his solicitor, who shrugged noncommittally.

Wild pushed his chair back. "Up you get."

Nathan made another silent plea to his solicitor, which went nowhere. "Alright. He's someone I grew up with. It's G for Guitar Man . . ."

Wild shifted in his seat.

"I just fell a bit behind." If Nathan thought he'd avoided a police cell he was sadly mistaken. In the absence of any timescale, his solicitor went off to support another stand-up member of the community.

DI Marsh regrouped her team upstairs. "Come on then." She clapped her hands like a weary schoolteacher. "What else do we know? Ben, any joy with the most dialled number?"

"Sorry, ma'am, not yet. I'm waiting for the mobile service provider to get back to me." He looked like someone whose new lottery numbers had come up the week before.

Wild decided to throw a theory on the pile. "Okay, both Alexander Porter and his son have bruises, but I can't see old man Porter putting up much of a defence. And going on the pathologist's report, are we looking at two separate events?"

Marsh's head wobbled in time with her thinking. "That would be quite a coincidence. Unless they were connected — same perpetrator?"

"Why go to the trouble of beating up Alexander Porter?"

Ben put his hand up. "To teach his son a lesson."

Wild shot him down, considering it a mercy killing. "Seriously? Pay me now or I beat up your dad? And so, what, Nathan steps in and then he also takes a hiding?" In the silence that followed, Wild played with the hypothesis in his head and found a golden nugget. Say it *was* true . . . "That would put Nathan down here from Kilmarnock before his father died, which is not what he's been telling us so far."

Marsh continued memorialising the team's output on a whiteboard. "In any case, the mobile mast data will tell us where the phone was, immediately prior to Porter's murder. And where is his bloody shotgun?"

Wild stood up again. "I don't see it," he blurted out. "I mean, yeah, it would make sense to take his gun if you used it, but how would it have gotten to the field in the first place? It'd have to be a burglary in advance or someone collected him and his gun. Either way, that'd be premeditated."

Marsh waggled her marker pen the way a cat flicks its tail. She closed her eyes. "Okay then, anybody . . . why take the bloody gun if it's not the murder weapon?"

Ben Galloway coughed. "I'll try the phone company again." He left them to it.

Marsh turned to — and on — Wild. "Have you been overworking him? He's not his usual chirpy self."

Wild seized the moment. "Maybe his car got scratched." The tension in the room was palpable. Wild allowed himself a sly smile. *And the case rests for the prosecution.*

Marsh snapped the lid back on her marker pen. "Right, chop chop. Let's move this investigation along. You," she pointed randomly, "bank records." She turned slowly, playing spin the bottle with orders. "You, speak to the local force in Kilmarnock. Find out whether Nathan Porter is known to them for anything, even as a witness. After all, we know he's not squeaky clean." As if cueing herself, she turned at last to Wild. "And you're with me — I have a special job for you."

Out on the stairway she issued her instructions. "Nathan's phone is unlocked, right, so get a message to this G-man telling him you want to make a payment in person."

"Isn't that entrapment?"

"No. We're not accusing him of anything at this point. But he might shed light on our investigation. Take a uniformed officer. Take Marnie along — she seems to be more tolerant of you than some at the station."

"Glad you've noticed that too. I was beginning to feel paranoid."

"Craig, you don't need a psychology degree to read people." She paused for a moment. "Sorry. That was inappropriate. Forget I said it."

"Already forgotten."

"See, DCI Rodin was right — you are a fast learner."

Wild swallowed his contempt. So much for Londoners sticking together. In his case, Rodin had just stuck him on a train.

CHAPTER 16

Wild kept the message short and sweet: *I have money, can we meet today?*

He figured the G-man would jump at the opportunity, and if his hunch was right that meant a second appearance from the courtyard musician. In the meantime he put Ben Galloway in charge of Nathan's mobile. "Let me know the second you get a response." Galloway didn't look too thrilled at babysitting a phone, but tough luck. On the plus side, the bank came through in a couple of hours with Nathan's statements. They showed a steady flow of mostly regular payments to the same account, usually in blocks of fifty pounds.

Wild's mobile bleeped for attention. Olsen had texted that she was going off shift. He rang her straight back. "Where are you? Have you left the building?"

"I'm heading out the door. I haven't forgotten about your IT issues."

"Wait there, I'm coming down." He took the stairs in twos, narrowly avoiding a collision with one of the admin staff. As he reached the car park, Olsen was fastening her biker's jacket.

"What was so urgent that it couldn't wait?"

He tried to catch his breath. "Two things. I might have an opportunity for you to do some real police work later." He grinned, still struggling. "And secondly, I wanted to fix a time for my computer. But the first thing might get in the way of the second thing."

"Will I need to change back out of civvies?"

"No, what you've got on is fine for blending in. You could say we're going on a stakeout." Yeah, he thought to himself, you could if you were desperate.

"Should I hang around, then?"

That was the question and of course he didn't know the answer, or how far away she lived. He mulled it over for two seconds. "Tell you what, I'll call you. Be ready to go — if you wouldn't mind."

She nodded, satisfied with his offer, and put her helmet on. Wild went back inside.

Galloway was practically incubating Nathan's mobile phone. Wild startled him. "Any joy?"

Galloway looked thoughtful for a moment, as if he hadn't quite made up his mind. Wild had seen that face before — on suspects. Galloway was hiding something, he'd bet his stripes on it. He checked that no one else was in the vicinity.

"Have you got something to say?" He followed Galloway's gaze to the phone, like guilty gravity. "Or do I need to put the mobile back on the machine?"

Galloway caved. "Can I trust you, Skip?"

Wild looked into his earnest face and decided to take a chance. "Is Nathan's phone fully charged? Let's take this conversation somewhere more private."

Galloway followed him out to the car park. Wild figured that even if they were on CCTV — in which case surely his car vandal would have been caught by now — at least no one could hear them.

"Come on then, out with it. What are you not telling me?"

Galloway's face hardened. "It's nothing. I think I'll leave it unless it becomes relevant." He handed Wild the mobile.

An email from the G-man had come in five minutes earlier: *7.30 tonight.* Wild did his thinking on the hoof and typed back *Where,* while Galloway looked on, open-mouthed.

The G-man wasted little time: *The Wheatsheaf. Ring me when you get there and I'll come outside.* The postscript was the real surprise: *Sorry about your dad.*

Wild offered the phone back to Galloway who declined. "I'll hold on to it then, and if you change your mind about talking to me, let me know."

Although the bank statements showed evidence of money being transferred regularly, they gave no clues as to the recipient. Wild already had solid suspicions — he was suspicious by nature.

DI Marsh was waiting for them inside. "I didn't think either of you smoked, so where have you been?"

Wild pushed Galloway on through with a hand at his shoulder and adopted the conciliatory tone that had never worked with his superiors in London. "I was spending a little quality time with one of the team."

"Well, make sure you remember which side of the divide you're on. I don't take well to my sergeants keeping secrets."

"Understood, ma'am. By the way, Marnie is off shift now and I'd really like the opportunity to speak to her before we go looking for the guitar man. Could you spare me for an hour? If anything comes up, I'm on my mobile."

She sighed through her nose, like an angry horse. "Fine, only be quick about it."

Wild was on the phone to Olsen before he reached his car. "Hi, it's me again — give me a call when you pick this up. I'm heading home now. Can you get there as soon as? Cheers."

CHAPTER 17

Perhaps Wild should have been surprised to see Olsen's motorbike outside his house when he arrived. He wasn't, though. He knew how keen she was to show her capabilities. And if that meant tear-arsing across town, so be it. Logically, she must have lived relatively close to his place, but that didn't stop him taking the piss.

"There's probably a career for you in traffic, policing the motorways."

She gave as good as she got. "I hope not. I'd much rather be a detective like you — the hours seem shorter and the expectations lower."

He let her have that one without comment and unlocked the door, flashing a grin so she knew he didn't have the hump. He went straight to the kitchen and put the kettle on. When he returned, she was looking at his bookcase.

"You must like your own company. Most of these books look like they've seen better days and you have an impressive DVD collection."

Own company. That was a joke but the right marriage to the wrong woman had eventually taken care of that.

"If I told you the truth you wouldn't believe me."

She turned and smiled. "Try me."

"Tell you what, you want to be a detective . . . you come up with a plausible theory while I make the tea."

When he returned she was seated in the armchair, hands threaded together like a mafioso.

He put the tea down and switched on his computer. "And your conclusion is?"

"I reckon you bought the lot at an auction, or maybe someone died and left them to you and you can't bear to part with them. I can't see otherwise how anyone would be into science-fiction, military history, autobiographies, and Jane Austen."

He handed her some chocolate. "Not bad, Miss Marple. Although the truth is sadder than that. One of Steph's many complaints," he enjoyed saying her name aloud, like tempting the Devil to appear, "was that I didn't read enough. Magazines sure, but never books. So what I did — and still do from time to time — is visit charity shops and buy three or four books, usually on the same theme."

"So why don't you take them back once you've read them?"

He took a sip of near-scalding hot tea and tried to look enigmatic.

"Because you haven't actually read them!" She blew sharply across her tea like a gunslinger.

"In my defence, I have two or three books on the go on my bedside cabinet. I can prove it."

"There is no need." She blushed and so did he. "Anyway," she stared at the floor, "what was so urgent that you needed me to come over straightaway?"

Wild broke off some chocolate. "I have this IT situation and I can't exactly ask technical support at work." He sipped more hot tea. "Supposing you wanted to track someone down on Skype, how would you do it? All I've got is a Skype ID — and her name of course." He could see Olsen's brows knitting furiously, like a grandmother in a handicraft competition.

"If this is some sort of online romance thing . . . only I'm really not comfortable—"

"No, nothing like that. This is genuine police work. Basically, I'm in contact with someone over Skype. She was a potential witness back in London and then she went into hiding somewhere. I'm concerned for her safety and all I have is her ID."

"Well, why don't you pass it on to your London contacts and let them deal with it?"

He saw how she scrutinised his face. She really would go far. "It's complicated. The woman in question, she Skypes me from time to time. She's a possible lead to a suspect in a case I was working on before my transfer. Call it unfinished business."

Her eyes widened. "And *that's* why they moved you on?"

He bristled. "How do you know it wasn't my decision?"

She bit into her chocolate. "It doesn't take a degree in psychology to know when someone's been press-ganged."

"You do know that comes from military history?"

"Yeah, I read books too!"

"Come on, Marnie, can you help me?"

He logged into his computer.

She waited for a signal before coming over to help. "I don't know how au fait you are with computers?"

"I just need it done. I'm not interested in learning how."

"Out of your chair then and stand back!" Without another word, she disabled his webcam and mic before going into Skype. There was a single contact, inactive but online. "That's a good start."

He watched, impressed and vaguely amused. If this was modern policing he belonged with the dinosaurs. He wasn't quite so impressed when his contact's status went from yellow to green. A message flashed onscreen in capitals: WHAT'S GOING ON? YOU SAID YOU'D ONLY USE THIS SKYPE ID FOR ME AND WE'RE NOT TALKING TODAY.

Olsen glanced to her left at Wild's incredulous face and quickly replied: SORRY NEEDED TO LET YOU KNOW MY COMPUTER IS IFFY.

"Iffy?"

"Sshhh, I'm typing." NEED TO GET IT REPAIRED SO OFFLINE FOR A COUPLE OF DAYS. An icon showed the other party typing, so Olsen used the time to access the full username and then check it on a Skype IP Resolver before the next message came through.

I'LL CONTACT YOU WHEN I HAVE SOMETHING TO TELL YOU. DON'T DO THIS AGAIN. I MEAN IT.

Olsen logged off while Wild was still doing a goldfish impression.

He peered at the screen. "Now what?"

"We enter the IP address here." She tapped in the digits with alarming speed. "Now see." A small map appeared on the lower half the screen.

Wild was no geographer but even he could tell it was London. "And is that definite?"

"Yes." She opened a word document and pasted in the Skype username and IP address. "But if she contacts you from somewhere else, the IP address will change because of the location."

"So, can you zoom in and get the street address?"

She laughed. "It doesn't work that way."

"So what's the bloody point then?"

"The point is that you know she's in London. More to the point," she opened another tab on his search engine, "people are notoriously lazy. They're creatures of habit, so unless she is very clever," and one look at his face told her that probably wasn't the case, "she'll keep that username or something very similar to it for other applications. You know, social media — that sort of thing. I'm assuming you've already searched her on the common social media sites?"

"Now and again," he admitted. "But I try to avoid breaking my part of the deal."

"And may I ask what information she has provided?"

"Not much really, truth be told. She said Tony — the bloke I'm interested in — was still at large in the London area, so she was keeping a low profile somewhere else. Makes it all the more strange that she'd be Skyping me from the big smoke." He glanced at his watch. "Not wishing to sound ungrateful, but how much longer will this take? Only I promised DI Marsh I'd get back to the station as soon as possible and I didn't expect it to be this involved — no offence."

Olsen rested her mug of tea on her knee. "I've got a friend from uni. Unlike me, she managed to get a job in computer science. You know, big data, that sort of thing?" One look at him told her that he was clueless. "Anyway, if you wanted — and no pressure here — I can ask her to do some online searches for similar usernames on all the major online applications and platforms. She can run AI bots to look at variants and key character replacements. It might save some time. I can't promise anything, mind, but if you wanted I could talk to her."

"Can she keep her mouth shut?" He cringed even as he said the words. It was a reflex, born out of the nagging sense that he was very probably pissing in the wind. "Sorry, that came out wrong. I'm sure you trust your friend. It's just that it's a sensitive situation and I'm not exactly on the case any more."

"None taken." She sipped her tea. "And don't worry about my friend — she works in the private sector and the firm has a contract with the Home Office. So really this is like an add-on to her day job."

He stepped back and finished his tea with a gulp. "Okay, ask your boffin friend and let's see what she comes up with. I don't want her discussing this with anyone else, and the same goes for you."

She scribbled away in her notebook without looking round. "Understood."

He thought she sounded pissed off. He could live with that. Maybe if she came up with something he'd tell her more. It wasn't as if he had many options left.

CHAPTER 18

Nathan's phone buzzed with another text: *Have the police spoken to you?*

Wild weighed up the odds. Delay too long and the G-man might ring, or suspect the worst. Give too much away and he might do a runner. He kept it short: *Yes. Can't say too much now. Can we meet earlier — six?*

Olsen was still getting her coat on as the reply pinged back: *Six fifteen. Still Wheatsheaf.*

"Marnie, we're on. Do you want to leave your bike here?"

He phoned DI Marsh to pass on the good news. She sounded less than enthusiastic, although she did assure him it was his call. The way that she showed her ire was to send Ben Galloway over as backup.

The three of them rendezvoused a few streets away from the pub at five thirty.

"What's the plan then, Skip?" Galloway talked like he'd been binge-watching the Dave channel.

"Nothing heavy." Wild paused to look at Galloway's lapdog expression — the heaviest thing about it would be his weight. "We simply want to eliminate him from our enquiries."

Galloway looked up to some unseen corner of his own mind. "Maybe we should all split up?"

Olsen stared at him, so Wild spoke for her. "Well, *yeah.*"

Wild studied Galloway's street map and did his planning on the hoof, surprised to find that he was enjoying himself. It reminded him of cases in London. That camaraderie when all the boys in blue were in it together, like the time CID and uniform had worked for thirty-six hours straight in order to nab a gang of card scammers. Happy days.

Mindful that he thought he'd already seen the G-man in the café courtyard, Wild thought it best to keep his distance. This guy was coming to collect some money so how hard could it be to collar him for questioning? "Tell you what, Ben, you cover the front so you can clock anyone on their way in, once I've rung him to come out again." He could see Olsen studying him, awaiting her turn. "Here." He handed her a fiver. "Find a corner in the bar and make that last. Stay glued to your phone and watch the door. Meantime, I'll hang about *here.*" He dabbed a fingernail against the map.

Olsen raised an eyebrow. "In the Crown?"

"It's a sacrifice I'm willing to make."

Wild pushed the pub door open and stepped into a world he'd known all his working life. Places where people like him found refuge from the pressures of the job and the strains of unhappy marriages. Steph had often remarked on his ability to compartmentalise. He'd never brought the job home, no, he'd kept it company in the pub instead. Conversely, one of the worst insults she had hurled at him before the big bang was that his work could be sloppy. Granted, he hadn't had her laser-like focus, but he put in the hours and did the right thing — most of the time.

He ordered half a pint at the bar, ignored the sneer and kept the change for himself. No chance of a window seat unfortunately. He kept his phone close, alternating between the blue glow of his screen and an unobstructed view of the window. If he was right and the G-man was indeed the same ponytailed bastard from the café, it was a fair bet he would use the same car park as before. And if that were the case this was one of the routes he might take on his way to the Wheatsheaf.

Wild spotted his phone had faded back to the screen-saver, so he woke it up. Galloway's text: *Nothing yet Skip* did little to calm his nerves. That familiar tension again. He deliberated for a nanosecond and then clipped a pill into his hand, washing it down with beer. He was on the point of replying to Galloway when a call came through from Olsen. She spoke casually, against a background cacophony of pub chatter, the clink of glasses, and second-rate jukebox music.

"It's me. Listen, I'm in the pub so I might be a bit late."

It took Wild a moment to figure out what she was doing.

"No, I won't stay long. Honestly, it's fine. I've seen another single woman here so it's perfectly safe."

He pulled the phone closer. "Does she look comfortable there?"

"Yeah!" Olsen laughed. "Of course. And waiting for some-one? Uh huh. That's easy, two glasses with different drinks. Hold on a second . . ."

Wild heard a chair scraping and then rustling before Olsen's voice kicked in again, a little distant this time.

"Excuse me, would you like my seat? I'm going off soon and you look like you're waiting for someone."

"No, that's okay." The other woman sounded nervous.

Olsen's voice became louder. "No, I said so," she played the part of a girlfriend under siege. "I'm talking to a girl — oh, for God's sake." She delivered her half of the imaginary dialogue perfectly before the sound dipped, suggesting she'd held the phone away from her face again. "My bloody boy-friend. Honestly, sometimes I don't know why I bother."

"If everything's okay there I'll clear the line for Galloway."

"Yeah, me too. See you later." She dropped the call.

Wild stared at the screen, willing Galloway to get his arse in gear and provide an update. When wishing didn't work, Wild finished his half of lager and returned the empty glass to the bar. As he glanced up at the pub window, a shadowy fig-ure ran past like a bat out of hell, away from the Wheatsheaf. It was a foregone conclusion. By the time Wild made it to the pub door he was left gazing into the middle distance. A younger and fitter cop, maybe someone like Olsen, would probably have been able to chase down the suspect. But Wild knew his limitations, down to the last kilogramme.

It had started raining, pub lights reflecting on the tarmac like a drinker's mirage. And still no word from Galloway. He took a slow, plodding walk up the street, pondering how best to receive Galloway's failure. Wild was no expert, but it didn't take a workshop on body language to realise that Ben Galloway looked shiftier than a burglar who's just spotted the CCTV.

In the few hundred steps over to the Wheatsheaf, Wild decided to lead the debrief with: "So what the bloody hell happened?"

Galloway stood before him, rain running down his face, as if he were too frightened to leave his post. "I dunno, Skip. I saw someone approach the top of the street and maybe he saw me — maybe I looked too obvious. Anyway, before I could even get a good look at him he turned and started running."

Wild phoned Olsen and she picked up on the second ring. "One question. Has the woman taken out her phone at any point? Or maybe she left your sight and went to the ladies?"

"No, she hasn't. Not for a second, thank you very much. As it is, I'm crossing my legs. Why, what's happened?"

"It's a no-show. Somehow the suspect got wind that we were there."

"Well, it wasn't me. Maybe he saw you at the Crown?" She paused and sighed. "What do you want me to do about . . . you know who? She seems pretty nervous now, keeps looking towards the door. The second drink is still waiting."

"Stay there. I'm coming in."

Wild hadn't planned on making a scene in the Wheatsheaf. On the balance of probabilities, the woman had been sent in advance, though she could be guilty of nothing more than arousing an overeager PC's suspicions. Galloway followed him in with all the reluctance of a forensic officer approaching a blocked toilet.

Olsen caught his eye straight away and directed him to the woman at the bar. Wild smiled to himself. He thought the voice had sounded familiar: Pauline Henderson, IT woman extraordinaire. She shrank back at the sight of them. As Wild reached her, Olsen pointed to the ladies and made a hasty departure.

Pauline looked first to Wild and then to Galloway.

"Hello again." Wild kept it informal, conscious that they were in a public place.

A muffled phone rang and Pauline immediately reached into her coat pocket.

Wild touched her arm and applied a light pressure. "Best not to answer that right now. You might want to finish your drinks — we're leaving shortly."

Olsen reappeared and, at Wild's cue, escorted Pauline outside. She stumbled on the cobbles and Wild rushed in to make the save.

"Steady now, Pauline, we only want to have a private chat. Have you ever been in trouble with the police before?"

She shook her head violently, as if she were shaking off a wasp. "No, never. I only sent an email on, that's all — I didn't mean any harm by it."

"Best wait until the interview."

Pauline brightened a little when she saw Ben Galloway, although he didn't share the sentiment as he escorted her while Wild and Olsen walked on ahead.

Wild kept his voice low. "Marnie, you're sure she never touched her phone?"

"Positive, Craig."

Interesting. Wild pointed along the street in the direction of the car, consumed by three questions: How had the G-man known to do a runner? Where was he now? And why he was so willing to leave Pauline behind if he'd only expected Nathan Porter? Then again, maybe they could use that to their advantage in the interview.

CHAPTER 19

Wild drove back to Mayberry police station with Olsen and Pauline Henderson on board, glancing periodically at Ben Galloway in the car behind. If it were possible for a police officer, Galloway had a permanent look of guilt on his face. Maybe he had something to feel guilty about. Wild was determined to find out one way or another. When they reached the station, he left Pauline in the care of the constables and zipped upstairs to see DI Marsh. She wasn't exactly thrilled by the fruits of his labours, more intrigued.

"Ma'am, perhaps you ought to lead the interview with Pauline Henderson? Marnie could sit in with you, given that she was present when we pulled Pauline in."

"And what, in the meantime you and Ben Galloway get your story straight about who's to blame for losing the actual person of interest?"

He knew what he should have said: 'No, as the senior officer I take full responsibility.' But he fudged it, saying he wanted to get Galloway's perspective and then talk to her about it afterwards.

"I still haven't made up my mind about you, Craig. You've either got hidden depths or you're playing some game nobody else is in." She opened the drawer and changed her glasses. "Go on then, I'll bite. I'll take Marnie in with me — it'll be good experience for her. You scoot off and have your little boys' chat and I'll see you when I'm done."

He thanked her on the way out. The changing of the guard downstairs was an awkward affair. Pauline waived her right to a solicitor. Wild figured, as he went back outside with Galloway, that she was probably terrified of getting her employers involved. Not good for business if your boss's business was the law.

Wild was beginning to enjoy the car park. He stood beside Galloway, surprised to see a lighter and cigarettes emerge from his jacket.

"I didn't know you smoked, Ben." He waved away Galloway's offer to join him at a future chest clinic appointment and waited until Galloway was engrossed in his fag. "Right, shall we cut the crap? The G-man was a no-show, except I saw him running the other way. So, either you stuck out like a sore thumb, or he recognised you somehow, or you warned him off. Because Pauline didn't even send him a text from the pub."

Galloway stayed quiet, drawing on his cigarette while he stared at his feet.

An idea came to Wild, as brilliant as it was poisonous. "Do you want to tell me what's going on, or would you prefer I confiscate your phone and stick it on the kiosk machine to see what calls and texts you've made in the past half hour?"

For a committed smoker, Galloway went a funny shade of green and started coughing his guts up. Wild let him get it out of his system.

"Is this going to cost me my job?"

"I dunno, not until you tell me what you've done."

Galloway took out another cigarette, faltered, and then shoved it back in the box. "Alright, so I sort of know this G-man. His name's Jeb Walsh. He was in the same school, two years above me. He's basically harmless."

"And you tipped him off, outside the pub?"

Galloway didn't respond, so Wild carried on fishing. "So what's the score — do you owe him money?"

Galloway shook his head. "No. He . . . er . . . well, he got me some grass recently."

"Congratulations, Ben, you are a complete moron."

"You telling me you've never tried it?"

"Not buying it from someone I went to school with, as a serving police officer."

"So what happens now, Skip?"

"I don't know. I can't see that there are many options."

"Look, I can take you to Jeb. I know where he lives. He's not dangerous — the two of us could go right now. That's got to count for something, hasn't it?"

Wild glanced behind them, where two coppers were heading through the door. "Okay, I'll leave word for Marsh at the front desk."

Wild drove while Galloway gave directions. Galloway changed before his eyes, no longer merely a nephew of a uniformed sergeant or the local boy who made CID. It wasn't exactly depth but another side to Galloway that at the very least made him more interesting. Besides, as Wild reflected on the largely silent drive over to Jeb's place, he was never happier than when he had a problem to solve.

CHAPTER 20

The house was much grander than the poky little cottage Wild had expected. The drive held two cars but had room enough for another three. Wild recognised Jeb's car from the car park, after he'd followed him from the Labyrinth café. There was no plan other than to gain access to the property and ask some questions, but the last thing Wild expected was for Jeb to answer the doorbell.

He didn't seem surprised to see them. "You'd better come in."

Galloway hesitated at the threshold. Wild nudged him in and a plaintive voice called out from along the hallway.

"Have we got visitors? We weren't expecting anyone."

Jeb eased a door open. "Just some friends of mine, Grandad. They're not stopping long." The television volume went up and a door closed.

"I, er, live with my grandparents — they brought me up. Come through to the kitchen, it's warmer there." Jeb stopped and squinted at Wild. "You're police as well, then?"

Wild was in no mood for friendly banter. "Well I'm not a bloody social worker. Nathan sends his apologies — unavoidably detained."

Jeb grinned. "I thought it was too good to be true — Nathan coming up with money at short notice like that, before the funeral and everything. I said as much to Pauline, only I never turn down an offer of easy money. You know that, right, Ben?"

Galloway sank into an old wooden chair that Wild had down as an antique. Jeb leaned against the cream-coloured range, hands behind his head, and stretched. He may as well have strutted like a peacock.

Wild wasn't in the mood. "You haven't asked what we're doing here."

Jeb's eyes dulled, the way a dog's face blanks when it looks like it's thinking. "Is Pauline okay?"

"She's in custody, if that's what you mean. We picked her up after your disappearing act." He spotted eye contact between Galloway and Jeb.

Jeb's face reddened. "Yeah, I was all set to meet up with Nathan, and Pauline went on ahead. Then I started having second thoughts . . ."

Wild thought he'd seen better acting in a third-rate soap opera. "You're full of shit. Get your coat."

"I'll just have a quick word with Nan and Grandad." Jeb didn't wait for permission.

Wild searched in his jacket pocket for a mint. Have you been here before, Ben? Recently I mean."

"No, Skip. Not for years."

Wild sucked hard on a mint. "Right, two things: one, for fuck's sake stop calling me Skip — it makes me sound like a sheepdog. And two, are you really telling me that you bought grass from Jeb out on the street?"

Galloway blinked slowly as if he'd been punched. "No, I'm not saying that. I met him up at the abbey ruins. We all used to go there in our teens." His eyes softened. "It was just a bit of puff."

"And when did this act of genius take place?"

Galloway gulped hard, as if he'd swallowed a brick. His hand gripped the edge of the table. "That's the thing,

DS Wild. It happened the night Alexander Porter was murdered."

Wild stared into space, rather than give in to the urge to knock some sense into Galloway. "And when you say the night . . . ?"

"I don't know *exactly*. But definitely after ten o'clock. I only came back from training that afternoon. I just thought what the hell, live a bit, you know? I didn't see as there'd be any harm."

By now Wild was leaning against the Aga, warming his back while he massaged his temples. "You do realise what you've done?" One look at Galloway confirmed the worst. Of course he didn't. Wild offered him a mint. "You've probably given Jeb an alibi for the time of the crime, and as soon as he puts that in a statement, you are royally screwed. On the plus side," he crunched his own mint, "at least it rules him out as a suspect, so your career sacrifice isn't a total waste."

Galloway looked up like a startled rabbit and for a moment Wild thought there would be tears. Not on his watch. "Pull yourself together. We have to figure out a way through this."

Wild heard voices in the hallway. He signalled to the door and Galloway followed him out. Jeb was waiting. As the three of them reached the front door, Jeb's grandmother poked her head out of the lounge.

"Don't forget your jacket, Jeb. We'll wait up for you. Is Pauline coming over tonight?"

Jeb became a twelve-year-old again, trying to save face in front of his mates. "No, Nan. Don't fuss, and don't bother waiting up."

"Righto," she beamed, as they were halfway out the door. "Have a lovely time."

Jeb let out a heavy sigh and turned to Wild. "*Am* I coming back tonight? If not, I'd like to let them know."

Wild took out his car keys. "We'll see."

By the time they were back on the road, Jeb had regained his self-confidence. Wild was half surprised he hadn't brought along his guitar for the performance.

"I dunno what you think you've got on me," Jeb leaned forward a little from the backseat. "Only, Benny boy and me, we've got a bit of a connection that might change your mind."

Wild shot a glance to Galloway and there was something in the response that prompted if not pity then a glimmer of empathy. He put his foot down as he navigated the lane, farm gates flashing by.

Jeb found it all very amusing. "Steady on, mate, you're not in London now."

Wild shifted down a gear and as he approached a pulling-in point muttered to Galloway, "Brace," before pulling sharp left and hitting the brakes. The car slid through muddy tracks and ended on the verge. A few seconds later a tractor rumbled by, the driver shaking his head in disbelief. Wild unclipped his seatbelt and twisted round to face the rear passenger.

"Shut your mouth or I'll come over there and do it for you."

Jeb's face took a puncture. He tried furiously to open the rear door, despite still having a seatbelt on. Nothing doing.

"Central locking, dumb arse."

Jeb paled and Wild followed his line of sight to Galloway's impression of acute embarrassment.

"Don't waste your time looking at him, it's me you need to worry about. Let's cut to the chase, shall we? You might say that Ben Galloway bought cannabis from you on the night that Alexander Porter died. And I'll say that Detective Constable Galloway was pursuing enquiries about alleged drug dealing in the local community. And while we are all busy arguing the toss, my detective friends will be ripping your lovely grandparents' house apart, along with their precious grandson's reputation. And that's just for starters. Do we understand one another?"

Jeb gave a feeble nod. Galloway's face resembled a dustpan without a brush. Wild turned round and put his seatbelt back on. He could still feel his nerve endings singing in unison, like a sub-dermal hallelujah chorus. He was back in the game.

He restarted the car. "So, Jeb, this is how it's going to go down. We will interview you about Nathan Porter and whether you can shed any light on the death of his father. For the purposes of the interview, I don't give a shit what deals you do as far as grass is concerned, as long as you're not supplying to kids. But don't think I won't come back to your house with just cause if there's even a hint that you are trading in or supplying anything else. Are we clear?"

Jeb spoke to the rear-view mirror. "I don't know anything about Nathan's dad's death. And that's God's honest truth. Well, I know they didn't exactly get on, what with his dad's drinking over the years and Nathan's gambling. But all I've done is lend them both money and then chase them up for payment. That's all I have to say."

"Save it for the police station."

* * *

Wild and Galloway were minutes into a formal interview, where Jeb had immediately waived his right to a solicitor, when somebody knocked on the door. Wild was pleasantly surprised to see Marnie Olsen enter the room with a folded note in her hand. He spoke aloud in a contrived voice for the benefit of the recording. "PC Olsen has entered the room with a note for DS Wild." He opened the paper barely wide enough to read it, as if shielding it from the CCTV. "This interview is now suspended while I attend to a related matter. PC Olsen will remain in the room until my return."

Olsen hovered by his vacated chair, uncertain whether she ought to sit down. He left her to figure it out for herself. As Wild closed the interview room door behind him, DI Marsh's frame filled the end of the corridor like a spectre. She beckoned him towards her with an icy finger.

"How are you getting on with Jeb Walsh?"

He tried to stay cool under her scrutiny. "So far he has confirmed he lent money to Nathan and also to his dad in the past. It seems that Alexander Porter was trying to help pay off his son's debts."

"And Nathan's bruises?"

"Jeb says that he and Nathan had a bit of a drunken altercation, that there was no assault because Nathan gave as good as he got, and that Nathan will back him up. Unless Nathan was too pissed to remember, in which case Jeb is fairly certain there were witnesses in the pub."

"And that pub was?"

"The Wheatsheaf, where we picked up Pauline Henderson." He tried his best smile. "I don't think you pulled me out of the interview to ask how it was going. What's up?"

"New information has come to light, following a disclosure by Pauline Henderson." DI Marsh waved a tired hand across her forehead. "Let's go get some machine coffee." She waited at the stairs so they could walk side by side. "I hardly know where to begin. According to Pauline Henderson, an email came to the solicitors where she works, a few weeks ago, enquiring about a US soldier who was stationed locally in the run-up to D-Day."

She waited expectantly at the machine until Wild cottoned on that he would be paying.

"With sugar, thanks. So, the relative of this GI emailed asking for any information about him. Apparently, Pauline hasn't exactly been 'discreet employee of the month.' She forwarded the email to Jeb and then deleted any record of it. Jeb smelt money and started communicating with the great-nephew, swapping emails and setting himself up as a private investigator."

Wild sipped his tea and extended a hand, palm upwards as encouragement. "I dunno, taking money under false pretences?"

"Ah, you see that's just it. We have no evidence so far that money has ever changed hands, but this," she waved her hand in the air, "distant relative has travelled all the way here."

"On the strength of an email?"

"That's what Pauline Henderson wants us to believe."

"Nah, I can't see it. There has to be more to it than that."

"And *that's* why I wanted you out of the room."

Wild did his thinking aloud. "So what's the relevance, if any, to the death of Alexander Porter?"

DI Marsh smiled. "Let's just call it an unknown factor. Maybe it's a coincidence and maybe it's nothing at all, but it's going up on the whiteboard. This American has been in contact with Jeb, and Jeb has loaned money to both Nathan and his dad, and Nathan's dad is dead."

"So you want me to go back into the interview and confront Jeb about this Yank?"

Marsh threw him a kindly smile, the sort a crocodile might offer a wildebeest midway across the river. "Not quite. I want to speak to Jeb myself to find out the Yank's whereabouts and then I want you to go and see him. I'm also thinking of releasing Nathan Porter, unless there's any more information on his phone that could assist our inquiry in other directions."

Wild's eyes widened. This was starting to feel like professional collaboration. "I say let him go, keep the other two in and put the pressure on Pauline. She has more to lose, both her reputation and her job at Hollings & Gresham where her aunt also works. All I know about Jeb is that he lives in a nice house with his grandparents — any idea what they did for a living, by the way?"

Marsh got up from the canteen chair. "Dr James Walsh was the local GP, like his father before him. Their son and his wife died when Jeb was still a toddler so they brought him up. Imagine how disappointed they must've been. He works when he feels like it and lives on their generosity the rest of the time."

Wild smiled. *If only you knew.* It took him a few seconds to realise that he'd been ousted from his own interview. So be it. He figured he'd use the free time to catch up on paperwork and continue his own research project: Operation Which-bastards-scratched-my-car.

He was professionalism personified when it came time to release Nathan Porter. As he'd anticipated, the good news caught Nathan off guard.

He sounded humbled, as though Wild had personally done him a favour.

"You . . . you're letting me go? Thanks, I really appreciate it."

Wild knew they had no evidence to charge him with anything. A lack of emotion was hardly a crime. If that were the case, Steph would be awaiting sentence in the case of the slaughtered marriage. He didn't bother explaining the extra communication with Jeb Walsh on Nathan's mobile — Nathan would figure it out soon enough. And if he wanted to make a complaint, so be it. On balance, though, Nathan would probably have his hands full with the funeral. Assuming the body had nothing left to tell the pathologist.

Wild wondered whether Nathan's release would spark an attack of conscience — not that he was expecting any last minute disclosures. His expectations were fulfilled. Nathan scurried out of the station and looked skyward. Wild watched him from the doorway, slightly distracted by a man at the desk complaining that in the twenty-first century he shouldn't have to produce his driving documents in person. There was always one unhappy customer.

Later, while Wild was updating the case on the whiteboard, a door swung at the far end of the room. He glanced to his left to see Sergeant Galloway approaching. For once, the team room was virtually empty, bar one of the admin staff feverishly inputting data. Wild nodded to the sergeant and they played a game of handshake top trumps.

The sergeant looked flustered. "Hello there, erm . . ."

"Craig or Wild, either is fine."

"So how is it all going, Craig?"

Against his better judgement, Wild stood to one side and introduced the board. "I feel like we're missing important pieces of the puzzle. That's why it's been invaluable working with Ben — you can't beat local knowledge."

Sergeant Galloway's chest visibly swelled. "That's good to hear. And like I said when we met—" He looked across at the admin person, who hadn't strayed from his task, and then lowered his voice. "We're all in this together so if I can be of *any* assistance . . ."

Wild murmured encouragingly. The last time he'd heard that they were all in it together was 2008, when a bunch of bankers watched the ship go down from the comfort of their luxury escape yacht. His mobile rang, delivering the name of a small hotel where the American visitor might be staying. He made a note of the details while Sergeant Galloway awaited his attention. "Listen, I need to go and speak with someone who's visiting the area of our investigation — an American tourist." He flashed a note in front of Sergeant Galloway. "I don't suppose you've run into him on your travels? It'd be helpful to get some background before I give him the knock."

The sergeant shook his head. "I can ask around the uniforms. It would be no trouble at all. I could even come with you if you like?"

Wild gave it a moment's consideration. "Yeah, alright then."

Sergeant Galloway liked to talk. And talk he did. About Ben and how he'd made the transition from uniform into CID, and all about the local communities, in ways that Wild hadn't expected. Twenty minutes in a car and Wild understood so much more about rural life in all its pettiness, its formality and the dignity it placed on tradition and the family. It was the next best thing to learning a foreign language.

He threw the sergeant a bone or two, referring to his years as a copper in London and, in a show of camaraderie and balance, reinforced all his colleague's preconceptions about metropolitan life.

"Now, don't get me wrong, Craig," Sergeant Galloway waxed lyrical, "I know that there are more opportunities in big cities, especially for people with ambition — like our

Ben. But I can't see as how so many people living cheek by jowl and squeezed into housing estates can do anything other than breed alienation and crime."

Wild would have conceded the point had he not prepared a comeback. "I've been here less than a month and I've seen vehicle theft, antisocial behaviour and much more." He fixed the sergeant with a momentary stare. "Not forgetting the murder of Alexander Porter."

"I hear what you're saying, Craig, but I'm still not so sure."

"Oh, it's murder," Wild insisted. "Don't you worry about that."

There were six cars in the hotel car park, and as they arrived a well-dressed couple were unloading cases from the back of a 4x4. Meantime, two darling children threw gravel at one another while Mummy and Daddy tried to ignore them.

"I know what you're thinking," Wild motioned towards the family as he drove past and parked. "Townies, right?"

Sergeant Galloway laughed like a dray horse. "I'm saying nothing without a solicitor present!"

Although they gave the parents a few minutes to get themselves organised and registered, the happy family were still at the front desk as they entered an ornate archway. Wild looked over at the receptionist, who stared back in quiet desperation, and raised his hand to confirm that they were in no hurry. After two rounds of 'Don't touch that' with suitcases getting knocked over, Mummy and Daddy handed over a credit card and then led the goblins upstairs. A middle-aged man in tweed followed them, lugging a case in each hand.

The receptionist glanced at Wild and the uniformed sergeant by his shoulder. "Just the single room is it?" She smiled impishly and Wild found himself smiling back, imagining the sergeant's discomfort.

Wild leaned a little over the desk. "Actually, no," he whispered. "We're here to investigate a crime in hospitality."

The receptionist laughed, the kind of unbridled laughter that only the young can lay claim to. The sergeant came forward and stood beside Wild, his face fierce and formal. The receptionist pressed her hands over the wide expanse of oaken desk. "Sorry. How can I help you gentlemen?"

Wild opened his notebook for effect, always more impressive than reading off the name by memory. "We are looking for an American visitor, who we believe is staying here. It's a Mr Aaron Kravers. Would you like me to spell that for you?"

"No need." She opened a leather-bound book and ran her finger down the two open pages. "Yes, we have Mr Kravers staying here, but he's been out all day." She looked first to the sergeant and then to Wild. "He's not in any sort of trouble, is he? Mr Paxton wouldn't like that."

"And he would be . . . ?"

She stood straighter and tugged a little at her jacket. "Mr Paxton is the proprietor of this establishment. He's just taking some cases upstairs. He'll be down presently."

Wild nodded and pointed over his shoulder, causing Sergeant Galloway to lean out at an alarming angle. "We'll wait over there." They crossed ornate floor tiles to wait beside the double doors. As Wild looked out at the car park and across the gardens, he saw birds darting back and forth, their black shapes reminding him of arrowheads.

Sergeant Galloway watched with him. "The larger ones will be swifts. The smaller ones — see the tails? Those are swallows."

Wild smiled on the inside. So much knowledge. They'd make a country boy of him yet . . . over his dead body. He swung round at the sound of footsteps on the tiles. Mr Paxton brushed dust off his trousers. Wild thought he had the benevolent look of a schoolteacher, if he'd been lucky enough to have teachers like that.

"Sandra tells me you are looking for Aaron Kravers." He walked up to them and gave the car park a cursory glance. "He must have taken his hire car out for a spin. Mr Kravers has been very interested in local history. He has borrowed all sorts of books from my library. I gather one of his antecedents might have been stationed here during the war, as so many of the GIs were."

Wild's curiosity was piqued. "Any thoughts on where he might be?"

Mr Paxton searched the middle distance for inspiration. "Let me see now, I believe he was interested in parish records and he did say he'd be visiting the museum in town. You're welcome to wait . . ." But the way he said it suggested that two police officers by reception, one of them in uniform, was not the image that Paxton's Country Hotel wanted to promote to its clientele.

Wild dispensed with subtlety. "That's okay, we can always come back another time and maybe bring a marked car to park at the front entrance."

Mr Paxton might have given the impression of a country squire who had fallen on hard times, but he was sharp as a fox. He directed his comments to Sergeant Galloway and kept his voice low. "I don't suppose there'd be any harm in letting you see his room, as long as nothing's disturbed."

Sergeant Galloway patted Wild on the back as he walked past to join the hotel proprietor, Wild trailing in their wake. "We appreciate your cooperation, Mr Paxton."

They climbed the stairs to the second floor, where Mr Paxton retrieved a set of keys from his tweed waistcoat. "It's bedroom number fifteen."

Wild followed along the corridor, noting — with some incredulity — that there was no room numbered thirteen.

Mr Paxton turned abruptly and caught his look of surprise. "Ah yes, that was like it before my time, so why change it? Of course it's a quirky talking point for our advertising — some customers can be dreadfully superstitious!"

Wild wondered if they had a ducking stool for the pond as well.

Room fifteen smelt of lavender and furniture polish, despite the bowl of potpourri on the chest of drawers. Some of the room furniture looked antique, or was made to appear so.

Wild took the lead. "Mr Paxton, would you mind waiting outside?" It wasn't up for discussion.

The proprietor swallowed. "Oh right, of course. I'll, er, be in the corridor if you need me. I trust you won't be too long and that you'll put everything back as it was."

Sergeant Galloway reassured him as he ushered him out. "Discretion is our watchword." He closed the door. "Right, Craig, what are we looking for?"

Wild made a start on the drawers, running his hand under the clothes to see what presented itself. "Try the wardrobe." Next, he scoured the three drawers and moved on to the bedside cabinet. In the top drawer he found a small Bible and beneath it some folded A4 pages bearing the hotel's letterhead. Handwritten notes detailed names, phone numbers and questions without answers. Wild laid the pages on the bedspread, photographing them on his phone without bothering to read the details.

Sergeant Galloway closed the wardrobe door. "Done."

Wild looked over his shoulder. "Did you check his shoes?"

Sergeant Galloway sighed and went back to the wardrobe without success. A quick tour of the bathroom — a receptacle for contact lenses, some cleansing solution, a toothbrush and a razor — and they were out of there.

Mr Paxton was waiting at the end of the corridor, a soul of discretion himself, relatively speaking. "We, er, don't have to make this official, do we?"

Sergeant Galloway knew his way around a difficult conversation. "Not at all, sir. Thank you for your time. A pity you weren't able to help us." He winked overdramatically. "We'll be on our way now."

Wild did his thinking on the stairs. "One more thing, Mr Paxton. How long has Aaron Kravers been staying at the hotel?"

"About a week. Actually, I think there have been a few calls for him. We can check with Sandra."

Wild raised an eyebrow at the timing. Downstairs, the receptionist checked the call log on her screen and swivelled it round so Wild could see. He photographed it on his mobile. "Saves time," he explained.

Sergeant Galloway didn't speak again until they passed the sign that thanked visitors and assured them of a warm country welcome. "Are we picking up this Aaron Kravers then?"

"Perhaps, if we knew where to find him. For now though," Wild patted his phone in its cradle, "we probably have what we need."

CHAPTER 21

Wild parted company with Sergeant Galloway on the stairs. He had just sat down at his desk to check and print the phone pictures when one of the team loomed in the doorway. Wild might have felt more comfortable if he'd remembered his name.

"Excuse me, DS Wild, have you spoken with Nathan Porter since you got back?"

"Hardly. I released him earlier."

The DC squirmed. "You might want to rethink that. The mobile phone company finally gave us positional data for Nathan's mobile over the past few days."

"And?"

"He was here the day his father died."

"Bollocks. Can you see if there is an interview room free and then meet me downstairs with a car?"

The DC started walking.

"Hold on a second. Let me make a call first." He dug through his notes and rang Nathan's mobile. "You lied to me — where are you?"

Nathan's tone was flat, dismissive. "I'm with the funeral director. Can it wait?"

Wild thought for a handful of seconds. "No, it bloody can't. You were here the day your father was murdered. Why didn't you mention it?" Wild heard a muttered conversation and then footsteps, followed by a door closing.

"Yes, alright, I came down to see Dad and we had words . . . about money. Years ago he promised me an heirloom and I suggested we sell it to pay back some of the money I owed to him and others. We had a massive row about it and I flew back to Scotland."

Wild's silence did the trick.

"I'll give you the flight details. You can verify everything."

Wild reached for a pen. "Oh, we will." He wrote down the bare bones and then gave Nathan his email address for copies of the mobile boarding passes. "You should have mentioned all this before." He looked over at the DC standing close by, staring into space. "If I find any inconsistencies . . ."

Nathan didn't rise to the bait. "You won't."

Wild shook his head at the DC. He was on the verge of ending the call when inspiration struck. "What exactly is this heirloom?"

Nathan cleared his throat. "It's an antique weapon." He swallowed. "A shotgun."

Wild blew out a long breath silently, and clicked his fingers to get the DC's attention again. They'd need that interview room after all.

CHAPTER 22

Wild's mother always said that nothing brought a family together like a wedding or a funeral, and of the two the latter usually brought out the truth. Consequently, he had high hopes of Alexander Porter's final send-off revealing *something*. From his perspective, the funeral ceremony would be like a suspects' reunion, since all three people so far interviewed — Nathan, Jeb and Pauline — were expected to attend. Nathan had explained — after his return to the police station to discuss a missing antique — that Jeb Walsh had agreed to accompany him on the big day. Hardly the actions of a murderer, Wild reflected, unless Jeb was a very clever one.

DI Marsh had approved a low-key police presence at the event, partly to smooth any ruffled feathers in the community. Although Wild hadn't planned on occupying a pew, he'd dressed up for the occasion with a black suit and tie, and he cleaned the car again the night before. He'd be the sole representative of the constabulary because Marsh made it clear that other officers were needed elsewhere.

Wild arrived early, having already forewarned Nathan he'd be outside. He loitered near the chapel gates, like a spare undertaker in search of business, and watched as Gordon Elleth and Edwin Causly — another tenant farmer Wild recognised from the whiteboard — entered to pay their respects. He recognised some faces from the George too, along with Pauline Henderson. Jeb and Nathan arrived together in Jeb's car, behind the hearse. Wild figured money was still tight and he couldn't see Jeb advancing any more, even in those sad circumstances.

Having kept a respectful distance at the arrivals, Wild held back a few paces from the coffin and followed it up to the threshold, remaining outside as the chapel door closed. He stood on the step with his back to the door, taking in the yew trees and ancient gravestones. It was certainly a fresh take on community policing. Church music filtered through cracks in the door, something suitably mournful that Wild recognised but couldn't name. The dirge faded and a minister, who Wild realised had already been inside, went through his paces. Wild moved closer to the doors, deciding — out of good taste — not to ease one door open. The minister welcomed the congregation, as he called them, and waxed lyrical on the mysteries of life and death. Wild would've called it a recruitment drive, but if Ben Galloway was anything to go by the church already had that pitch sown up.

* * *

Gordon Elleth spoke next. Wild recognised the voice. The eulogy stuck to the Bible, courtesy of Ecclesiastes 3:2 — a time to be born, a time to die. Then again, it was hardly going to be a comedy turn.

After a speech from the late Mr Porter's other tenant farmer, Edwin Causly, and a couple of hymns, the minister cued the congregation up for the procession to the graveside and committal.

Fearing he'd outstayed his welcome, Wild eased his shoulder from the door and trod a path around the chapel to a side gate. So much for his plan. It had always been a long shot, expecting Aaron Kravers to put in an appearance. He paused where he could just about see the funeral procession as they gathered like crows around the abyss, and rang DI Marsh.

"I don't think there is anything more to gain here."

"Fair enough." Marsh's tone conveyed the opposite message. "I can think of better ways to spend taxpayers' money."

He took it on the chin and glanced at his watch. Even coppers in the doghouse were entitled to a tea break, and he knew the perfect place.

The Labyrinth's courtyard was emptier than on his previous visit, especially without Jeb's strolling minstrel act, seeing as he was at the funeral. Wild found no queue inside, only a clear path to the counter and a friendly face. For five seconds, anyway.

"I've got a bone to pick with you!"

He caught the glint in her eye. "What, in a vegetarian café?"

"How come you never called me?"

He felt his cheeks burning. "Sorry?"

"I left you my number on the napkin — opposite the smiley face?"

He fronted it out, rather than admit he'd accidentally squished cake over the napkin and obscured her number. "I've been busy — with work." He smiled sheepishly, but only because he realised the hole he'd just dug. The next question would inevitably be about where he worked, and that would leave a choice of lies or the shutters coming down. He was still wondering how to play it when she saved him the bother.

"I suppose that comes with crime-fighting." She did him the courtesy of watching him flounder. "Word gets around, er . . . ?"

"Craig," he replied. "Or Wild."

She rubbed at one of her earrings and then raised an eyebrow. "And are you?"

"Not by nature." *Not any more, anyway*. He placed an order for tea and cake, and waited to collect it.

"I'm Caitlin, although you'll remember that from when I gave you my number. Actually, I'm due a break soon. I'll come and join you." She passed him his tea and cake.

This was novel. "I'll be upstairs." He still wasn't sure whether she was taking the piss, but he entertained the possibility that she wasn't. He'd just sat down when he heard footsteps by the open doorway.

"Room for a small one?"

He tried to do the smiling thing, only it wasn't his strong suit. Truth be told, after Steph had parachuted out of their matrimonial nosedive he hadn't given any thought to other women. A shame he hadn't been as focused during the marriage.

Wild had chosen the same table as on his previous visit. As soon as Caitlin sat down, he leaned back casually towards the window. "Much quieter here today." He gazed down at the courtyard. "No sign of that musician either." He felt that what he lacked in social skills he made up in guile.

She nodded slowly. "The guitarist? Yeah, very popular is Jeb, especially with the ladies." She sipped her tea, implying it was the only answer on the table.

"What's his story, then?"

She smiled and her eyes crinkled in a way he found very appealing. "Coppers are never off duty, are they? Even an incomer from London!"

"Only after hours."

"Well then, Craig," she said his name as if it were a dare, "maybe we'll put that to the test sometime."

"So, what about el musico?" He thumbed behind him at the window.

"Jeb Walsh? He is mostly harmless. Unless you're ovulating."

Wild paused the fork's journey from cake to mouth.

"He's a bit of a Peter Pan, is Jeb. There are a few lasses locally who have enjoyed his company, and at least two that I know of are paying the price. I doubt his grandparents are aware that they have great-grandchildren in the county. Don't get me wrong, he's not so different from any man, given half a chance." She gave him a beady-eyed stare from the rim of her teacup. "So why the interest in Jeb?"

He went with a half-truth, trusting that Old Man Elleth would forgive him for bearing false witness. "There was a report of two men fighting. From the description, one of them sounds like Jeb."

"Yeah, that top hat is a definite giveaway. From what I heard, the other party gave as good as he got. Now, are we going to spend my break discussing community policing or are we going to fix a date for that drink?"

He fumbled a piece of cake and it bounced off the table to freedom.

"Cat got your tongue, Craig?"

"No, it's, er . . ." he flustered. His finger itched where his wedding ring used to sit. He wondered what Olsen's psychological insight would make of that.

"Let me guess . . . divorced? Back on the dating scene and out of your depth?" She took another sip of tea. "No, wait a minute . . ." She raised a finger like an am dram detective. "You're still adjusting. Well, let me spell it out for you, Craig." She sat back confidently and held up her fingers, palms towards herself. There were two silver rings on her right hand on the index and middle fingers. Apart from three narrow bracelets on her left wrist there were no other adornments. "Divorced and over it. No attachments, not looking to be rescued, and remarkably free of baggage for someone of our age."

He forked some cake, reflecting that this was turning out to be the best tea break of all time.

"So, Caitlin, can you give me your number again? And I'll give you mine too." He took a scrap of paper out of his back pocket and led by example.

By the time Caitlin's fifteen minutes were up, Wild's day had improved significantly. He had some background intelligence on Jeb — insubstantial in itself although it helped build up a picture — and a probable date.

CHAPTER 23

Wild had barely sunk his arse into a chair before the call came through. The only thing that made it stand out from a job for uniform was the complainant, a Mrs Walsh, and the allegation that an American or a Canadian has assaulted her husband. With DI Marsh and Ben Galloway indisposed, and Wild disinclined to buddy up with any of his other detective colleagues, he rang down for Sergeant Galloway.

They took a marked car and the sergeant did the driving. And he did most of it in fourth gear.

Mrs Walsh was standing at the front of the house staring up the drive. "Quickly," she insisted. "He's in here. Didn't you bring an ambulance?"

Sergeant Galloway touched her arm to reassure her. "Is he badly injured?"

"I suppose not." Her voice faltered. "He says he doesn't want any fuss in any case, but an assault is still a crime."

Wild had spotted the hire car in the drive. It wasn't hard to miss. Somehow, to his jaded eye, it seemed inevitable that an American would choose a BMW. Then again, maybe they were all out of Mercedes.

"And what about the other man?" Sergeant Galloway eased past her.

"I don't understand it. He was politeness personified when he came here before. Chatted with James for an hour, he did. I left them to it. So interested in local history and wanting to know all about the families hereabouts and *their* histories."

Wild thought back to his search of the hotel room. "And where is this . . . visitor?"

"Mr Kravers? Well, after my husband regained his wits we pretended to make our peace with him and then locked him in the study."

"What about the windows?" Wild answered his own question when he recalled that the hire car was still there.

"Those old windows haven't opened in years. I won't let James smoke there any more on account of it — filthy habit."

Sergeant Galloway called him. "Craig, in here."

Wild rushed in to find James Walsh leaning back on the sofa, hands on his knees, motionless but for his breathing. As he tilted forward Wild saw the mark on his head.

"Are you alright, sir? Can you tell me what happened?"

James Walsh blinked slowly. "Mr Kravers returned my father's diaries and I'm afraid we had some cross words. He accused me of keeping something from him. After that it's all a bit of a blur, I'm afraid. I'm quite alright really, just a little dazed."

Wild signalled to Sergeant Galloway to stay put. "And Mr Kravers?"

"My wife . . ." James fell silent.

Wild frowned at Galloway. "Tell you what, sir. I think we'll get an ambulance here anyway — to be on the safe side."

"Oh, I didn't hurt our visitor. At least, I don't think I did?" He looked up at Wild for the answer.

Mrs Walsh came into the room and handed Wild a key.

Wild would have found his way to the study by the shouting alone. Aaron Kravers was rattling the doorknob with some gusto and making threats.

Wild announced himself and then unlocked the door. Kravers had decamped to one of the study chairs, as if some other red-faced assailant had been making the racket. Wild flashed his warrant card and slowly took out his notebook. It had the desired effect.

"Hey, Officer, I think there's been a misunderstanding. I borrowed some books on local history and I enquired about another book. Dr Walsh became quite agitated, and in my efforts to settle him we might have tussled a little."

Wild knew a first-class bullshitter when he heard one, on any side of the Atlantic. "So how did you come to be locked in the study, sir?"

Kravers levered himself out of the chair. "Well, that's just the thing, Officer. I think they are both a little, how shall I put it, off the wall? I guess it's that famous English eccentricity." He grinned for effect.

Wild turned his attention to the room. Drawers were not closed flush, presumably in haste, piles of books teetered precariously. It looked, to Wild's trained eye, as if someone had been trying to cover up their treasure hunt, maybe in the moments between his arrival and the unlocking of a door.

"Did you find what you're looking for?" He saved Kravers the bother of lying. "Another diary, wasn't it?"

Kravers strained every muscle not to respond, like a politician's wife in a photocall after a scandal. "So, is the good doctor going to press charges?" There was something about the face and its suggestion of a smile that made Wild dislike him even more, if that were possible.

Wild wrote a line in his notebook and then looked up. "Dr Walsh says it's all a misunderstanding. However, I'm not convinced, and I have sufficient grounds to question you back at the station."

Kravers stood his ground. "You know what, Detective? I think you're making a big mistake. But, hey, it's your funeral."

Wild stopped in his tracks and, in what he would later consider a lightbulb moment, realised that Aaron Kravers visiting the Walshes when Jeb was away at Alexander Porter's funeral was either a happy coincidence or the result of some careful planning.

CHAPTER 24

Aaron Kravers didn't go the traditional route of protesting his innocence in the car, and Wild had taken the decision not to use handcuffs. The assault evidence was slender at best. Despite that, he was eager to get Kravers in an interview room for a fishing trip.

Sergeant Galloway said nothing on the drive back to the police station, so Wild took the opportunity to dangle some hooks. He directed his comments to his colleague. "These diaries must be pretty important if they can provoke a fight between strangers." He didn't check for a reaction in the rear-view mirror. "No, what am I saying? They met once before, didn't they, when Mr Kravers here first asked to borrow the diaries."

Kravers let out a heavy sigh. "Look, guys, I know what you're trying to do here. And I know my rights. So you'll pardon me if I wait until I get my brief before I comment on your little show here."

Sergeant Galloway piped up. "As you say, Mr Kravers, you are well within your rights. You'll also have the right to remain silent, although . . ."

"Yeah, yeah, I know how court systems work."

* * *

If DI Marsh was pleased at the latest development, she had a funny way of showing it. First, she gave Wild a rundown of the difficulties they had getting hold of a solicitor at short notice — because it was obvious from Wild's update at the arrest site that Aaron Kravers would only be as cooperative as he needed to be.

And second, as she put it herself, "I'm drowning in paperwork about people whose only crimes so far seem to be keeping secrets and being habitual liars. What I need is a serious suspect we can *work on*." The way she said *work on* implied she would have preferred a more summary method of justice.

You can take the woman out of Glasgow . . . thought Wild, and kept his thoughts to himself. It was inevitable that one of the local solicitors would answer the call, and Wild felt uncomfortable at the sight of Mr Hollings when he appeared at the front desk to represent his new client. It was all getting incestuous. Naturally, Hollings was entirely professional, but it didn't stop Wild wondering whether he was hiding something too.

After a twenty-minute confab with Kravers, Hollings emerged to announce that his client would be happy to assist the police in any way he could, and to that effect, Aaron Kravers had prepared a statement for the interview. It sounded to Wild like a speech printed on a card. Well, Mr Hollings had to have something in that briefcase.

The party of four took their seats and Wild went through the preliminaries. Everyone seemed to perk up a little at the sound of the beep. Wild refreshed everybody's memory with the contents of the emergency call, which recorded Mrs Walsh's distress at the assault she said she'd witnessed on her husband. After that little appetiser, Wild read out Mrs Walsh's assault complaint and reminded them of how she had both identified and captured the alleged assailant.

Hollings raised a hand, like a schoolboy in need of the toilet. "Before you go any further, my client wishes to make the following statement in an effort to clarify what happened." He gazed at a sheet of A4 paper and read from the florid writing. *I have been on vacation for a few days, visiting the sites that my ancestor, Melvin Kravers, would have seen when he was stationed here during the Second World War. Melvin Kravers died during the D-Day landings and I have been researching his life as part of a family genealogy project.*

Wild was amazed at how much could be squeezed into a twenty-minute consultation and yet still say nothing of relevance. He made some notes to show he was paying attention and gave the required response. "That's all very well, but it doesn't explain—"

Hollings cleared his throat to cut him off. Kravers stayed motionless, staring at them from behind a stony facade.

"If I may continue, Detective Sergeant?" Hollings smoothed the piece of paper for effect. "He goes on to say: *In the course of my research, I identified the family name of the local doctor during that time and thought I would call there in case there was any record of my great-uncle Melvin's unit. Naturally, with the passing of years, I did not expect to find Dr Walsh still alive, but fortunately his son, James, had carried on the family tradition and shared anecdotes that had been passed on to him. In addition, to my surprise, the late Dr Walsh had kept journals, detailing that crucial period of history. Dr James Walsh kindly loaned me some diaries, and it was only on reading through them that I realised one of the volumes was missing. When I returned the diaries, I mentioned this to Dr Walsh and he became extremely agitated, and may have been accidentally injured in my attempts to calm him down and discuss the missing diary.*"

Wild sucked a tooth. "That's not how Dr Walsh's wife reported it."

Aaron Kravers found his voice. "Look, Officer, with the greatest of respect, Mrs Walsh was not in the room with us at the time, and we both called out for her due to Dr Walsh's distress. I can easily understand why Mrs Walsh may have drawn the wrong conclusion."

Marsh turned a folder to Wild, angled so that neither Kravers nor his solicitor could read it. She had underlined a single sentence: Email to Jeb.

Wild made himself comfortable: he loved this part too. "Now, Mr Kravers, having understood your part in the altercation with Dr Walsh, which is still under consideration, I'd like to talk you about another matter. I understand that you and a private investigator were in communication by email before you made the journey to the UK. Is that correct?"

Kravers stalled, looked to his brief and rebounded from the blank stare like a tennis ball off a wall. "I, er, yeah, I guess so. What's your point?"

Wild took that as a yes. "How did you first find them?"

"I'm not sure I follow. I did a search for the oldest solicitors in the area and emailed the first one. I guess I got lucky because next thing I know a private investigator contacted me on behalf of the solicitor."

Wild saw Hollings flare into recognition as he worked out that his practice would have been the one contacted, and that he knew nothing about it. Wild watched his face slide and decided to help it on its way. "And would you have any objection to letting us see those emails?"

Kravers thought for a moment. "Hey, is this about the DNA match?"

Marsh took over. "I think this would be a convenient moment for us to take a break. I remind you that you are still under caution." She paused the recording. "We just need a few minutes — can we get you some tea or coffee?"

Kravers rose to his feet so quickly that his chair threatened to topple backwards. "What's going on here?"

Wild raised a critical finger. "You wanna watch a temper like that. People might get the wrong idea."

Hollings dabbed at his forehead with a handkerchief. He looked as if the world had nothing left to surprise him. "It is a little stuffy in here. Some tea in a side room will give everyone a chance to cool off. And perhaps a biscuit?" he added, with a twinkle in his eye, as if he knew what a dick his client had become.

"Of course," Marsh replied curtly. "I'll ask one of the PCs to bring it down for you. If you'd care to follow me."

By now, Wild knew that carefully controlled voice, which meant things were about to get difficult for him.

After depositing the visitors at the far end of the corridor, she turned abruptly to Wild. "Back in the room."

He nodded dolefully. No tea for him then. He followed her in and closed the door. She looked pissed off.

"I don't like surprises, Craig."

Back in London he would have said something glib about the Secret Santa. He knew better here. He glanced up at the wall clock. "Give me five minutes. I'll see if I can get hold of Jeb. Hopefully he's sober, but you know how it is with funerals. Maybe we should get an update on his grandad and see whether Mrs Walsh still wants to press charges?"

Marsh nodded and her face softened. "Good point." Her tone made it sound like *good boy*. "Don't mention the alleged assault to Jeb though. Fair enough if his grandmother has already told him, but we can do without his involvement. I think we need to build bridges with Aaron Kravers. There is more to this — you mark my word."

Wild took his leave of her and went back to his desk. Before he rang Jeb, he tried to fit the pieces together in his head. Kravers had said nothing about UK relatives. Quite the opposite. He wondered idly whether there'd be some record of all US servicemen who were stationed locally before the D-Day landings. Meantime, there were more pressing matters at hand.

Jeb's voice seemed to echo at the other end of the line. Another voice in the background sounded like Nathan's, and Wild heard the clink of glasses.

"I need to talk to you. Now."

"You've got some nerve. You know we had the funeral today. Can't it wait?"

If Wild had thought it through, he would have planned exactly what to say. But if he had been that sort of copper, he would have made DI by now. "It's about DNA, Jeb." He was answered by silence. "Now, are you going to find somewhere quiet so we can talk in private or would you prefer I speak to Pauline instead?"

The next sound he heard was the clunk of a laden glass against a hard surface, followed by the scurrying of footsteps through a swing door and outside.

"So, what's all this about?"

"Spare me your feigned offence. I don't have time for it. And to be honest, your bohemian minstrel act is wearing a bit thin as well. Tell me about the DNA match with Aaron Kravers, or so help me I will come there, arrest you myself and then charge you and Pauline with obstruction."

"Hold on a second. Pauline doesn't need to know any more about this. It is a private business arrangement between Mr Kravers and myself. Alright . . . I know this is going to look bad, but I wanna get it off my chest, okay? I might not be a qualified private detective, whatever that is. But I have provided Mr Kravers with a service."

"You told me that no money changed hands."

Jeb's sigh sounded like the truth escaping. "I offered to do some local research on his behalf. After all, I had access to my great-grandfather's records. That's got to be worth something. Anyway, I wanted to be thorough, so I read my great-grandad's personal diaries as well as his notes . . ."

Wild stared across the room. "Did Kravers know you had access to family diaries?"

Jeb laughed. "Course not! He was paying me by the hour! I set up a Gmail account in the name of Jay Investigations and told Kravers I did this as a sideline."

"So, he doesn't know you're related to Dr Walsh?"

"You London boys catch on quick, eh?"

Wild was still shuffling ideas in his head when he realised he hadn't said anything for several seconds. "Right, DNA. And make it quick. I need to be somewhere."

"The thing is . . . well, I haven't broken any laws or anything. Well, not intentionally."

Wild waited.

"Okay, so there's probably something you ought to know . . ."

Wild heard the office door behind him and turned to see Marsh pointing at her watch, as if he were an imbecile.

"Better make it quick, Jeb."

"The Yank's relative fathered a child when he was over here during the war."

"I'll get back to you." Wild cut the call and returned to the lion's den, updating Marsh on the way.

When the four of them were back together again, Aaron Kravers was more conciliatory. Either he'd had a successful personality transplant, or his solicitor had managed to inject some sense into him.

"Can I just start by apologising for my manners earlier? I'm not sleeping well, and jetlag makes me cranky."

Wild remembered something that had been bugging him. "Out of interest, where did you keep those dairies you borrowed?"

Kravers smiled. "You'll think I'm crazy! I didn't want to trust them to a hotel safe. And I didn't feel comfortable leaving them in my room, so I put them in the trunk of the car for safekeeping."

Wild nodded. One mystery solved. "Tell me about the DNA."

"I suppose it was a couple of weeks after I first starting communicating with . . ."

Wild glanced at his notebook. "Jay Investigations."

"Uh huh. They emailed me to say they might have a possible DNA match and gave me a site to use. I knew that couldn't be right although I was intrigued. So I uploaded a sample like they said and I got a match. I'll be honest, I thought it was a scam, but up to that point everything had been done electronically so unless they had someone working for them Stateside it didn't make sense."

"What about contact details for the matching sample?"

"Not a chance, which the investigator obviously knew in advance."

"And I presume their fee increased significantly at that point?"

"You bet your ass it did."

"So, when you next contacted your private investigator, did they give you details of this alleged relative?" Wild noted the glimmer in his eye. Kravers might have been intrigued, but he wasn't stupid. He would have figured out that he could probably complete the picture for himself and save some money. Wild tried fishing again. "Presumably you've been looking at parish records?" He smiled at Kravers, but only because things were starting to make sense at last.

Kravers folded his hands in his lap. "I fully intended to pay, only he got greedy. The money he wanted covered my flight, accommodation, spending money, and then some."

Marsh cast a glance at Wild. He chose to see it as a mark of respect. Then again, she may have just been waiting to have her say.

"And what about this relative? Have you met . . . ?" Another look at Kravers pre-empted the rest of his sentence.

"No, not yet. I guess you could say I still have some loose ends to tie up. I'm nearly there."

"Like the missing diary you argued about with Dr Walsh?"

Kravers tried to look inscrutable, which Wild knew was not easy to pull off under pressure. "Yeah, one of those books was definitely missing from the set. Dr Walsh Senior refers back to some event in the later books, without giving any details. He mentions turning to religion a few times — that shows how much it affected him."

Marsh scribbled furiously and then held the note under Wild's nose. He read it and then took it from her, laying it face down on the table.

"You think it was a secret birth?"

"Maybe. Or a secret marriage. Before Melvin Kravers was shipped out, he managed to get two letters home. In one of them he talks about a local girl that he thinks his ma and pa would approve of."

Wild stared blankly, killing time.

"His folks were farmers, so I'm thinking this girl — whoever she was — you know, similar background."

Marsh tapped the desk politely. "And what about the second letter? You said he sent two."

Kravers was in his element now. Whatever he did for a living, which Wild would have laid money on being something corporate, he was clearly comfortable holding court. "It was more of a telegram and all it said was that he had *big* news." He held his hands apart, as though describing a fish he'd caught. "It took several months after D-Day before his folks received word that he died in action. Somewhere in the family archives there's a letter from the captain of his unit, sent after the war ended, and it says he'd been involved in some sort of mission that had been essential to the war. I guess a lot of that kinda thing went down."

Marsh used her uncanny knack of cutting to the chase. "I don't suppose you have these letters with you?

"Sure, I have copies of his letters home. I didn't think I'd need the captain's letter because I've already confirmed his credentials. He's dead now, of course."

Wild fought to stay deadpan. Kravers stopped speaking and reached into his jacket, only to come up empty-handed. "I must have left the copies in the trunk of my hire car — will that be all?"

Marsh tapped the table with a single lacquered nail. "For now."

They had just handed over Kravers to the desk sergeant for release when the investigation took another turn for the worse.

CHAPTER 25

Wild relied on London driving and a blue light. Everyone else could fuck off. While his sympathies lay with Mrs Walsh and even Jeb, his overriding thought was that he should have been more diligent. Mrs Walsh had been near hysterical on the phone, according to the call handler. Information was scant. She had returned from a shopping trip and found her husband dead in his study.

By the time Wild arrived, with DI Marsh and Ben Galloway on board, the ambulance was already on site, blue lights still turning. Wild was disappointed to find it was a different crew to the previous callout, otherwise it would've made the inquiry a little more straightforward.

DI Marsh opened the car door. "Remember what I told you. You speak when you're spoken to and you say nothing that cannot be corroborated. Chiefly, you do not express opinions or theories. Is that understood?"

Wild nodded. This was bad. Worse even than the London bank job that resulted in the loss of £50,000 and a bullet to a member of the public.

He followed Marsh in like a student copper, through the front door and into the kitchen where one of the ambulance crew was making Mrs Walsh the obligatory cup of tea. Wild wondered where Ben Galloway had gone, but presumed he was waiting outside for the forensics team. Marsh nudged him towards the kitchen table and gently drew the paramedic aside.

Wild sat down beside Mrs Walsh and waited for her to speak. They usually spoke, despite the trauma or perhaps because of it. A basic human need to make sense of the unfathomable.

She looked as if she were forcing herself to breathe. "I don't understand. He said he felt fine and the ambulance staff said there was no serious injury. I even asked them if it would be okay to pop out — he likes his magazines, you see. I did ask." She stared across the table and held onto her cup like an anchor.

"Would you like us to notify anyone?"

Her gaze lowered and she started crying. Wild didn't say any more. He crossed the room and tapped Marsh on the shoulder. "I'm going outside to ring Jeb Walsh — I won't be long."

As predicted, Ben Galloway was standing a little way out of the front door, staring up the drive. "Forensics are on their way, Skip."

"We need to tell the grandson."

"Okay," Ben said quietly. "I think it will be better coming from me. I'll ring him now."

Wild agreed, although there would be no way of making this better. By the time he returned to the kitchen, Marsh was done talking with the paramedic.

She directed him to another room. "It's a suspicious death. Looks like a blunt force trauma to the head. Some sort of angular surface, like the edge of something. We'll know more when forensics get here."

"I'll check for signs of forced entry." He knew it was beyond the realm of coincidence, just as surely as he knew that Kravers hadn't slipped out of the police station to finish the job.

Marsh nodded, sending Wild on his way. His first port of call was Ben Galloway and the news wasn't good – no answer from Jeb Walsh. As they discussed Galloway's findings, or lack of them, the forensics team put in an appearance. Wild gave them an update and then left them to it so he could check the perimeter and the outside windows.

He had nothing to show for his efforts by the time he'd circled the house and returned to the front door. No scratch marks on the frames and no convenient footprint beneath them. It looked like an inside job. That unpleasant thought accompanied him back into the house, where the ambulance crew were finishing up and handing over to forensics.

Wild caught up with Galloway. "I need you to do something for me. Find out from Mrs Walsh exactly where she went shopping and then get down there to confirm her movements. Do it now."

Galloway all but saluted and Wild recalled, with some relief, that he would probably have met the family in the past. Fingers crossed he'd had his sensitivity training.

Wild put on his shoe covers and entered the crime scene. Marsh finished conspiring with the pathologist and faced him. "Craig, come and have a look at this. Tell me what you think."

The pathologist and his photographer made space for him. It wasn't pretty. They never were. The pathologist held up a clear bag with a tiny flake of black material. "I extracted this from the wound with tweezers." He sounded disproportionately pleased with himself, but hey — who didn't respect someone who had found their passion in life?

Wild quickly realised that the late Dr Walsh still had the one head injury, only now it was gaping.

Marsh drew his gaze away from the corpse. "Well, we know that Kravers wasn't responsible for this."

Wild felt sand in his throat, like tiny grains of conscience. "Nothing to say he didn't have an accomplice."

Judging by the look on her face, Marsh wasn't used to being contradicted publicly. "Where is Galloway?"

"I sent him out to check on Mrs Walsh's alibi. We can't make any assumptions and it doesn't hurt to be thorough."

Ouch. Even the pathologist flinched. Marsh turned to the pathologist and his photographer, who had lowered her lens. "Could you give us a couple of minutes?"

Wild backtracked. "Look, I'm sorry if I spoke out of turn."

Marsh's smile set his teeth on edge. "Not at all, Craig. But this tragic event complicates things." She glanced down at the body. "Particularly for you."

"Hold on a second, I don't see how we could have prevented this."

"Quite so. But it's reasonable to conclude the two deaths are connected, is it not?"

He hated rhetorical questions. "So we expand the current investigation and work on finding the link."

"The thing is, *Craig*, we both know this doesn't look good for the team. Now, obviously, I will bear the brunt of it, as befits my senior rank. However, it doesn't reflect well on you as my number two. I mean, someone looking in from the outside might well conclude that if we'd apprehended whoever is responsible for Porter's death, then Dr Walsh might still be alive."

"With respect, ma'am, that's bollocks and we both know it. We are pursuing all lines of enquiry. What more could the team or I have done?"

She stared right through him. "Maybe you could have caught the bastard."

Wild's career-ending reply never made it to his mouth, thanks to the intervention of his mobile phone. "Excuse me." He took off for the front door and directed the forensics team back in behind him. "DS Wild," he growled.

"Skip, it's Ben Galloway. I've spoken to the staff at the newsagent and they confirm Mrs Walsh's story and that she paid by card. Don't worry — I didn't let the cat out of the bag. Anyway, I'm on my way back now. Over and out."

Wild found a smile. If there was still a place on the force for earnest coppers like Ben Galloway — recreational cannabis use notwithstanding — then there was hope for the world. It was only after he cut the call that he realised they could have asked Mrs Walsh if she'd kept the receipt and saved themselves the bother.

Lacking a reason to return to the crime scene, Wild returned instead to the kitchen where Mrs Walsh was still in her chair, frozen in time. "Can I make you some more tea?" It was hardly compassionate in action, but it was all he had.

She shook her head slowly. "I've tried to get hold of Jeb but he's not picking up. I didn't want to leave a message." She looked up at him, eyes dulled and empty. "I wouldn't know what to say."

"You leave that to us, Mrs Walsh." It occurred to him that Galloway hadn't said any more and Jeb hadn't returned home. Probably still with Nathan Porter, paying their respects together in a pub. "Mrs Walsh, can I ask you . . . prior to today, had your husband had any serious disagreements with anyone?"

She blinked slowly, as if she were sifting through her memory. "Everybody loved James. He was a pillar of the community."

Wild heard a car outside then excused himself, and nipped out to catch Ben Galloway. But it was Marnie Olsen getting out of a marked car. "What the bloody hell are you doing here?"

She narrowed her eyes at him. "Nice to see you too, Wild. DI Marsh phoned the station and requested a female officer for Mrs Walsh. She said it required the gentle touch."

Wild took it like a bullet. "Do you know what? I'm out of here. If the DI wants me, I've gone to follow up a lead." He slid past her and got into his car, vaguely aware that she'd called out after him. He started the engine and bellowed, "Shit!" in the privacy of his car. Less than a month in a new team and the wheels had already come off.

CHAPTER 26

Wild made himself scarce for an hour by sitting at his desk. There had been no more updates from Ben Galloway, although hopefully he'd taken the initiative to find Jeb. In the meantime, Wild had gone back through Jeb's phone logs to see if there was any traffic between him and Kravers. It seemed that all communications were by email, unless he had another mobile phone. It made him wonder whether Kravers knew Jeb's identity and by extension whether they had ever met in person. As he worried that one out on paper another thought came to mind: did Jeb even know that Kravers was in the country? And while he was collecting unanswered questions, what about the missing wartime diary — where might Jeb have hidden it for safekeeping?

He picked up his mobile phone, dialled Hollings and Gresham and started walking. The secretary answered with a careful balance of politeness and superciliousness. Clearly, the firm did not give any truck to peasants. Her attitude quickly changed when he reminded her that he was a detective sergeant. She couldn't do enough for him then, especially when he explained it was actually Pauline Henderson he was after. Not literally, of course, although her tone seemed to infer something similar.

A quick blast of Vivaldi and then Pauline came to the phone. She sounded nervous even before he'd said anything. He put that down to the fear of what he might say to her employers.

"How . . . how can I help you?"

"Pauline, I think we need to have a little chat. I'll get over to you in about twenty minutes." He heard her gasp and then let her off the hook. "Make some excuse and take a walk up the road."

"Which direction?"

"I dunno. Take a left and I'll park up somewhere along the road."

"Well, it's a longer road to the right . . ."

He rubbed one of his temples. "Fine, turn right then." Anything for a quiet life. "I'll see you in twenty."

Wild wasn't a great believer in anything except Sod's Law. Consequently, he wasn't particularly surprised to see DI Marsh and Ben Galloway pull into the car park as he left the building. Marsh blanked him. Galloway still wore that puppy dog gratitude face that evoked a mixture of pity and disdain.

He kept on walking. "Any joy with tracking down Jeb?"

Galloway shook his head.

"I'll deal with it myself then."

Marsh paused on the tarmac like a delayed flight. "Case review in ninety minutes. Don't disappoint me, Craig."

He got into the car and did the thing adults are never supposed to do — he turned off his phone. The radio blared out local news and he listened to it without care or interest. Thanks to a broken down bus, he arrived to find Pauline already at the end of the street, feverishly smoking a cigarette and gazing intently at passing traffic. He waved slowly as he passed and looked for a space, opting for a single yellow line. To make life easier for himself.

He wound down the window. "Put that out first and get in." He tried to smile, to make it seem less like in order, but there had been very little to smile about today.

She flicked the cigarette into the road, closed the passenger door and fiddled momentarily with the seatbelt before deciding to leave it in peace. "I can't stay long. Mr Hollings needs some work caught up on after I was away this morning — on account of the funeral."

"I'm going to ask you two questions and to make it easier, you are not under caution and you can get out of the car any time you like." He saw her left hand edge towards the door handle. "But if you choose to leave now, or if I think you are hiding something from me, I will get out of the car with you and speak to Mr Hollings about the company email account. I have no doubt Mr Kravers has kept a record of everything."

She fixed him with a beady stare and said nothing, which he took as compliance.

"Right. Where will I find Jeb right now? He's not in trouble — not this time, anyway."

"He's probably up at the ruins. It's where we all used to go."

"Thank you." He watched her face soften. "Right, next question — do you know where Jeb has hidden the missing diary?"

He watched her face betray her. There was no telling if she had read the diary herself. He could only be certain that she knew what he was talking about.

"It's locked away in my drawer at work."

"Well, you'd better get it then, hadn't you?"

Pauline's eyes widened. "You said he's not in any trouble, so why are you coming to me like this?"

He played opposites and spoke quietly, blinking softly to try and build rapport, like the books said. "I can't go into that right now. It's for the investigation."

She caved at the magic word. "Does Jeb have to know about this?"

He thought for a second. "Not right now. Tell you what, Pauline, you give me the book and I'll copy it and get the original back to you. That way, everyone is happy."

Contrary to his assurances, she didn't look happy at all when she got out of the car and returned a few minutes later with a jiffy bag.

Wild felt the weight of circumstance on his shoulders. He didn't really *do* touchy-feely emotions — it hadn't taken the marriage guidance counsellor half an hour to suss that. And, surely to God, Ben Galloway could have figured out where Jeb had got to, after a quick tour of the pubs. Well, whatever the truth, the bearer of the black telegram was him now. He put his foot down, less out of consideration for Jeb and more to fit in with the DI's timescale.

The fractured carcass of Montford Abbey ruins slipped in and out of view as he navigated the main country road and then its tributary. There was only one vehicle when he got there — Jeb's. He hoped Nathan Porter had stuck with Jeb. They had a lot in common now.

He parked close to Jeb's car and felt the bonnet — barely warm. Evidently, they'd been there for some time. Nought out of ten for Ben Galloway's detective skills. He found them resting against the remnants of a wall, a six-pack of beer at their feet. A gentle breeze stirred. From where they sat you could take in the land farmed by Elleth and Causly, and the bracken wasteland of Fortune's Field.

Nathan made a half-hearted attempt to raise an unopened can. "Care for a drink, Detective?"

Wild waved it away with a flick of his hand. "Still on duty, thanks all the same."

Nathan brushed away at the grass. "Come and join us, why don't you?"

Wild decided that his bad news would be better delivered standing up.

Nathan drank greedily from his can. "Back in the day, the Porter family held wealth and power. Now look at us." He squeezed the can as if he could extract more from it by force of will. "Mind you, it was already a bloody ruin then. We're not so lucky with money — you might have noticed that."

No one had asked why Wild had turned up. He was hoping one of them would make it easier for him. No such luck. He took a deep breath and stood to attention. "Jeb, we've been trying to find you. I'm afraid I have some bad news. Your grandfather was involved in an incident today, and I'm sorry to tell you that he died as a result of his injuries. I've come to fetch you so you can be with your grandmother."

Jeb didn't move for a few seconds. He sat in silence, gazing out at nothing in particular. His next words surprised Wild, but he didn't place any store by it. "Was it an accident?" Who wouldn't prefer a random tragedy to someone else's malice?

Nathan pushed against the wall and struggled to his feet. "Well, answer him then. He has a right to know."

Wild would have told him to mind his own business, but it was the day of his father's funeral so he cut him some slack. He moved round to face Jeb directly. "We are treating the death as suspicious, pending enquiries."

Nathan lurched forward and for a second Wild thought he was going to take a swing at him. He balled a fist and edged back out of reach.

"That's what you said about my dad, for all the good that's done."

Wild relaxed and extended a hand to Jeb. "I think we should go now — your nan is waiting. Give me your car keys." He helped Jeb to his feet and then turned back to Nathan. "You're in no fit state to drive. Where would you like me to drop you?"

Jeb found his voice again. "He can come back to mine."

Wild left them at the top of the Walshes' drive. He figured Olsen was still at the house and didn't wait to find out. He had an appointment with the boss, and more importantly the photocopier. If everything went to plan, he'd keep his promise to Pauline.

CHAPTER 27

Wild checked his watch on the stairs — still around fifteen minutes before the team huddle or whatever they called it here. He noticed Marsh's glassy gaze as he walked past her office, but she didn't stir. He avoided the rest of the team and checked the paper trays of the photocopier. After a couple of trial pages, he adjusted the copier settings so that he could actually read the good doctor's writing.

Partway through the copying one of the admin staff came over with a small folder of paperwork. "Hi." She smiled awkwardly, and he returned the favour. "Are you going to be long? I only need four sheets."

He stalled for a moment, caught between team spirit and the task at hand. "Sorry, I really need to get this done. I'll be as quick as I can. Maybe another five minutes . . . or so."

She nodded, tapping the folder against her palm as she walked away. Another Christmas card he wouldn't be getting. No great loss, he hadn't been a fan of Christmas since he was a kid.

He printed the last pages with the admin woman (another name to learn and write down) loitering on the periphery like a timeshare agent in a holiday park. He checked his watch again. Bollocks. No chance of getting the book back to Pauline for a while. The only saving grace was that Jeb would have other things on his mind.

The team's mass migration to the briefing room gave him no chance to return to his desk. He folded the A4 pages into the jiffy bag with the diary and kept it close.

* * *

DI Marsh treated him with the same disdain she showed the rest of the team. Maybe that was her take on equal opportunities. She directed Ben Galloway to a second whiteboard, and he seemed to revel in the chance to be pen monitor. Marsh pointed around the room, seeking updates from the team while conspicuously leaving Wild untroubled. He knew his turn would come though.

Finally, this loaded game of spin the bottle pointed his way. He approached the whiteboard so he could face them all. If he were getting a grilling, he'd do it on his own terms. The first thing he told them was that Jeb Walsh had been located and informed of the death of his grandfather. Ben Galloway's face lowered a few inches. "I left him and Nathan Porter at the Walsh household before returning here."

DI Marsh threw him a glimmer of a smile, more — he reasoned — for his chutzpah than his detective skills. The room fell silent and tunnel vision kicked in. Although he wanted to reach for a pill, he knew there'd be questions. Maybe he could ride this one out. His mouth turned to sandpaper.

Marsh cleared her throat. "Whenever you feel ready."

A ripple of laughter flitted around the team. He forced himself to make eye contact, remembering the war films that cautioned the troops not to shoot till you saw the whites of their eyes. It didn't help, and the pounding in his head grew so loud he wondered whether the others could hear it. The team started to get restless, their whispered side conversations a more polite way of turning their backs on him.

Say something. He took a gasp of air and gripped the pen until his knuckle whitened. "I've not been a popular choice for DS!" He laughed at his own joke — he was the only one laughing. "I know you would have much preferred someone local in the role and to be honest this hasn't been a bed of roses for me either. This case is all about extended families and historic loyalties. People around here seem to care more about the past than they do about the present. I dunno, maybe it's me — maybe *I'm* the one who's out of step."

Marsh scratched her head. "Detective Sergeant Wild, is there a point to all this? Beyond the entertainment value, I mean."

Wild began to extract the photocopied pages from the jiffy bag. "The point, Detective Inspector Marsh," he enjoyed watching her bristle, "is . . ."

He felt the team lean in closer to watch the car crash. Bollocks to them. He stuffed the copied pages back into the jiffy bag. "You know what? There is no point — none at all." And as he said the words, he saw Marsh's face harden like a malfunctioning Medusa. He started walking.

"And where do you think you're going?"

He voted with his feet, one hand slamming against the door so that it careered backwards in his wake. By the time he reached the bottom of the stairs he'd made a decision.

At Hollings and Gresham he asked to see Pauline and returned the envelope, minus his copy, thanking her for the loan of a book on local history. Afterwards, he drove to the supermarket, picked up six cans of lager and then went home. He thought about taking one of his pills — the daily medication his last GP had prescribed for anxiety — and then decided against it. Besides, lager ought to do the job just as well.

The house seemed less inviting than usual, which wasn't saying much. Maybe he'd get a cat. He laughed at the idea. Yeah, a cat would make all the difference. It was only when he reached the kitchen that he realised he'd forgotten to change into slippers. Sod it, what did it matter? What did any of it matter?

He popped a can and raised it to himself. "Congratulations, Craig — you've finally achieved what the Met couldn't. By this time tomorrow, you will be officially unemployed. On the plus side, think of all the leisure time." That's when he remembered Caitlin from the café. He dialled her mobile phone and left a message, promising to ring her again once he'd dealt with some work stuff.

He wondered whether DI Marsh would ring first or simply put in the disciplinary papers. And for the first time in ages, he didn't care. It was liberating not having to worry whether anyone was critiquing his performance, or what the bosses might say, or if his work colleagues found out how spectacularly he'd screwed up in London. No, this way the hand on the dagger was his own. Well, the counsellor had talked about the need to take back control of his life. He figured they'd junk him on health grounds and that way he'd still get his pension. Life would go on, somehow, with or without a cat.

He quit at two lagers and made a sandwich before sitting down to watch television. It didn't so much numb the pain as make him wonder whether he was staring into his future. What was left of the afternoon dragged itself into evening like a dying creature looking for a final resting place.

Having had his fill of antiques shows, garden makeovers, and quizzes for the masses, he turned on his computer. A gaggle of emails offered him funeral plan insurance, Bitcoin investments, and introductions to fun-loving singles in his area. Unlikely, he reasoned, as his new address looked set to be up Shit Creek.

His eye was drawn to the Skype icon along the bottom of his screen. He clicked on it. His lone contact showed as offline and she'd left a text message for him.

Craig, it's Jackie. I need to talk to you. I don't feel safe any more. Can we meet? I'll explain everything in London. Here's my new mobile number. Text me when you get to London. Jackie.

The screen galvanised him into action. There was only one thing to do — the right thing. He packed a bag and turned his mobile back on. DI Marsh deserved that, at least. Part of him hoped he could get away with leaving a message, but when had he ever been that lucky? She picked up on the third ring.

"It's Craig Wild. I just wanted to apologise for my behaviour. I think we can both agree that this little experiment hasn't worked out. I, er, I need to go to London. I'm sorry to let you down."

"Is everything alright, Craig?"

He smiled at the phone. How often had he heard that line in the past few months? "I've got some personal stuff to sort out. Sorry, it can't wait. I can sign whatever papers you need me to when I get back."

There was a pause on the line and then Marsh took a breath. "Papers? Look, maybe you came back to work too soon. I can spare you for a couple of days. I'll tell the DCI it's on compassionate grounds, and I'll speak to the team as well. Go sort your head out. And take my advice: leave your ex-wife well alone. DCI Hutcheson does not need the aggravation. And neither do you. I'll see you in two days' time."

"Thanks, boss." He cut the call and spoke to an empty room. "Well, that was unexpected."

CHAPTER 28

Wild kept his bag to a minimum — change of clothes, warrant card, collapsible baton . . . the usual. All being well, he could see Jackie, finally get some useful intel and then pass it on to the shitbags in the Met that he used to call colleagues. Granted, he wouldn't get the glory but there'd be the personal satisfaction of seeing their faces when he came bearing gifts. He didn't bother booking overnight accommodation. There was always the faint possibility that he could wrap everything up quickly and catch a late train back. Failing that, maybe he could kip at one of one of his old oppos' places. Spoilt for choice with shelves of unread books, he grabbed a Stephen King and chucked the photocopied diary pages in his bag for good measure.

He got a cab to Swindon station, tried to barter down to the cheapest train tickets possible, and waited on the platform. A train arrived — late for others but bang on time for him — and he had the strangest feeling that rather than returning to the big smoke to prove them wrong, he was actually making a farewell performance. Then again, his departure had not been so much under a cloud as washed away by a monsoon.

The train crawled along. It took a few chapters of *Cujo* before he remembered to check his phone, and when he did, he was glad. Marnie Olsen had left a message — her breathing so laboured it sounded as though she had run up a hill for a signal.

"Wild, I heard about what happened today. Well, not exactly, but DI Marsh said you were going to London. I hope you're not planning on seeing your ex-wife. Anyway, I need to talk to you about Jackie. Ring me when you get this. It's Marnie, by the way."

He stared up at the onboard display: only three stops to London, if they ever got there. The train arrived at Didcot Parkway and took up residence. An announcement cited technical problems and promised an update in the next few minutes. He moved out of the carriage and called Olsen back.

"Where are you?" She sounded desperate.

"What's up, Marnie? Are you okay?" He hadn't expected to give a shit about another human being quite so soon.

"It's not me, it's you, Wild. Did you get my message?" She huffed at herself. "Of course you did, or you wouldn't be ringing now."

"That psychological insight of yours is really paying off."

"Now is not the time. My friend got back to me about Jackie, your witness. They ran her details through their searches, and she's been lying to you, probably."

"Probably?"

"I told you before that her IP address for Skype was in London. I think she's always been in London."

He filled her in on Jackie's latest message and the fact that she'd given him a new mobile number.

"She probably bought that one specially for the occasion. I bet if you asked to see the receipt it would be from London. My friend — the one I was telling you about — she said there's a secure data warehouse for all active mobile phone numbers."

He moved his bag out the way to let someone get to the toilet. "That can't be right about Jackie. She's been avoiding London for months because of Tony. She wouldn't even tell me where she's been living." He pressed the mouthpiece closer. "What's that about a database?"

"Shit. I shouldn't have said anything. Forget it — it's inadmissible. The point is, she's been lying to you."

"Well, we'll soon know, won't we? I'm going to London to meet her."

"I think it's a mistake."

"Bit late for that as I'm on a train." The train lurched forward, prompting a chorus of sarcastic cheers from the other passengers.

"You still there, Wild? I'm serious. Could you get local backup in case it's a ploy?"

"I think we both know that's unlikely. Listen, Marnie, I appreciate your concern, but I can look after myself."

"I think you're blinded by this need to prove a point."

"And is that your considered psychological perspective?"

"Don't be a dick. Look, I'll meet you in London. Send me details of a pub where I can find you."

"Marnie, don't be stupid. I've been on the train for at least half an hour. I'll be in London within the hour — God willing. It would take you ages." He smiled for an instant because he realised she had his back.

"I'm already part way up the M4. Text me. And you're paying for my petrol."

The line went dead and he found another seat to put his phone on charge. He stared blankly out of the window at distant horizons, at farmland where no one was being murdered, and at his own blurred reflection. What if Olsen was right? In the cold light of day, all Jackie had ever given him was the promise of something useful. Sure, she'd confirmed things he already knew, about Tony's past trips to Spain and the feud with his brother, and his propensity for violence. But despite their little chats over Skype these past few months, what did he really have for his time *and* his money?

He opened his wallet and dug out a small piece of paper that looked as though it had intended to stay hidden. "Kieran? Hi, it's Craig. How's life in the Met? Yeah, you're never going to believe this but I'm on my way up to London. Fancy a quick drink later?" He rattled off his sentences without a pause, aiming to browbeat Kieran into submission. Just like old times.

Sergeant Kieran Byrne wriggled a little, as expected, and then he caved. "I can squeeze in one drink — I need to be somewhere afterwards, a social thing."

Wild didn't dive in straightaway. He took his time, like a predator weighing up the strengths of its next meal. Kieran's silence could only mean one thing.

"Are you likely to run into Steph there?"

"Christ, let it go, Craig. She has moved on with her life, why can't you?"

Kieran didn't sound defensive, so no suspicions on that front. But the gauntlet had been thrown down and Wild knew he wouldn't get any peace until he had the full picture. And Kieran knew that too.

Wild dug the truth out of him like a splinter, until finally it glistened red raw. Not a party this time, a gathering. Now where had he heard that before? He smiled to himself, recalling the get-together for Steph's promotion, the one he gatecrashed after a mini pub crawl.

Kieran sighed. "Don't do it, Craig. Have some self-respect."

"I've got nothing left to say to Steph. And if I had, we do all our talking through lawyers." He wanted to ask if there was anyone in her life, but what difference would it make? "I'll see you in about an hour and a half. Where do you want to meet?"

"The World's End."

It seemed fitting, given that his world had pretty much ended when he left North London.

* * *

As soon as he reached Paddington Station, Wild sent a text to Jackie and then took a moment to soak it all up. He'd missed the ebb and flow of a meandering crowd at the terminus, and the way the evening heat of the city enveloped him. The London Underground seemed like the United Nations on wheels and he realised he had missed that too. He embraced his anonymity and joyfully entered the maze of walkways and tunnels to make his way to Camden Town.

Kieran was already at a table, two pints in front of him. Conclusion: he wasn't stopping long. Wild tried to make it easy for him and summoned all the fake bonhomie he could muster.

"I got you your usual."

Wild splashed a smile across his face and proffered a hand. "Thanks, it's been a while." All bullshit of course. In reality it had only taken a few months for his relationship to fold, the job to have gone tits up, and for him to be signed off sick before someone on high intervened to truck him out of London. But, hey, what's a white lie between friends?

He took a sip of lager and waited for the inevitable questions.

"You look well, Craig. How is the . . ." Kieran looked at Wild's face, and seemed to realise he'd dug himself a hole, "er, transfer working out?"

Yeah, let's call it that. "Pretty good. Already involved in a major case — a murder."

Kieran stood up awkwardly. "I need to take a piss. When I come back, you can tell me what you're doing back in London."

Wild waited until Kieran had disappeared and then sent his location to Olsen. It was odds on that Kieran was ringing someone of a much higher rank. Only now did Wild notice the wet circle where another pint had rested. Dutch courage before the visitor arrived.

Kieran looked glum on his return. Wild cut to the chase. "You remember the Tony Weston case?" Of course he remembered it. A spectacular clusterfuck of an investigation, in which Weston did a runner and his ex, Jackie, asked for protection in fear of her life, but wasn't able — or willing — to trade information in return.

"What about it?"

He treated himself to a sip of lager. "I've kept in touch with Jackie."

"You always were an arrogant sod. What makes you think you could do a better job than the entire team?"

"It's not like that. Somehow she heard about me being shunted out of London. So she gave me her Skype ID and we've been talking ever since."

"And you didn't think to pass this intelligence over to the Met? No, of course not, because you're the sort of stupid bastard who thinks they can make this right all on your own."

"I needed to win her trust. You know how jittery she was . . ."

Kieran stared daggers at him. "So, what do you want from me?"

"Jackie said she had information for me, but she'll only give it face to face. It would be helpful to have someone I can rely on as backup."

Kieran lifted his hands from the table, as if it were electrified. "Sorry, mate, whatever you think you're doing here you're on your own. You've caused enough damage."

Wild fought the urge to lean across and smack his face clean off the chair. But one copper knocking seven bells out of another didn't really exemplify team spirit.

Kieran sank half of his pint in one hit. Wild knew what was coming.

"Look, Craig, it's been good to catch up but I have to be somewhere. If you've any sense, you'll pass on whatever you have to the Intelligence Team."

Wild rested an elbow on the table and cradled his chin. "The meeting's either tonight or tomorrow. By the time wheels are in motion Tony would be long gone."

"If he hasn't gone already."

Wild shrugged. They managed a few minutes of neutral conversation, mostly about the state of Wiltshire pubs. Then Wild suggested a game of darts.

"Go on then, for old times' sake."

* * *

Olsen ordered a lime and soda water and made herself comfortable. It had always fascinated her to watch strangers. Maybe that had been part of psychology's appeal. Craig Wild hadn't noticed her, of course he hadn't. He was lost in the moment, and from where she sat that moment was unbridled nostalgia. It was sweet in its way, watching the boys play darts. But she hadn't come all that way for a case study.

She left the bar, glass in hand, and walked towards the dartboard. "I hate to spoil the moment . . ."

Wild turned towards her and broke into a broad smile. The other copper turned, made fleeting eye contact and then looked her up and down — about as subtle as a nosebleed.

"Hi." Wild half-extended a hand and then realised he didn't really know how to behave around her in company. He lowered his hand. "Marnie, it's good to see you. This is Kieran Byrne — from my old team."

Olsen stepped into the space and proffered a polite if noncommittal handshake in Kieran's direction. "Marnie Olsen, from Craig's new team."

Kieran's smile slid off his face. He spoke directly to Wild. "What's she doing here? Please tell me you haven't involved her in your redemption game."

Olsen glared at him. "It isn't a game. The data suggests that Jackie has been in London for some time, so she's probably in regular communication with Tony Weston." She enjoyed the satisfaction of putting an idiot in his place.

Kieran half-turned away. "No offence, love, but this isn't some countryside feud. You're a bit out of your depth here."

Wild jabbed him in the shoulder, rocking him on his feet. "Hey, who do you think you're talking to?"

Kieran turned back to her, read the fire in her eyes and took a breath. "You're making a huge mistake. I don't know what he's told you, but Tony Weston isn't stupid enough to get caught by *data*."

Olsen smiled faintly. "No, but perhaps Jackie is. You know, what with her being a woman." One glance at Wild told her he was enjoying the moment.

Kieran shrugged his arm free. "You know what? You do what you have to do. As far as I'm concerned, this conversation never took place." Solemnly, he packed away his darts and downed what was left of his pint. "Don't call me again, Craig."

Olsen and Wild stood together and watched him leave. "And for the record, Wild, I don't need you to speak up for me. Thanks, anyway."

"He has always been a bit of a prick. Good copper, though, albeit an average darts player. Right, take me through everything and then we'll decide how to play it."

Olsen laid it out, referring to her notes when she needed to.

"And this is proof that Jackie has been in London the whole time?"

"Pretty much. The IP address has remained in the London area, according to the log my friend saw. And there's a variation on her username on two social media accounts that reference London locations. Not many friends, though."

"Why wouldn't she be more careful?"

"I told you, people get lazy. That's what makes police work easier than it should be — most of the time. Plus, if she was never in any real danger, the only risk would be you finding out."

"So why does she want me up in London?"

Olsen took a sip of her lime and soda. "How much does Tony Weston hate you?"

Wild considered the question as he carefully eased his dart flights into the case. "Enough, I s'pose. Which means he could be part of the welcoming committee."

"What is he wanted for?"

Wild finished putting the darts away and replied, matter-of-factly, "Armed robbery."

Olsen gulped. "I know how much you want this, but perhaps Kieran has a point. We are out on a limb here."

"Maybe not. I think I know someone who will help us."

"Why?"

"Because she owes me."

CHAPTER 29

Olsen sat beside Wild on the Northern Line train, watching the darkness of the tunnel slip by. "I'm still not sure about this."

"Relax, it'll be fine." He tried to ignore the churning in his guts. "Besides, she's already started divorce proceedings and exiled me to the shires — no offence. What else can she do to me?"

She tried to lighten the mood. "How do you even know her new address?"

"I am a detective! Don't worry, I'm not stalking her. It was somewhere in the paperwork. I'm not going to make a habit of this."

They exited Barbican Tube station, Wild navigating his way with ease.

"Have you been here before?" She eyed him suspiciously.

"Only on my computer. We want the third block." Wild glanced up at the flats. Nice work if you could get it, and Steph had. He allowed himself a scintilla of jealousy, or maybe it was regret. Perhaps if he'd applied himself a bit more and . . . no, who was he kidding? He'd been happy with his lot. He just hadn't read the signs.

He wavered a little at the entrance, relieved to see the door was on the latch. Probably intended for the invited guests of tonight's little gathering. He chose the stairs, partly to clear his head and partly because lifts still gave him the creeps — thanks to one unfortunate junkie, who had taken her last hit on the way up. Or the way down.

Olsen dutifully followed him. She wondered what sort of reception they'd receive, and how on earth Wild would get his ex-wife to take him seriously. Maybe everyone was a little more sophisticated in London. She thought about how her university relationship broke up, and how they'd never spoken again.

"Right, this is it. Would you rather wait outside?"

"Are you kidding? I'd pay money to see you pull this off."

He was still laughing as he rang the bell.

"One minute."

He pictured Steph reaching for her earrings. She'd always done that last minute. He heard footsteps and then a pause behind the door, presumably taking a peek through the spy hole. "What are *you* doing here?"

Olsen crowded in beside him and looked straight at the glass.

"I don't want any trouble, Steph. I just need to talk to you."

"Jesus, Craig. We've been through this."

"It's work, Steph. Five minutes, that's all I'm asking for. We can do it through the door if you want but your neighbours . . ."

He stepped back as the lock chunked and felt Olsen's shoulder pressing against his. The door arced back to reveal DCI Stephanie Hutcheson, arms limply at her sides, unconsciously emphasising her baby bump.

"So now you know."

Wild scratched around for a response while his brain played with dates. Olsen saved him the bother.

"Congratulations, ma'am."

DCI Hutcheson cast her a weary smile. "Steph, please. You'd better come in. Five minutes, you said? I have people coming round." She led them inside and left Olsen to close the door.

Wild fought the urge to say 'nice place' — or what he really wanted to say, which ran along the lines of 'what the fuck?' "Excuse me, I need to use the loo."

Olsen thought that Steph was on the verge of tears, or rage, and stepped into the void. "It's a lovely flat."

"Thanks." Steph swallowed and then fiddled with an emerald earring. "I don't want to be rude, but I have caterers arriving soon. It's an unofficial engagement party."

Olsen felt herself blushing.

"Sorry, too much information? Where did you two meet?"

Olsen made a split-second decision and stuck with the script she'd been given. "Through work. I'm a constable, uniformed . . . It really is about work. The Tony Weston case? A witness contacted Craig." The look on Steph's face disappointed her.

Steph sighed and pressed her hands together. "You do know that Craig was on medication? He probably still is. You can't always rely . . ."

Wild appeared in the doorway behind her, the aftertaste of his prescription meds as bitter as Steph's comments. "Shall we talk somewhere a bit more private?"

Olsen shared a moment's eye contact with Steph. "No need to on my account."

Wild glared at Olsen. "Fine. Anyone mind if I have a drink?"

Steph flicked a hand at the window. "Scotch is on the side. Help yourself but make it a small one — you're not stopping."

Wild poured a small glass of whisky, carried it over and sat down on the white leather upholstery. "New sofa. Nice. Not really suitable for Junior, though."

Olsen sat next to him and elbowed him hard. His arm jerked to one side.

"I'll get straight to the point. Tony Weston's ex — Jackie — got in touch . . ." He winced at Steph's raised eyebrow.

She always knew how to get so much from so little. "We've been communicating for a while now, over Skype. The point is that she wants to meet tonight and she says she'll give me information that will help convict Tony Weston."

Steph folded her arms. "What makes you think you can trust her . . . this time?"

Olsen leaned forward a little. "The thing is, ma'am," she didn't wait to be corrected, "there is data confirming Jackie has been in London for several months, so it could all be a set-up."

Steph's lips pursed. "Craig is *still* going though, of course he is. So, what do you want from me, Craig — absolution?"

Wild swirled what remained of his whisky. "Some backup would be preferable. If it goes well, I'll pass any evidence on to you, or Kieran Byrne, and then I'm out of it. Job done. And if it is a con, hopefully someone can stop me taking a beating."

Steph shook her head. "That's not funny, after the last time."

Olsen scratched the back of her hand. "He's not joking though."

Steph stood up abruptly. "I bet you haven't told her the full story, have you?" She turned to Olsen. "He spent three weeks in hospital afterwards."

Wild figured he should have been embarrassed, but he was a practical sort of bloke. "All I'm asking for is some support. Preferably armed, although I'll take whatever's going." He could see Steph getting agitated and he was sorry for that. When it came to Steph, he was sorry for a lot of things.

She shook her head dismissively. "You stupid bastard. I don't know which of us you're trying to impress." She pressed her hands together again, as if in prayer. "If I do this, regardless of the outcome, I never want to hear from you again."

"Agreed. Marnie will give you her number to contact us when you've put something in place. Goodbye, Steph, have a good life."

He waited as Olsen hastily wrote down her mobile number. “Come on, we’re leaving.”

Steph didn’t see them to the door. She called out, “Good luck,” but it sounded hollow, and Olsen couldn’t be sure which of them she was talking to.

CHAPTER 30

Wild's mood brightened considerably when they got outside. He gazed skyward to watch a plane's blinking lights cross the sky. Sure, Steph's pregnancy had been a kick in the face, but it didn't change anything. In some ways it made things easier — no way back.

"What are you smiling about?"

He looked across at Olsen, aware of the sound of London's thrum again. "Dunno."

Her face twitched. "Is it true, about the meds?"

"It's only one a day and my doctor has reduced the dose. But when I start to feel . . ." he raised a hand as if to grasp the right word, ". . . overwhelmed, I take these herbal tablets instead and they sort me out right away."

She narrowed her eyes for a moment. "You *do* realise that pills don't work like that — instantly, I mean. And especially anything non-prescription. What you're experiencing is a placebo effect."

"Who cares, if it works?"

She didn't bother replying. There was no point.

They hadn't reached Barbican Tube before a text came through on Olsen's phone: *Report to Charing Cross police station*

— *ask for Inspector Laghari.* Wild looked up the address on his own mobile and checked a map. Result.

Wild didn't know what to expect at the front desk, but a welcoming committee wasn't high on his list. Inspector Laghari was waiting for them, easy to spot by his shoulder pips.

"Detective Sergeant Wild?"

"Sir." Wild kept it short and sweet. Chances were that Steph had used considerable influence to strong-arm the Met into helping a fellow officer in his hour of need.

Laghari took them both upstairs to a side room where four black-clad officers waited like a blagger's nightmare. He heard Olsen gasp and wondered why being in a room with SCO19 — the Met's specialist firearms unit — didn't bother him. Then he remembered the pill he'd taken at Steph's.

The inspector didn't waste time on introductions. "How long before you meet your witness?"

Wild looked at his watch. "I have about an hour, unless she changes her mind."

Laghari shook his head sternly. "Let's hope not. DCI Hutcheson went to a lot of trouble to set up your support. You need to get a result."

Yeah, Wild thought to himself, she must have made all of two phone calls. He listened as the firearms team walked him through the plan. He didn't baulk at wearing a wire, even though they freely admitted it could make him a target if things went pear-shaped. Meanwhile, he tried to ignore Olsen's glare. He was at risk anyway and if Olsen was right, at least they'd hear him calling for assistance. He smiled darkly at the thought.

After the briefing from SCO19, DI Laghari spoke again. Wild noted that he didn't make eye contact and he looked like he had somewhere else to be. A rogue thought ran through Wild's head that maybe Steph and Laghari knew one another rather well. He dismissed it out of hand, not because he didn't believe it but because he was past caring.

"We'll keep PC Olsen informed at every stage of the operation. Perhaps you two would like a few moments together?"

Olsen nodded, eyes on the ground, while Wild stared at her incredulously. He didn't speak until the last of them had left the room. "What's going on?"

"Steph thought you and I were an item. I let her believe it. It didn't seem fair that she saw you as a total loser and this way I'm kept in the loop."

She looked so pleased with herself. He couldn't see how it was a benefit to either of them, but he liked the idea of her listening in. She went in for an awkward hug and ended up slapping him on the shoulder, like a much-loved horse.

"Good luck, Wild. Assume that everything Jackie says to you is a lie. Because it will be. And let the firearms team know immediately if you think you're in danger."

"You think I'm really stupid doing this."

Olsen matched his candour. "I think you're trying to prove something — whether to yourself, or the Met, or even Steph is anyone's guess. Just remember there are two murders waiting to be solved in Wiltshire."

Wild had to admit, as far as pep talks went it was light on sentiment, although it still packed a punch. He was all psyched to go when his mobile pinged. *I'm in a hotel. Room 406. Booked under Jackie Collins. Click the link for map.*

Funny girl. He relayed the name and link and waited while they updated their plan. Olsen sat beside him, oblivious to the tactical decisions being made on his behalf. She leaned in towards him.

"Shouldn't you be wearing a stab vest at least?"

Laghari broke off suddenly from his discussion. "It might tip Jackie off that he doesn't fully trust her. The team will be able to hear everything and they'll be near enough to respond."

Wild caught the look on Olsen's face and forced a smile. They knew what they were doing. Probably.

* * *

He opted for the hotel stairs, partly for the illusion of space and free choice. The steps were shallow but he was puffing by the fourth floor. "I'm on the last flight," he announced to an otherwise empty stairwell.

* * *

Inspector Laghari craned forward a little in the unmarked police car parked a couple of streets away. Olsen sat beside him, poised like a child waiting for fireworks, a mixture of dread and anticipation. Her feet rested awkwardly on Wild's bag. Laghari turned to her as the firearms team confirmed that they were ready to seal off the hotel and nodded at the dashboard.

"You can relax now, Olsen. No one else is getting past them."

"And what if Tony Weston is already there?"

Laghari's face froze. He turned back to Olsen, who had already opened the passenger door.

* * *

Wild heaved open the fourth-floor fire door, grateful for level ground again. He wasn't unfit as such, he'd just never been the athletic type. Sure, he'd chased down his share of villains, buoyed up by adrenaline and peer pressure. Now though, the uncertainty of what awaited him clung to his legs like weights. Added to that, he was knackered.

For no reason at all he started whistling 'Walking Back to Happiness' — an old tune he remembered from the Labyrinth café. Then he stopped in case his colleagues at the other end of the wire thought it meant something. "Soz," he whispered.

Room 406 looked no different from its neighbours. He knocked three times, as arranged, and looked along the corridor to a discarded dinner tray three doors along. Room service sounded like a great idea.

Jackie took her time opening the door. One part of his brain still wanted to believe the charade and told himself she was ultra-cautious. Another chunk of grey matter had processed every ounce of Olsen's evidence and found Jackie guilty of conspiracy, perverting the course of justice, and taking his money under false pretences — arguably the biggest crime of all.

She stood in the doorway and looked around him, her voice as staged as her performance. He wondered where the audience was. "Hello, Craig. I wasn't sure you'd come."

He thought the text messages they'd shared had been a strong clue. She deserved an Oscar for this. He followed her in and the door closed of its own accord.

"Can I get you a drink?" She waved a bottle of *Teacher's* in the air as if it could ward off evil spirits.

"Actually, tea would be nice." He had it at the back of his mind that a hot drink might be a useful weapon if — or when — Tony Weston put in an appearance.

She seemed thrown off balance by his reply but she made good with the miniature kettle and two teeny plastic sachets of milk.

He sat in the desk chair and manhandled it round to face her. "How have you been, Jackie?"

"Oh, you know." Her face looked flushed on one side, like it had been recently slapped.

He didn't comment. He set his cup down. "You asked me to come here . . . ?"

Her whole body tensed. "Alright. Give me a minute, will you? I'm taking a big risk talking with you. If Tony was to find out . . ."

He was getting Skype déjà vu. "I have already said that we'll protect you. Mind if I write this stuff down?" He reached slowly into his pocket, as if extracting a gun. The look on her face suggested that pen and paper could be just as deadly.

"Start with the Logan Brothers' snatch. Talk me through what you know."

He cupped his tea and watched her dancing for ideas. If she refused, it would leave him open to ask what else she had instead. And if she responded he would flush out the truth like a ferret in a rabbit warren.

Jackie started slowly, wasting his time. He stood it for a few minutes before heading off to the bathroom. To his relief, Tony wasn't hiding in the shower. He heard the TV through the bathroom speaker and was grateful he had an empty bladder now. Her demeanour had changed when he emerged. She'd kicked off her shoes and now sat perched on the edge of the bed. He smelt perfume in the air and, unless he was mistaken, her hair seemed a little mussed up. He retreated to his chair.

"Finish your tea then, before it gets cold."

He went to take a sip and looked up at her, stark fear in her eyes.

"Nah, I think I'll leave it."

"Please, drink your tea." Her voice seemed shrill.

He pushed the cup away. "Why, what will happen if I don't?"

"Don't play silly buggers, Craig." Her gaze darted to the door, and two loud raps made them both jump.

He was halfway across the room when a truck smashed into the back of his head. As he fell to the floor, he heard a disembodied voice.

"You idiot, you shoulda taken the easy option."

His head lolled to one side and as he opened his eyes, he felt Jackie stepping over him to get to the door. He tried to move but someone had filled his head with cement. His eyes fought to focus as she scrabbled at the door guard and unlocked the door.

Marnie Olsen stepped forward at the sound of the door unlatching and gave it a hefty shove with her shoulder. She heard a woman swearing and then a muffled thud. The door hit something solid and refused to open any further.

"Wild, you in there?"

He struggled to his knees, one hand at the back of his head protectively. "Yeah, I'm here. Watch your step: she has a cosh."

Olsen appeared from behind the door, one hand out in front of her. "Well, I have a baton. Jesus, Wild — did she slug you?"

Jackie let go of the weapon and sat up, dazed. She looked like she was thinking very slowly and then opened her mouth to speak.

Olsen closed the door behind her, an extendable baton at her side. "Save your breath, Jackie. Tony Weston is in custody. The firearms team caught him coming down from the fifth floor. What did you do, leave your mobile on?"

Jackie slumped back a little. "Look, I still have information to trade — as a witness."

Olsen retrieved the cosh carefully, watching Jackie all the while. "You must be kidding. Assaulting a police officer — that's got to be at least six months. And then there's assisting an offender . . ."

Wild hauled himself up to standing with the aid of the chair. His head felt twice its normal size. He reached back. No blood, which was always a bonus.

Jackie stayed kneeling. "Please, Craig. I didn't mean to hit you so hard — I panicked."

"What was the plan then? Give me the truth now." His confidence came from the wire on his chest and Laghari at the other end.

"It was Tony's plan. Drug you. A few photos with me . . ." She slipped a strap off her shoulder for effect.

"You were going to blackmail him?" Olsen fingered her baton.

Wild touched his head again. "Or proof of a bent copper if Tony got caught. It'd make any subsequent conviction unsafe and torch what I have left of a career. And the Skype calls?"

Jackie gave her best impression of contrite. It wouldn't win any awards. "All Tony's idea. He used to sit off-camera and listen — I never had a choice. His mum's ill so he can't stay hidden for ever, and you were an easy option."

Wild nodded gently, blinking as his brain sluiced around inside his head. Lazy. He should have checked the family connections again.

"Handcuffs, I think." Olsen took the lead and Wild didn't argue. She clicked them on despite Jackie's compliance and then said to Wild, "Your arrest, I believe."

Wild raised his palm. "No, she's all yours. I was busy testing the carpet. You've earned it, Marnie. Well done."

CHAPTER 31

Wild said his goodbyes to Olsen at Charing Cross police station, declined a trip to A&E to get his head checked over, and went off to complete his statement. In some ways it was a relief not to have to worry about Jackie any more. And as for her and Tony Weston facing justice, that would be someone else's problem.

It read less like a statement and more like a confession. He held nothing back: the Skype calls, the payments by PayPal, and his own testimony about the events in the hotel that he knew would be corroborated by the sound recordings. If he felt good about anything, apart from the fact that the throbbing in his head had abated, it was that Olsen would get some recognition. She did well under pressure, a world away from Ben Galloway's performance on the stakeout. He'd definitely put in a word for her with DI Marsh when he got back.

He had hoped someone could have driven him to Paddington Station, but fair enough there was still a lot of work left on the case. And yeah, he would've loved to sit in on an interview with Tony Weston — if only to see the look on Tony's face. Still, the journey on the Tube helped him get some perspective. His contribution now was as a witness, who would no doubt be called to court when the case went to trial. Beyond that, for the first time in a long while, he felt free of Steph and his old life, as if he were finally leaving London on his own terms. He made it to Paddington Tube station with time to kill and treated himself to half a lager at a nearby pub. A darts game was in full swing and he toyed with the idea of trying to muscle in. Best not.

The train boarded ten minutes before departure, which gave him time to find a table seat with no one else in close proximity. He opened the overnight bag that he wouldn't need now and took a chunk of chocolate from the bar. Yes, they really had rewarded him for his efforts and injury — with a large bar of bastard chocolate. The adrenaline rush had long since left him so cocoa and sugar were all he had to fall back on. Keen to stay awake so that he'd sleep properly later, he took up the photocopied pages from Jeb's great-grandfather's diary and started reading.

The pages spilled their secrets like poison being drawn from a wound. The good doctor had used his diary as a confessional. Nothing strange in that, except the secrets all belonged to other people. Wild read slowly and carefully, falling back on procedure by making notes. Dr Jacob Walsh was a master of self-justification. He wrote earnestly about being telephoned for an emergency near some farmland. And how, when he arrived, there were two men there to greet him, and only one of them was alive.

'George Porter was hysterical, weeping like a child. I found myself disgusted by his weakness, unworthy of his Home Guard uniform. This is war, after all. I recognised the young GI from an earlier brawl between a group of soldiers and some local men. Perhaps he'd sustained a more serious injury than I'd first realised, or he could have been attacked a second time. It mattered little, there was nothing to be done for him.'

Dr Walsh confirmed the death and immediately made contact with an American base captain who he'd had dealings with earlier. Porter had been left to stand guard over the body.

Wild looked up from the page and rubbed his eyes. He had questions that would probably never be answered. Who was in the earlier fight and how did Porter come to find the body? He read on.

'Captain McAllister came out to take control of the situation, such was his arrogance. He ordered us to remain with him and stood awhile, smoking while he formulated a plan.'

Now Dr Walsh digressed, weighing up the pros and cons of a decision he insisted was never his to make. The unexplained death of a serviceman would have had severe repercussions on everyone, he said, and would have driven a wedge between the Americans and the locals. The captain proposed that they bury the body in secret. Porter had the perfect place — a small medieval graveyard in a parcel of land that belonged to his family. Dr Walsh recorded that he, George Porter and the US Army captain had said a prayer for Private Melvin Kravers and then hidden the body temporarily in a ditch.

With the pact assured, the captain now played his part. As the GI had been found — quite by accident — on a path that was seldom used, Captain McAllister returned to base and told his commander that Private Kravers was missing. He ordered a detailed search of the base and confined everyone to their barracks. It was then up to the doctor and George Porter to dispose of the body by nightfall.

Wild became aware of a pair of shoes in his peripheral vision.

"Sorry to disturb you, sir, may I see your ticket please?"

Wild offered up the necessary without bothering to read the man's name badge.

"Thanking you. Must be a good book you're reading."

"Yeah," Wild mustered a half-smile. "It's a killer." He waited until he couldn't see the conductor's head over the seats, dug out more chocolate and reconnected with 1944.

Dr Jacob Walsh had been vague about where they'd buried the body and said they hadn't been able to mark the spot. Wild reckoned a jury would have found that convenient. In the days that followed, Dr Walsh moved swiftly from guilt to acceptance, aided perhaps by a realisation of possible consequences. There had been no post-mortem for one thing, so what if it hadn't been an accident after all? An entry five days later showed the *good* doctor livid that Captain McAllister had telephoned and arranged a meeting of the three conspirators. At the meeting the captain revealed that he had confided in his base commander. The commander authorised the captain to let it be known that Private Kravers had been selected for a mission that was vital to the war effort.

In the days that followed, Dr Walsh's diary entries were little more than impersonal memoranda of his daily life and those of his patients. Then, uncharacteristically, a gap of weeks was followed by a summary that bordered on melodrama. Dr Walsh presented a problem, a girl of seventeen who had discovered she was pregnant. Maybe the doctor had learned from his last experience because this time he avoided facts and kept his reflections to his own judgement of the situation. He had spoken with the girl's mother when she brought the girl to him. Only at the end of the long passage did Dr Walsh mention her name: Constance.

Wild added that to his notes. It wouldn't be hard to trace the name through parish records. He remembered the photographs he'd taken at Paxton's Country Hotel and sifted through his phone, expanding the image and sliding it around the screen so that he could read names. Constance Elleth was one of a handful of names that Aaron Kravers had identified as possible connections with his great-uncle.

The next section in Dr Walsh's diary read like a Greek tragedy. While Constance had refused to name the father of her unborn child in the presence of her own mother, she had been more forthcoming when she spoke to the doctor alone. All she knew about Melvin Kravers was that he was missing and, in the opinion of Dr Walsh, unlikely to return. Only a few days before, the neighbouring family, the Causlys, had learned that their youngest, Peter, had perished at Normandy. Dr Walsh's solution was to name Peter as the father. Constance had known Peter all her life so where was the harm? No, as Dr Walsh pointed out to history, doing this would bring comfort to the Causlys in their time of grief. Dr Walsh then spent half a page absolving himself of Kravers's secret burial by the way he'd provided for the unborn child.

Wild looked up at the window and smiled to the darkness. It sounded like what Dr Walsh needed most was a priest. The tannoy announced Didcot Parkway as the next stop in ten minutes' time. Wild took out his phone.

"Hi, is that Caitlin?" He frowned — of course it was. He'd made a point of entering her number into his phone very carefully so as not to make a tit of himself.

"Hello, Craig, I wasn't expecting your call so soon — and so late!"

"Sorry. Bad time?"

"No, no." She yawned and then apologised, laughing. "Where are you — some sort of echo chamber?"

"Close. I'm on a train." He winced. He sounded like the sort of person he hated. He raised his head like a meerkat and glanced around a near empty carriage. "Coming back from London."

"You sound pretty pleased about it."

"I am. Tied up a few loose ends. I, er, wondered if you were busy later?"

"What time does your train get in?"

"It's scheduled to reach Swindon around ten."

"Fancy a curry?"

"You're on!" He tried to temper his enthusiasm.

"I'll see you at Swindon station then. Make sure you wait if I'm not there when you arrive."

"Brilliant." He cringed. Too eager. "Yeah, looking forward to it."

"See you soon, Craig."

A text came in from Olsen, sharing her plaudits from the Met. He sent one back to tell her she owed him a drink.

He used the time stuck at Didcot Parkway on a red light to apply some critical thinking. So what if Constance Elleth's child had been a cuckoo — what bearing did that have on a murder seventy-odd years later? And yet . . . and yet

Alexander Porter's murder happened within days of Aaron Kravers arriving in the area. And what about Jeb Walsh — where was his place in the domino sequence?

Caitlin was waiting at the exit. He had wondered if she'd change her mind, what with the time and everything. She nodded as he approached the exit and he floundered for a greeting. A kiss seemed presumptuous and a handshake ridiculous. He muttered, "Hi," and raised a hand like he was stopping traffic.

She smiled. "Do you have an Indian restaurant in mind?"

"No, sorry, I thought you'd know somewhere. I could look one up on my phone . . ."

"It is a bit late . . ." Her voice dipped.

He smiled. *But here you are*. He clicked his fingers. "Got it! I know where we can get a curry, only it's a bit of a mad idea."

"Try me." She steered him across the car park to her car.

Wild directed them to a twenty-four-hour petrol station close to where he lived. She waited outside while he rummaged through the ready meals, holding them up so she could see them through the window and give him her approval.

They drove to his house in silence. It felt strange to have a woman in his orbit again. Steph had started off as a competition. Most of the lads in the station had fancied her and he went out of his way to stay aloof, watching with glee as her would-be 'suitors,' for want of a coarser word, fell by the wayside. It all seemed like a long time ago now.

By the time Caitlin turned off her ignition it was nearly 11 p.m. They sat for a moment, still saying nothing in the orange glow of a streetlight.

Okay, Craig, easy does it. He invited her in and put the microwave to work. A few minutes later they were enjoying a nondescript curry and making conversation.

"So, what was your trip about? You didn't say much on the phone."

He revelled in the attention. "I helped out colleagues in the Met and I ran into my ex-wife. Turns out she's pregnant and getting engaged."

"Ouch!"

"Yeah, you could say that, I s'pose." He broke off a piece of naan bread, split it in two and offered her half. "Then again, it was only a matter of time."

She nibbled at it delicately. "Who's the lucky fella?"

"I didn't stay to ask." He dug around in his curry to avoid her pity. "She's moved on and that's the right thing to do." When he looked up again, she was staring at two wooden doors on the wall.

"Do you play, then, Craig?"

He laughed, following her line of vision to the dartboard. "Well, it's not up there for show."

"No, I mean, are you any good?"

"Madam," he conjured up pomposity, "I'll have you know I've won prizes. I'll show you." He opened one of the cardboard boxes edging the room and lifted out a couple of plastic trophies, one of a darts player and the other in the shape of a dartboard. While she was looking at them carefully or feigning interest — he couldn't tell which — he took his darts out of his jacket and inserted the flights. Then he stood at the oche, which he'd marked on the carpet in faint chalk, and unleashed hell. If hell were three darts thrown with precision: treble twenty, single twenty, and double top to finish.

She uncurled her knees and stood up. "Can you teach me?"

He felt his mouth drying. "Sure."

She stood beside him and he tasted lamb curry in the space between them. He retrieved his darts and handed one to her.

"Keep your movement fluid and don't lower your gaze."

Thud. Seventeen.

"Not bad. Can I just . . . ?" He stood close enough to see the hairs on her neck. "If you stand like this . . ." He pushed a hand lightly between her shoulder blades and felt her bra strap under his palm. "Now, try it."

She hit an inner. "What's that worth? Twenty-five? God, this is easy. Where's my prize?" She sank the last dart in the five, just over the border from the twenty.

"You're getting there." He crossed the carpet to extract the darts. No expectations. And no flirtations either. He liked her well enough, but it didn't seem that kind of night. She called it quits about half an hour later. On the plus side, she suggested returning for a rematch.

He saw her to the door, disappointed in himself. Had he missed a cue? It was too late now. As he stood at the step, watching her reach the gate, she turned and walked smartly back towards him to plant a small, deliberate kiss on his lips.

"Thanks, I enjoyed tonight. Call me again — soon."

He waited until she was safely in her car before closing the front door. "Christ, what a weird day." Weird or not, sleep came easily and this time without tablets.

CHAPTER 32

Wild woke around seven, the musty smell of last night's meal haunting the house like the ghost of curries past. He'd planned to surprise Marsh by turning up bright and early at the station, but she beat him to the punchline. He picked up her message when he exited the shower.

"Wherever you are, whatever you're doing, ring me as soon as you get this. It's DI Marsh."

He loved the unnecessary qualifier, as if he knew loads of insistent Scottish women. He called her back still wrapped in a towel.

"Good morning, ma'am. Sorry, I was in the shower. I'm back home now. Everything is sorted."

"No, it bloody well isn't. We have a situation at the Elleth farmhouse. Edwin Causly has gone there to make trouble. As both families have a direct connection to the ongoing Alexander Porter case, I want you over there pronto."

He recalled the explosive contents of Dr Walsh's 1944 diary. "I might have an idea what it's about. Leave it with me."

"Well, get off the phone and get on with it. Top priority."

He took her at her word and picked up yesterday's clothes from the floor, grabbing his jacket off the back of the chair on the way out.

He radioed in from the car to get more details. Edwin Causly had turned up at the Elleths' in a rage, but Marsh considered it a low-risk situation until there was some evidence to the contrary.

Wild was surprised to see a marked police car at the farm gate. Sergeant Galloway started walking down towards him. Wild could also see Ben Galloway sitting in the car.

Wild wound his window down for the sarge.

"Morning to you, Craig. This'll turn out to be some farming dispute."

"Then shouldn't you be up there?"

Sergeant Galloway's face reddened. "Detective Inspector Marsh said to wait for you and you'd take charge. She couldn't come herself on account of a shoulder strain — playing squash, would you believe?"

Wild played his best poker face. After the previous day in London he was prepared to believe anything.

"What do we know?"

"The call came from a distressed female, Elleth's wife we think. And then the line went dead. It's out of order now."

Wild started walking up to the house. "I'll call you if I need you. In fact, you might as well take off and leave Ben with me.

"Right you are, Craig. If that's what you want."

Ben Galloway got out of the car sharpish as Wild approached, eager as a collie. "Morning, Skip. The curtains are all drawn and we've not heard anything."

Wild glanced at the house. "Let's get on, then. It's hardly going to be the Siege of Malta." He stared at Galloway, amused by his ignorance. Clearly, not a history scholar. It wasn't yet eight o'clock, so what could have riled Causly so much at this hour? He could guess the *why* but not the *when*.

He knocked on the door and stepped back, addressing the house. "Mr Elleth, it's DS Wild. I'd like to come in and have a chat." No response. He moved closer and poked the letterbox. "It's DS Wild. I'm sure you'd all prefer I talk inside rather than shouting your business to the four winds. Especially *you*, Mr Causly."

He heard scraping and creaking, like the movement of heavy furniture, and then Causly's voice called along the passage.

"You get on and mind your own business. It ain't anything to do with you."

Wild tried the front door for the first time — locked. The sound of a door slamming and someone shouting sent him back to the letterbox.

"Look, I'm not going anywhere until I've spoken with Mr Elleth."

Now there were footsteps echoing upstairs, then he heard a window opening.

Edwin Causly did the talking. "We can hear you fine from up here. Say what you've got to say and be on your way."

"That's not how it works."

"Is that a fact?" The window opened a little further and the barrel of a shotgun poked through. "Well, why don't you tell me . . . ?"

Wild gazed up at the barrel as it waved around. He felt his throat constricting and leaned forward to try and breathe easier. Bloody guns. He squeezed his fists tightly and then released them, exactly how the counsellor had shown him. It took a few times before he sensed his chest opening a little more and as the air filled his lungs, he felt his fingers tingling.

He straightened up. "You open this fucking door right now or I'll have an armed response team here in fifteen minutes and you can discuss it with them. Do you understand me?"

"No need for obscenity, Detective Sergeant."

He heard the strains of a conversation and then the window came down. Footsteps thudded down the stairs and up to the front door. A key turned and a heavy bolt retracted. The door swung back slowly to reveal Causly and his gun.

"You wanted in. You got your wish." The gun twitched. "Now, move."

Wild went inside. Causly's gun hand wavered although his finger wasn't on the trigger. Wild wondered where the dogs were, and a sickening feeling rose in his guts. Causly saw him looking at the basket.

"Dogs are outside in the yard, don't you worry about them. Get in the kitchen and sit down."

Gordon Elleth didn't look too pleased to see him.

Wild sat where the gun pointed. "Mr Causly, I think I know why you're here."

Causly leaned on one edge of the kitchen table, the small shotgun nursed in one arm like a grudge. Wild's attention was fixed on how compact the gun was. Small enough to fit into your mouth and reach the trigger.

Causly faced him down. "So, what are you going to do?"

"I'm here to keep the peace."

"You're too late for that. There'll be no peace here in this world or the next."

Wild realised that Mrs Elleth was missing. Come to that, so was the black cross on the wall. Maybe she'd taken it for comfort.

"Where's your wife, Mr Elleth?"

Causly patted his pocket. "She's upstairs, safely under lock and key. This concerns him, not her."

Wild adjusted his chair. "I know about the child — the GI's child."

Causly turned to him and his body sank a little, as if the truth had suddenly become harder to bear. "My whole life has been an obligation, lived in my father's shadow." Tears welled in his eyes. "And without him, I grew up fast. Had to. And all that time I had no business being there, worked like a dog. The Elleths could have claimed me and my mother, but instead they abandoned us."

"My father was not a forgiving man," Gordon Elleth conceded.

"We might have had a better life in America. Not tied to the land every waking hour. And all that time the Elleths were lying to us. Lying to me."

Wild decided against pointing out that Constance also knew the truth. Better not to antagonise a man with a gun.

Elleth looked genuinely contrite. "I'm sorry, Edwin. This all happened before I was born. Constance was nineteen when I came along and we lost two brothers in the cradle before then. I learned about her secret eventually, but it wasn't mine to reveal."

"Well, it's out now." Causly moved around the table to a spot midway between Elleth and Wild. The sadness had passed and there was a coldness in his eyes.

Wild thought he looked capable of anything. "Could I get some water, or some tea? I need to take a tablet." He opened his jacket and Causly snapped the gun towards him. Wild eased the box out slowly and rattled it. "It's for anxiety. Otherwise I get dizzy and sick." He held the packet out.

Causly leaned across to take a look and nodded. "Tap's over there."

Elleth made to stand. "I'll get it."

"You'll stay where I tell you to, Gordon Elleth. We might be blood but that's never counted for anything before. No reason I can see to change that now."

Wild got up very carefully, arms away from his sides, and moved towards the sink, turning his back to Causly.

"How did you find out about the GI?" Wild played for time, turning the tap slowly and letting the pipe shriek.

"That American chap came calling. Said he was looking into local history. Wanted to know if we had a Constance in the family. I said no at first because my mother's first name was May, although no one used it — Constance was her middle name. Then this Aaron Kravers starts talking about DNA and a family secret, and a lot of things began to make sense. So here I am, asking Gordon for the *truth* of it."

Wild glanced over his shoulder. Causly was mostly rambling now, the gun swinging as he moved. He'd never make that distance, not without a distraction.

"You gonna be all bloody day, Detective Sergeant Wild?"

Wild's chest pressed in. *Not now.* As he bent forward, he felt his darts wallet against his ribcage. He leaned over a little more and coughed dramatically, as if he might retch in the sink, then he slipped a dart from the case. "Just coming . . ." He teased a flight out and slipped it into place. As he went for another, he fumbled the case and it fell into the sink, clattering against crockery.

"What are you playing at, Copper? I'm not afraid to use this. You won't be the first bugger I've taken a shot at."

Wild pressed the dart flight in place, feeling the narrow edge against his palm. He took a breath and as he breathed out, he span around and hurled the dart at Causly. It arced across the kitchen table and lodged in the side of Causly's head.

Causly screamed and lurched backwards, discharging the weapon into the ceiling as he fell, scattering unused shotgun cartridges on the floor. Wild was on him in seconds, wrestling the weapon away, not that Causly put up much opposition. Blood pumped rhythmically from the wound in his head.

A plaintive cry echoed from upstairs. "Gordon, what's going on? Are you alright? Oh my dear Lord!"

Gordon Elleth bellowed at the top of his lungs, "I'm fine, my love. Edwin Causly has had a bit of an accident, is all. I'm coming up to you now." He went over to Causly, reached into his pocket and took out some keys. Then he glanced down and leaned closer, like he was sharing a secret. "I forgive you. You had a shock and it's unsettled you."

Wild was already on his mobile, calling for an ambulance. Elleth stood up. "There was no need for you to come here today, DS Wild."

Wild choked back bile. "Are you taking the piss? He threatened us with a loaded shotgun."

"That's not how I see it. My nephew came over to visit me and his licensed shotgun accidentally went off. It'll be your word against mine." He glanced at the wall where the cross had hung and went upstairs to his wife.

Causly appeared groggy as he sat up. Wild fetched a tea towel from the range and held it under the tap, wringing it out a couple of times before passing it to Causly. "Apply some pressure. You should be good at that."

"Bloody fool. You could have had my eye out."

Wild fashioned a smile. "Only if I'd wanted to." He picked up the dart from the floor, wrapped it in a handkerchief and moved it out of reach, where he'd already placed the gun. "Evidence."

He sat with the Elleths and Edwin Causly to wait for the ambulance. No one said anything, their silence interrupted by the sound of the dogs barking for attention outside and the distant sound of a clock.

When the ambulance crew arrived, Wild let them in and exited the house. He held up the shotgun and bloodied handkerchief as Ben Galloway came running towards him.

"You okay, Skip?"

"Yeah, no thanks to you — where were you?"

"You told me to wait here."

"Oh yeah, so I did. Right, I want you in there to get statements from the Elleths and then get one from Causly — you might have to see him in hospital."

"Do I need a statement from you as well?"

Wild looked up at the clouds drifting by. "Sure. Once we see what they've got to say for themselves."

CHAPTER 33

Wild rang DI Marsh from the car to give her an update and then headed to the police station. She'd said little on the call, other than to clarify a couple of points, but he could tell she wasn't impressed. It was a sombre drive back, interspersed with glances to the passenger footwell where he'd stashed the weapons.

As he pulled up, a couple of uniformed officers stopped in the car park and glanced at him — or his car — before going about their business. He noted one of the copper's collar numbers and added it to his car scratching suspects. It had become a sizeable list.

As he climbed the stairs one of his junior colleagues — he thought her name was Rose but he couldn't be certain — paused and smiled. "Great work, Skip." Her earnest expression implied she probably meant it and it wasn't sarcasm. Come to think of it, he *had* done well: he'd resolved the situation without any significant harm. He thought back to Edwin Causly leaving in an ambulance. Maybe not Queen's Police Medal material.

Marsh sat at her desk, chair set back. She had one arm in a sling, which made her seem even more buttoned up. Her face reminded him of Queen Victoria, and not on a good day. "Shut the door." She didn't wait. "First, I want you to take me through the events of this morning in more detail and then you can tell me about this diary you've been carrying around for two days."

He talked about the incident at the farmhouse for longer than felt comfortable, finishing with a flourish. "That mad old bastard was lucky an armed response team didn't lay him out for Dr Bell."

Marsh had barely moved a muscle and when she spoke he wished she hadn't. "Maybe you should have rested after visiting London . . . Marnie Olsen came back while you were playing *Bullseye*. I gather you two had quite a time there."

"I'm totally fine." He read her face and retraced his steps. "I mean . . . having recently been assaulted in London in the line of duty, I may have overreacted today in a moment of crisis, after being confronted by an unstable man with what I thought was — and turned out to be — a loaded weapon."

"Very good. We'll make a politician of you yet."

He resisted replying, 'Hopefully not,' and changed tack. "Marnie did really well in London. She saved my bacon."

"Interesting. She tells it a little differently. I think you may have a fan there. You might want to speed up your charm offensive on the rest of the station though."

The second topic of conversation attracted more audience participation. He laid it all out for DI Marsh — the brief history of Melvin Kravers and the entanglement his death had created between the Elleths, the Causlys and the Walshes. When he'd finished the only questions were the ones in his head. He sat for a moment and pondered where they'd go from there. How did the past help them catch Porter's killer? Or Dr Walsh's, come to that?

Marsh took a sip from coffee that was at best tepid, while Wild shuddered a little. "Go and book in your evidence and then we'll have a team review. I think we're gonna need a bigger whiteboard."

* * *

Wild treated himself to a vending machine visit after booking in the shotgun and one of his precious darts. Booking in all three was a step too far and he expected — well, *hoped* — that Edwin Causly would let the matter drop. Thankfully it wasn't his best set of darts. Tungsten was too good for Causly.

As he reached his desk with a hallowed cup of coffee, he saw Sergeant Galloway and Marnie Olsen approaching from the opposite direction. He cracked a smile and she barely acknowledged him, following the sergeant's lead to DI Marsh's office.

They went straight in and the door closed quietly. Clearly, they were expected. Wild sipped his coffee and tried to read the situation. Olsen had been her usual focused self but there was something else, a sense of tension that hinted at triumph or disaster. Maybe this was the royal handshake after the London debacle. Why Marsh, though, and why not say something to him beforehand?

Wild tapped his desk rhythmically to accompany his thoughts. Logically, it had to be connected with the Porter investigation. Maybe he'd missed something or screwed up somewhere down the line? "Nah," he assured his darkened reflection in the screen, "you'll be fine."

A few minutes later, to no surprise at all, a hand poked through Marsh's office blinds and beckoned him. He didn't bother knocking, especially as they'd have company. A man had his pride if nothing else.

"Ma'am?" He nodded to Sergeant Galloway and then Olsen, whose flicker of a smile suggested it wasn't a bollocking party for one with guests.

"Sit down, please."

He pulled a chair in from one of the cube walls.

DI Marsh turned to Olsen. "You have the floor."

Olsen blushed but quickly regained her poise. She spoke aloud to the room, although Wild would have laid money on this being the repeat performance for his benefit. "On Sergeant Galloway's instructions, I have been looking into known collectors of firearms across the county — including some who prefer to purchase with no questions asked."

Sergeant Galloway gave a chuckle, and Wild glanced his way, remembering their conversation on the first day after Porter's murder. *Collectors* — a byword for dealers and fences of illegal weapons. Clever girl though, sharing the credit for her progress report with her sergeant. Wild awaited the good news and she awaited his full attention.

"We put inquiries out in all the usual places and the search drew a blank. It didn't help that we lacked a picture of the weapon."

That rankled with Wild a little, but he was in mixed company so he let it go.

"However, having become aware that Mr Porter's firearms cabinet had been ransacked, I wondered if the shotgun had actually been there when the burglary took place."

Wild nodded, having shared the same conclusion with her at Porter's house. He couldn't blame her — when he was a uniformed PC, he took every opportunity to blow his own trumpet. How else was he supposed to trade up to plain-clothes, hard work aside? He realised that Olsen was still talking.

". . . So, I made some other inquiries through gunsmiths. On the day of the murder, Mr Porter's antique shotgun was being cleaned and refurbished. I struck lucky."

DI Marsh beamed. "You did more than that. You thought like a detective and applied some lateral thinking, thereby tracing the weapon to a gunsmith over the border in Dorset. Wouldn't you agree, DS Wild?"

"I would, ma'am." He didn't begrudge Olsen her moment in the spotlight, especially as it validated his early theory that the murder weapon may have belonged to someone.

Marsh gave a heavy sigh. "Our Dorset colleagues are meeting us halfway. Sergeant Galloway, perhaps you'd be willing to collect the evidence?"

"Of course, ma'am."

"Excellent. Right then, that will be all. But I'm very impressed, Marnie. I'll be keeping my eye on you in future."

Wild watched them file out from the comfort of his seat. He figured Marsh had invited him in for more than that. He wasn't disappointed.

She removed her glasses and rubbed the bridge of her nose. "Did you and Ben Galloway have a little man-to-man chat before you went up to London? While you were away, he asked to see me and talked about putting in for a transfer. Is that your doing?"

Wild felt a familiar adrenaline rush. No more histrionics in work time though — that was his deal with himself. He gave himself some breathing space before responding, and stuck as close to the truth as he needed to. "Yeah, I did have a chat with Ben a few days ago. I think this case is a little too close to home for him. He went to the same school as half the suspects and his family knows Mrs Henderson at one of the solicitors. It wouldn't hurt him to get some distance once this case is concluded."

"When I want your help with staff management I'll let you know, okay?"

He knew not to reply. It was her show and her stage.

She put her glasses back on. "I need to know I can rely on you, Craig. No more stunts like the one you pulled in front of the team before you buggered off to see *old friends,* or delaying sharing vital evidence — and yes I do realise we'd not have that diary without you — or giving puncture wounds to suspects. Clear?"

"Crystal."

"Right, what's your assessment of Mr Causly? And before you start, his brief has already spoken with me and in light of the fact that Gordon Elleth has decided not to pursue a complaint against him . . ."

Wild sneered. He knew what was coming.

". . . After thoughtful discussion, we have decided that it's not in anyone's interests to take any further action over the events at the farmhouse today."

"I'd still like to interview him about the family situation. It might have a bearing on the Porter case."

"Agreed. After the case review, then. I want to make sure everyone is up to speed on developments, especially you. Shall we?"

CHAPTER 34

The team gathered in the only room large enough to house two moveable whiteboards, plus an array of chairs and tables. Other notes had been stuck to fixed boards with magnets. DI Marsh took centre stage, her slinged arm reminding Wild of Admiral Nelson in his latter days.

The DI reached behind a whiteboard with her good arm and retrieved a bamboo cane. "Okay, settle down, people." She waited all of fifteen seconds before speaking to the room. "What do we know?" After a momentary silence she tapped a whiteboard with more force than needed and waited expectantly.

Wild lurched into the breach. "Alexander Porter, aged sixty-eight, found dead in one of his own fields. Superficially, the crime scene looked like a suicide." He paused to make a point. "However, we quickly established this was a murder." He glanced around. Incredibly, some of the team were writing this down.

Ben Galloway saw his moment. "No weapon found at the crime scene — no great surprise there," he paused for laughter, "and also no obvious mode of travel to the field." He stopped talking.

Marsh cast him a weary smile: C for effort. "Given the location, we know he didn't walk there and — thanks to DS Wild and PC Olsen — we also know he ate at the George on the night he died. The only witness so far to confirm he was there is the landlady."

There was disappointment in her voice and Wild welcomed it with open arms. Maybe if he'd been a *local*, then the pub clientele might have been more forthcoming. However, he seriously doubted that. He tapped the top of a pen on the table in front of him. "The place where Porter died marks this out as personal. We still don't have a clear motive, but the perpetrator is someone who knows Porter or knows about him."

Marsh received the pass and ran with it. "You can see our list of suspects on the board: Nathan Porter, son of the deceased — racked up debts that his father was helping to pay off. Although Nathan was down from Scotland on the day his father died, they had a row and Nathan's phone confirms he was heading north when Alexander Porter died. We are awaiting CCTV from the airline in case any smart alec wants to suggest his phone went home without him."

Marsh's bamboo cane moved across the whiteboard. "Jeb Walsh, went to the same school as Nathan Porter although a couple of years older. Jeb lent both father and son money at different times. Had a fight with Nathan, presumably over money, but the best of pals now. A shady bastard, not a suspect — especially since the unexplained demise of his grandfather, Dr James Walsh, which we are treating as related. Incidentally," she looked directly at Wild, "I forgot to mention that Dr Bell confirmed the bruising on Alexander Porter's body was due to his medical condition and not the result of an assault." She did him the courtesy of a three-second hiatus. "As you suggested. Also of note, Pauline Henderson — Jeb's girlfriend — works at Hollings and Gresham, so she may have known about the first will. May have."

Ben Galloway fidgeted a little until he found the courage to speak up. "What about this email business?"

Marsh flicked the end of her cane at Galloway. "Thank you, Ben. Now this, ladies and gentlemen, is where things take a turn for the strange." She handed out a stack of papers to the person nearest to her. "Pass them on, please." She didn't bother waiting. "For those of you who aren't up to speed, this will help. Jeb Walsh learned that in 1944 May Constance Elleth got pregnant by an American GI, who later died, and was persuaded to pass off the baby's father as Peter Causly, who died at Normandy." She paused and stared over her glasses. "Obviously, this goes no further than this room and if I hear otherwise there will be severe repercussions."

The room turned to stone. Ben Galloway managed to break the spell.

"No, that can't be right. Constance Elleth was married to Peter Causly. There's one headstone for the pair of them."

Wild craned across the table. "That's just it, Ben — she wasn't. Constance took his name and moved into the Causly household before the birth, as *if* they'd been married. The Causlys welcomed her with open arms. Why wouldn't they? And I suppose the locals fell into step." He sat back in his chair. "Is this a motive to murder Alexander Porter over seventy years later?"

Ben Galloway stopped speaking and looked at the printed page. Something that passed for recognition swept across his face. "Did Alexander Porter know? I can't see as anyone has anything to gain from this getting out, especially all this time later, although the Causlys wouldn't like it. Nor the Elleths, I imagine. What with both families being church folk and all."

Wild blew out a breath. Galloway had a point, relatively speaking. He looked up at the whiteboard, where three names awaited attention: Gordon Elleth, Edwin Causly, and Aaron Kravers — a relative of the very late GI. "What about the Elleth and Causly families? Extended families, I mean."

Marsh turned teacher. "The Elleths use agricultural labour for the hard graft on the farm, although Gordon likes to keep his hand in. Sergeant Galloway interviewed Edwin Causly for us while DS Wild was in London. Incidentally, Edwin Causly stuck to the same script as Gordon Elleth – that of not seeing Alexander Porter in the George on the night he died. It's all in the notes." She flicked through a couple of pages. "Now, where was I? Right, there is a Causly heir, but unless he arranged an assassination from Canada, he's out of the frame. There's a second cousin as well," she waggled her cane, "or something like that, who helps with the harvest. Otherwise it's a mixture of regular and seasonal labour. Oh, and a daughter, although she apparently has no interest in the farm." Marsh eased herself around to face the board.

Wild nodded to the back of her head. Neatly done. "What about Aaron Kravers?"

Marsh drew a question mark beside the name. "He's the curiosity. I mean, he has a reason to want Porter dead . . . sins of the father and all that. Plus, it would fit DS Wild's profile of this being personal."

Wild decided not to mention it had been Olsen's idea. "Where would he get a shotgun from, given that he's been here for, what, a couple of weeks?"

One of the silent wonders Wild had been forced to consider teammates cleared his throat. Harris, if Wild remembered correctly.

"At our last review, after DS Wild had to leave suddenly," he shot Wild a glance like an arrow, "you said Porter's house was probably broken into after the murder in order to find his gun? That means the killer had to know he *had* a gun." He sat back and folded his arms.

Wild could feel the stripes' envy from across the room. "You're assuming the killer and the burglar are connected. Who's to say word about Porter's death didn't get around sooner than we think and someone chanced their arm? Especially as we now know Porter's shotgun was a valuable antique. Other people might have known that." Wild dropped his pen on the table with a satisfying rattle. Chew on that, Harris.

Three staccato raps on the door broke the tension. Olsen stepped in and handed DI Marsh a piece of paper. As she turned to leave, Marsh called her back. "Why don't you sit in and join us, Marnie?"

Harris kicked a seat out for her, and Olsen deftly moved past it to find a space by herself. Wild found himself smiling.

Marsh glanced at the paper and passed it back. "Marnie, perhaps you'd share what you've learned."

Olsen sat up straight, aware that all eyes were on her. "As you thought, ma'am, there was a third will, superseding the one that benefited Edwin Causly. It was made over a year ago in Chippenham, so the solicitors weren't local. In the event of Mr Porter's death all his land goes to a wildlife trust." She reread her own notes and tried not to stumble over the words. "There's a stipulation that the middle field — Fortune's Field — is left undisturbed. They can grow wildflowers there and treat it as a nature reserve as long as they don't do any digging. The other two fields," she squinted at her own scrawl, "can still be farmed."

Marsh beamed. "There you go then."

Wild stared at her, waiting for an explanation.

"Why would Porter have left land first to Elleth and then to Causly? Come on people, what do we know about him?"

Wild felt her eyes boring into him. "He's skint."

"Bravo, DS Wild. Okay, so hypothetically he has borrowed money from them in the past, presumably offering the land as a payback, so he could settle some of Nathan's debts or his own. It's a pound to a penny that there are other debts we haven't uncovered yet." She fixed her gaze on Galloway. "Ben, go back to Porter's bank and see if you can match up any payments to when the first two wills were made, and any unusual transactions immediately before or afterwards."

Ben Galloway got up and headed for the door. Marsh stared at him, incredulous, and then looked to Wild who slowly shook his head. She could humiliate him another time. Besides, he had something else to say.

"What about Dr Walsh's demise? That can't be a coincidence."

Marsh pointed to the second whiteboard where a timeline had been established. She put down her cane and took off her glasses, flicking them from side to side like a cat's tail. "Jeb Walsh lends money, so could it be some other debtor?"

Wild felt like they were the only two people in the room. "The timing is key. We had Aaron Kravers in custody. I don't fancy Nathan Porter for this — no way . . ." He stalled, all out of ideas, and his attention drifted to the other whiteboard where Porter's life and death were revealed in a series of photos, documents and marker pen lines. "What about the farming families?"

Marsh snapped to attention. "The men are both in their seventies . . . Harris, look into the actual farmers, and the daughter. See if you can track her down."

Harris took flight as if she'd kicked him up the backside, scraping back his chair in his eagerness to do her bidding.

"That's us for now. I'll go see this third solicitor in Chippenham. Marnie, I'd like to see you in a couple of minutes — will you wait for me outside? DS Wild, I need a word."

The room cleared, leaving Wild and Marsh together. Wild came up to the front. He could see Olsen lurking outside. "Pet project, boss?"

"I need a driver and yes, why not? By your own admission she hauled your arse out of the fire in London." She arched an eyebrow as if it were a weapon. "Here's what I think you should concentrate on when you speak to Edwin Causly . . ."

CHAPTER 35

Wild galloped down the stairs. Marsh had given him some direction and he intended to listen to most of it. The sharp-suited solicitor, Corey, had agreed to come straight over from Santers in order to *support* Mr Causly, and Ben Galloway — Causly's designated driver — would be riding shotgun in the interview. It promised to be a fun-packed hour.

Ben Galloway was waiting by the swing doors when Wild descended the last flight. "Mr Causly is having a quick chat with his brief. He told me in the car that he's happy to cooperate in any way he can."

Yeah, Wild thought, short of telling the truth.

"One more thing." Galloway's face grew as serious as a child's. "He's pretty self-conscious about the injury he sustained at the Elleths' place. Best not to mention it. And no need to, I suppose, as no one is pressing charges." His voice carried all the gravitas of a school nativity speech.

Wild smiled and nodded, the way he did with old people when he wasn't really listening. "Give them a knock and tell them we're in interview room four when they're ready, and wait outside to escort them."

The first sight that greeted Wild, as he stared at the door from his uncomfortably spongy seat, was Edwin Causly's head, sporting gauze and plasters. He felt the urge to laugh and pushed his tongue against his bottom teeth to give his face something else to do.

Causly sniffed, as if looking for a bad smell, sat down and turned to the door. The patch on his head moved in an irresistible arc. Wild heard words being exchanged outside and felt his shoulders fusing together. Ben Galloway had a lot to learn.

The solicitor entered next, greeted Wild and took his place beside Causly. They both seemed relaxed, which surprised Wild because last time he'd seen Corey he'd had him marked down as a cocky sod. Maybe he'd been working on his deskside manner.

Ben Galloway closed the door and sat down, hands folded in front of him. Wild hit the switch, explained that Causly was under caution and free to leave at any time. Causly glanced to his brief, a faint smile on his lips.

"Thank you for coming in today, Mr Causly. As you know, we are still investigating the death of Alexander Porter." He paused to see how that landed. It didn't. Causly remained stone-faced. "However, as you know, there was an incident today — a misunderstanding — that we think may have a bearing on the case."

Causly leaned back until his brief laid a reassuring hand on his arm.

"Mr Causly, how would you describe your relationship with Gordon Elleth?"

Causly looked confused. "Well, he's family. Constance, my late mother, was Gordon's older sister. Yes, the Elleths and the Causlys have farmed side by side for generations."

Wild let the statement hang there for a moment or two. The solicitor scribbled a note and Causly nodded to him. Galloway stared ahead like a border collie awaiting instructions. Wild went in gently for the kill.

“I don’t wish to be impertinent, Mr Causly, but who was your father?”

Causly swivelled to face his brief. “Do I have to answer that?” The brief whispered something in his ear and Wild let it go because he knew the answer.

“Mr Causly, what would you say if I told you that evidence has come to light which strongly suggests your biological father was a man called Melvin Kravers — an American GI stationed here during the war?”

“No comment.”

Wild coughed. Bloody hell, no comment in a voluntary interview — a new low. “I mention all this as it may have a bearing on the death of Mr Porter. We now have credible information that suggests Mr Porter’s father may have helped conceal the death of Melvin Kravers back in 1944—”

The solicitor opened his mouth to speak but Wild headed him off at the pass. “And a relative of Melvin Kravers has been trying to research his family history. Has Aaron Kravers been in touch with you recently?”

Causly’s face contorted. “He came up to the house. Bloody cheek of it. Insisting we were related and talking some ole nonsense about him matching a DNA sample on the internet. I couldn’t make much sense of it so I sent him packing.”

“But not before you put two and two together? Perhaps you spoke with your, er, daughter?”

Causly folded his arms. “Well, I took in some of what that Yank said and the more I dwelt on it the more certain I was that the Elleths were at the bottom of it. And I remembered, see, how it was between my mother and her family. We only saw them in church — till my mother stopped going — and on Boxing Day. Rarely otherwise, unless it was farming business. When my mother,” he touched his sternum, “God rest her soul, became ill, her parents wanted nothing to do with her. Only at the end did her father come down with his Bible verses and his black cross . . .” He stalled, seemingly lost in memory.

Wild brought him back to the present. "Alexander Porter also had one of those crosses on his wall." He saw the way Causly's eyes enlarged. "What's that all about?"

Causly's chest lifted. "At the end of the war, the people in our parish held a renewal of faith. The vicar ordered iron crosses from a blacksmith—"

Wild fought the urge to smirk: iron crosses at the end of the Second World War.

"—To raise church funds and help some of those who had suffered with their menfolk being overseas or lost. Most of the *old* families round here will have them. Them's as still believes, anyhow." He turned back to his brief, who started to put on his coat. "I've answered your questions, Detective Sergeant, them as were fit to ask in the first place. Can I go now?"

Wild stretched his hands behind his head. "Thank you for your time. One last thing. Were you aware that Mr Porter made a new will, superseding the one naming you as the main beneficiary?" He stared at Causly's face, hoping for a flicker of emotion — rage, shock, sadness — he'd take anything on offer. There was nothing, and that could only mean this wasn't new information.

Causly stood up, arms limply at his side until Corey helped him on with his coat. "Is that a fact?"

* * *

Wild checked his watch as Causly and his solicitor left the building and loitered together in the car park. Forty-five minutes from start to finish. And what did they have to show for it? Causly had no-commented, deflected and obfuscated. But Wild could smell blood now, he was sure of it. He let the door swing shut and went upstairs to see Ben Galloway.

He found him at his desk, puzzling over some paperwork.

"Someone's keen!"

Galloway looked up, startled. "Sorry, Skip, I thought you'd be a few minutes. This is another case." He blushed. "Well, not a case exactly. I was speaking to some of the lads in the canteen and a few of them have had their cars scratched, like yours. No one's bothered to make a formal report but I thought I'd see what I could do with it. Common denominators and the like."

Wild felt the moisture evaporate from his mouth. "Don't, er, spend too long on it, commendable though your initiative is." He tried not to sound like he was taking the piss. "Low-level vandalism like this is notoriously difficult to prove. That's why I didn't report mine. How far have you got, anyway?"

Galloway lifted his arm reluctantly, the way a schoolboy shares hard-won test answers. "I got four cars noted, plus yours."

"Any common factors?"

Galloway huffed under pressure. "Other than it's all coppers? Not really." He looked back at his handiwork. "The only thing is that it's all happened in the past few weeks."

Wild leaned closer. "Since I arrived at the station."

Galloway seemed flustered. "Yeah, I suppose so. And I'm not implying anything, Skip. No offence . . ."

He patted Galloway on the back. "None taken. I'd be interested in anything you come up with — if you'd like some feedback?"

"Nice one, Skip. That'd be very helpful."

Wild didn't breathe easily until he got back to his own desk. No more evening drives for a while, even though he had one more copper on his list. Win some, lose some. As he logged back in, he wondered how Marsh and Olsen were faring together on their road trip. He thought about texting Olsen for a laugh. Then his personal phone started ringing.

"Craig speaking."

"Cheer up, might never happen! It's Caitlin — from the café? I'm, er, free tonight if you fancy a rematch? Takeaway curry and darts practice," she laughed. "What do you reckon?"

He freed up his tongue. "Yeah, sure. That'd be great. See you at mine, say seven fifteen?"

"Right you are, then."

* * *

Olsen paid close attention to the DI. How she spoke, her use of language, even the way she sat. The solicitors had kept them waiting for fifteen minutes and DI Marsh had stayed poised and focused, devoid of small talk.

"Ma'am, what should we be asking?"

Marsh looked at her kindly. "Well, I'll be asking how Mr Porter first contacted the solicitor and when. And I'll ask the wildlife trust the same questions."

Olsen glanced up at the reception desk, where a woman in a tweed suit had just arrived. The woman turned to meet her gaze, raised a hand in greeting and approached them.

"Hello, you must be the police. I'm Becka Desai. Sorry to keep you waiting, a meeting overran. Come on through." She carried on talking as they cleared the shiny metal doors and passed along the corridor. "Tragic news about Mr Porter. An interesting client, actually. I offered to see him at home because I was in the area and he wouldn't hear of it. Insisted on coming to the office the following day." She turned a handle. "We're in here. Can I get you a tea or coffee?"

Marsh answered on autopilot. "No thanks, we're fine. You said on the phone that there was a matter you wanted to discuss, regarding the will?"

Becka sighed. "It's a little embarrassing actually. Mr Porter added a codicil that if a mobile mast were to be placed on the land then any rental income should be paid to his son, Nathan. As you can appreciate, that complicates matters somewhat. One of our junior staff — now no longer with us, for reasons that will become obvious — pre-empted that eventuality by contacting a mobile network company. I think it was an honest mistake. They were probably trying to show initiative by prospecting for future business. Anyway, a network representative went out to look at the land and was chased away by a rather angry farmer with a shotgun." Her smile shattered in the fierce light of Marsh's gaze.

"And was Mr Porter informed of this?"

Becka looked away for an instant. "No, the senior partners felt that it would not have reflected well on our practice and showed a lack of professionalism, hence the dismissal. The mobile network company agreed not to pursue the matter because they recognised they had inadvertently trespassed."

Marsh stood up. "Thank you for your time, Becka. I think we're done here. PC Olsen will collect whatever paperwork you can release, and I'd appreciate any printed or electronic correspondence pertaining to the mobile mast miscommunication."

Olsen waited by the reception desk while DI Marsh stood at the door. She received a small bundle of paperwork and followed the DI out to the car.

Marsh had a look of sublime satisfaction spread across her face. "There's your motive, Marnie — in black and white. The question is: *whose* motive?"

CHAPTER 36

Wild took the call, realising as it progressed that he couldn't remember the forensic officer's name. No matter, as long as he heard something useful.

She spoke quietly and precisely, as if she were used to being heard and simultaneously misunderstood. "It took longer than expected to match the residue in Dr Walsh's tissue sample."

He translated that to 'the victim.' "I don't suppose you found traces of iron? An educated guess."

"Iron residue? No, I think we would have identified that relatively easily." Her voice raised at the end of her sentence in the way he hated.

He smiled, amused at being patronised by someone who sounded half his age. "And your findings?"

"I confirmed the presence of dimethyl siloxane, dimethicone, and other compounds commonly found in spray polish. I'll email you over the results. That material taken from the wound was a fleck of dried blood from a previous injury, nothing significant."

He doodled a tick on his notepad. "Thanks. And can I take your details again in case I have any further queries?" He opened a desk drawer and took out an indexed book, flipping the pages to F where he wrote *forensics* and her number. "Okay, Eloise Palmer, thanks again."

"Any time." She cut the call.

He added her name to the page, checked his emails and then followed it with her email address. And to think he'd scored poorly on interpersonal skills at his last performance evaluation. Piece of piss. The report provided enough details to satisfy a scientist or a prosecution team. A chemical analysis laid it all out, along with a graph for the linguistically impaired. Iron would have been a better fit for his emerging theory, but spray polish could be just as instructive with a little more detective work.

He printed off the report and took a stroll to the second whiteboard to add the highlights under Dr James Walsh, late of this parish. Then he checked in with DI Marsh. He heard the background roar of road travel.

"Hold on, Craig. We're in the car on our way back. Right, you're on hands-free. Go."

She sounded buoyant, which unnerved him a little. He tried his theory on for size and he liked the fit. "When I informed Edwin Causly that there'd been another will after his, he didn't react — this wasn't news to him. Suppose Edwin Causly and Gordon Elleth got talking some time about farming and money and Alexander Porter. If Gordon Elleth had mentioned *he* was a beneficiary, all Causly had to do was ask when that will had been made and he'd know who was first in the queue."

Marsh murmured, "Aye, until the new will was made, anyway. *Cui bono*, as they say, is no help to us this time. It's not about *who benefits* . . ." She paused.

He knew what she meant but he allowed her the moment. It'd be a shame to waste her education.

". . . But who doesn't benefit? In this case, either of them." Now it was her turn to grandstand, and she talked him through their meeting with Becka Desai.

"Causly did say I wasn't the first person he'd taken a shot at."

"That's not proof, though. Listen, we'll be with you in about twenty minutes. Anything else to report?"

He stared at his screen. "Whatever was used to assault Dr Walsh had been recently polished."

"Come on, Marnie, put your foot down. Sorry, Craig, you mean like an ornament in the house? That would tend to preclude premeditation."

"Depends whose ornament it was."

"Hmm . . . okay, I'll see you in my office in twenty and I expect a risk assessment and a plan." There was no smile in her voice.

* * *

Wild stared at the guidance notes for inspiration. Neither Gordon Elleth nor Edwin Causly were flight risks. They both had shotguns, though. Maybe he'd need to carry a second set of darts! He heard himself laugh, a hollow cackle that belied the sense of terror he'd felt at the sight of Causly's firearm in the farmhouse kitchen. Always listen to your instincts . . . He added a few lines on the page, changed the font to Arial 13 so the text took up more space, and then turned his attention to the plan. Two suspects who seemed to have a strange symbiotic relationship, stranger still given their family dynamics. In his considered opinion both men needed to be questioned again and potential evidence seized from their homes.

He rested his hands on the desk. As plans went, it was weaker than a day-old kitten, but no doubt Marsh would knock it — and him — into shape. He shut his eyes for a moment and thought about the gaps, the things he still didn't know — even if they didn't have an obvious bearing on the cases. He was still writing out a list when he heard Marsh's voice as Olsen held the door for her.

"Craig, the fact that you aren't already in my office suggests you are still working?" She breezed past into her office, Olsen trailing in her wake. "If you're ready?"

He printed the document, gathered his notes, and prepared for scrutiny. Inside, he passed the paperwork over and Marsh clutched at it like a straw, while Olsen looked on in bewilderment. Wild cast her a sideways glance, as if questioning her presence. It was a look that Marsh did not appreciate.

"I thought Marnie's psychology training might provide some insight."

He nodded, realising simultaneously that Marsh had changed her tune and that it wasn't his place to point it out.

Marsh's head rocked from side to side as she read his notes. "Hmm, rudimentary. I'll work it up." She took out a pen from a desk drawer. "Now, this is more promising." She held up Wild's unanswered questions as if looking for a watermark and read out each point slowly and deliberately.

"1. Aaron Kravers said he found a DNA match on a website, just as Jeb Walsh predicted. Whose DNA did Jeb put online and how did he obtain it?"

"2a. If Gordon Elleth or Edwin Causly killed Alexander Porter, why would the other one provide an alibi for the night of the murder?"

"2b. Who else could corroborate or refute their alibi?"

"3a. Why was Dr James Walsh killed?"

"3b. If it was accidental, why confront Dr Walsh in the first place?"

"3c. Dr Walsh murder weapon — blunt object, heavy, polished."

Marnie — your thoughts please. There are no wrong answers."

Wild knew that was patently nonsense, but he was curious to see what Olsen came up with. She rubbed at her neck and blushed a little.

"It would make sense to arrest Elleth and Causly simultaneously." She swallowed. "Assuming there's enough evidence. And best to have paramedics on standby."

Wild wasn't sure whether he was still part of the conversation, so he thought he'd find out. "First thing tomorrow morning would be favourite. Gives us time to organise, and it's not as if they're going anywhere." He smiled for an instant, although probably not for the reason that Marsh smiled back. If his shift ended on schedule, he'd still make it for dinner with Caitlin and perhaps more.

CHAPTER 37

Wild had planned for all eventualities. He'd managed to find the spare set of darts that hadn't seen the light of day since Steph moved out. Not the good ones, obviously. There were two local takeaway menus to choose from, ready and waiting on the table. He had even stashed a bottle of white wine in the fridge beside two cans of beer. Choc ices lay in wait in the freezer. And last but not least, he'd bought a packet of condoms — not because he thought he was God's gift to women but, as his mum used to say, fortune favours the brave.

Caitlin phoned around six thirty so he ran through the menus with her. Not exactly Shakespeare, or foreplay, more of a tension breaker. Curry house delivery and meals selected, he said his goodbyes, put on his least offensive aftershave and played a couple of 501 games to steady his nerves.

The food arrived before she did, by design, and after plonking everything in a warming oven he went through his meagre collection of CDs and put on *The Very Best of Simply Red*. With Mick Hucknall as a wingman he wouldn't go far wrong.

The doorbell rang at a quarter past, on the dot. Caitlin radiated warmth, her face a sunshine smile of blusher and glitter. The next thing he noticed was her cheesecloth blouse and then he tried to pretend he hadn't. As he lowered his gaze, he spotted her tightly laced purple pixie boots and decided not to invoke the shoes-off rule.

"Food's ready and waiting."

Her face fell. "Oh God, am I late? I spent so long trying to find the right footwear." She did an impromptu dance.

"Nah, you're fine," he spluttered. "I mean, it's fine. I ordered early to save time." He heard his voice like a stranger's. *God almighty — stop talking.* "Come in." He took her coat, showed her to the table, draped her coat on a spare chair and waltzed off to the kitchen, swiftly returning with two plates held in oven-gloved hands. "Drink?"

"Not right now, maybe later." She made it sound a tantalising prospect, which was a hard sell for his supermarket plonk. "This smells great."

He loved the way she ate with abandon. Steph used to go through a napkin routine that drove him to distraction. It was like eating with a Buddhist monk. Caitlin, on the other hand, got straight to it. He wondered if that came from working in a café.

She broke off a piece of poppadom and scooped up some curry with the shard. "How was your day — solve many crimes?"

"Less than the public would like to think! Same old, same old."

"Are you on the big case — the one everyone is talking about?"

He choked a little and picked a caraway seed out of his mouth. "I can't really say anything . . ."

"Sorry, didn't mean to put you on the spot. I imagine your job must be fascinating. The high points of mine today were locating a child's missing soft toy — on a chair pushed under a table — and seeing two teenagers fall in love over chocolate cake."

The way she said it, he could almost picture it.

"I nearly forgot," she cut a point off a samosa, "your guitarist friend did a guest spot in the courtyard for half an hour. Surprised to see him really, after his family tragedy."

Wild's interest was piqued. Had she been keeping watch on his accord? "You've the makings of a good detective!"

"Is that what you always wanted to be? A detective, I mean."

"Not exactly." He took a mouthful of jalfrezi. "Before I joined up, I was a postman."

She toasted him with a samosa. "Quite a career change."

He smiled noncommittally. He'd heard them all before: a first- or second-class policeman, a man of letters, did he get the sack from his old job . . . ? Oh yeah, and had he abandoned his post? When he arrived at CID no one cared about his previous jobs. He'd reached the hallowed ground of becoming a plain-clothes detective. No one really noticed him at all until Steph came along.

Wild became aware that no one had spoken for a while. Time to breach the silence that even Mick Hucknall couldn't fill. "What led you to working in the café?" He tried to sound sincere and congratulated himself on avoiding the 'how did you end up' bear trap. One glance at her face, as the walls went up, told him there was a story there but maybe some other time.

"Oh, you know. Things happen and before you know it you are somewhere you never expected to be. No complaints in that regard tonight, by the way. We have food, we have wine and we have darts."

"And choc ices."

Mick Hucknall's became the only voice again, declaring that he'd wasted all his years. Wild loved that song with its mixture of melancholy and hope. After Steph left, he'd played that album to within an inch of its digital life, and that particular track became an anthem. Hearing it now, he felt only mild embarrassment.

"I, er, dug out a spare set of darts if you do still fancy a game later?"

She finished chewing. “Sure.” She smiled. “If you’re feeling lucky?”

He blushed and she seemed to take delight in it. Normally on a date, if that’s what this was, he expected to feel less tense as the evening wore on. Not here though. Caitlin wielded her confidence the same way she had in the café, like an acrobat’s baton. Dinner led to a glass of wine on the sofa with more chat and a change of music. She chose the Beatles’ red compilation from his meagre collection.

They skipped dessert in favour of the dartboard, punctuating their banter with metal points. He won the first game easily, of course he did, but she stepped up for a rematch undaunted. She was about to play again when his mobile bleeped at full volume from the other side of the room.

“Sorry, it’s my work phone.”

She carried on throwing her darts.

Marsh’s text wasted no words. *Arrests at seven thirty. Be in at six thirty*. He glanced at the clock on his phone. Already after ten. Tricky.

“Everything alright?”

“Yeah.” He felt his face betraying him. “Boss wants me in especially early tomorrow, before seven.”

She looked impressed. “Sounds ominous. Maybe it’s a manhunt. Perhaps I’ll see you on the telly!”

He didn’t answer, which somehow felt worse than a denial. He racked his brains to try to remember whether he’d said *anything* about what he was working on.

She subtracted her score on the chalk tally. “We can always finish this some other time.”

He let his darts do the talking, extending his lead — reluctantly — to a three-dart finish. “Tell you what, I’ll make it up to you — dinner at the weekend, anywhere you like. Well, except the George. I’m not too popular there!”

“I’d take that as a compliment. It’s an old fogeys’ pub — from what I hear.”

Somehow, by the time she edged towards the door, he was less certain about her than ever. Were they mates or were they dates?

"Look, Craig, sorry again about the work thing. Didn't mean to pry. Let's get together soon, yeah?"

"I'd like that."

She seemed to be waiting, hand on the door handle, so he moved towards her and closed the gap. One kiss that made his heart pound in his chest and then she slipped away like a phantasm.

CHAPTER 38

Wild half-remembered a dream about a fire alarm interrupting some sofa time with Caitlin. He opened and closed his eyes with effort, as if building up the muscles. His bedside alarm screamed at him and he realised he hadn't dreamt it — this was the second act, after the snooze button. He scrambled out of bed and got ready, making do with a wash before he found a shirt that didn't need ironing. Well, not much. A jacket hid the worst of it.

He needed food but what he wanted was caffeine. Plates, glasses and takeaway trays littered the kitchen table. He ignored them and grabbed a cup of instant coffee, topped up with some cold water to save time, and then a quick run with a toothbrush and he was good to go.

Although the car clock read 06.10, traffic was non-existent. That made for plenty of thinking time, mostly about Caitlin. She seemed so devoid of baggage it unnerved him. Must have been a painless divorce — so they did exist. No mention of kids, which put them at level pegging. A momentary thought about Steph embarking on that path and he banished it with the radio.

Mayberry police station shone out like a beacon. As he dragged himself up the stairs his stomach sang at the sweet and salty aroma of bacon. He followed his nose to the briefing room where DI Marsh presided over the banquet.

"Right, come on, settle down. Tea or coffee and grab a roll — bacon or egg."

Wild commandeered a bacon roll and a cup of tea and accompanied them to an empty space. Marnie Olsen appeared out of nowhere and sat beside him.

"Morning." She tilted towards him. "I need to have a word with you, Craig. Not here."

DI Marsh tapped the top of her pen on a table. The seven people in the room fell silent.

"Okay, thank you for giving up your beauty sleep, ladies and gentlemen. We have two objectives for this morning. Firstly, the arrests of Gordon Elleth and Edwin Causly, in connection with the death of Alexander Porter and for further questioning about the death of Dr James Walsh. Secondly, the gathering of evidence at their home addresses. DS Wild, DC Galloway and PC Olsen will attend at the Elleth farmhouse. I will go with Sergeant Galloway, DC Harris and PCSO Wishaw to pick up Edwin Causly. Two vehicles apiece to contain the suspects and effect the search. Any questions?"

DC Harris glanced around him before tentatively raising a hand. "What evidence are we looking for?"

Wild's mouth slipped into gear. "Shotguns, obviously, and any coats. If either suspect was present at Porter's death, there may be blood specks for forensics." He looked over at Marsh, who nodded slowly in encouragement. "There should be a black cross on the wall in each house somewhere, downstairs probably — bag them up. Could be others in other rooms. Expect some grief on religious grounds but take them anyway." He fancied he could see the backs of Ben Galloway's ears reddening.

The PCSO waggled a pen. "What about other people at the house?"

Marsh raised a finger towards Wild and he realised her arm was out of the sling. "Elizabeth Elleth should be no trouble. If anyone comes in from the field, keep them at arm's length. Arrest is a last resort." The fateful finger swung round to PCSO Lisa Wishaw. "As for Edwin Causly, there's only agricultural labour. Same deal." Marsh finished her tea. "Okay, downstairs in five minutes."

* * *

Wild drove with Olsen, Ben Galloway following them in a marked car. "What did you want to say?"

Olsen flipped down the sun visor mirror and glanced back at Galloway, noting his fingers on the wheel at the recommended ten and two positions. "I forgot to tell you that I burned your Skype details, in case you were wondering."

Wild's blank expression surprised her.

"Remember your trip to London, when I rang you on the M4? Didn't you wonder how I knew Jackie had been in touch and what she'd said?"

Come to think of it, he hadn't. He pursed his lips. Sloppy.

"You *must* have wondered . . . Wild?"

He hunched in his shoulders a little. "Slipped my mind at the time. I had other things to think about." He changed tack and moved the spotlight. "So, had any job offers from London?" He smiled to soften the sarcasm. It didn't seem to help any.

Her lip curled. "Not yet. How about you?"

Touché, Ms Olsen. "I expect mine's stuck in the post somewhere."

Olsen laughed and the muscles in her face softened. "Looks like we'll be on the same team for a while, then. I suppose I've worked with worse."

* * *

Wild pulled up and waited for Ben Galloway to join them. In the meantime, he radioed through to Marsh. "We're in position, ma'am." He glanced in the rear-view mirror. "Ben's coming up the track."

"Give it four more minutes and then go. And, Wild, try not to make any more enemies."

"Understood," he lied.

Ben Galloway looked distinctly uncomfortable as he got out of the car. Wild let him open the gate and the three of them walked in a line towards the farmhouse. It reminded Wild of a dodgy cowboy film. He watched the smoke rise up from the flue, pale as poison in an otherwise cloudless sky.

The dogs barked long before they reached the front door. Only a cry for attention, Wild judged — pepper spray not required. He rapped the heavy door knocker twice, sending the dogs into a conniption. A woman's voice rose above the din and the house went eerily silent before a key stiffly turned.

Mrs Elleth faced them. She seemed, to Wild, both weathered and majestic. As if nothing he had to say mattered to her. He put it to the test, introducing his fellow officers and stating the reason for their presence so early in the morning.

She took her hand off the door and headed back towards the kitchen. "Gordon's not here. He left not long after sun-up."

Wild applied some charm. "Is he out in the field?"

She stopped walking and the two dogs gathered at her feet, eyeing her intently. "Shouldn't think so. Said he had something to attend to and went out. Didn't even have his breakfast."

Wild felt a sudden feeling of dread. "How . . . how did he seem?"

She carried on into the kitchen. "Seemed alright when he left."

Wild gestured for Galloway to go outside and ring DI Marsh with the bad news. Olsen squeezed past him with a plastic box containing evidence bags.

Mrs Elleth stood by the kitchen range. "You be wanting tea before you go?"

Olsen glanced at Wild and nodded, deciding it was a good way to keep her occupied. "Yes, please — all three, milk and one sugar."

Galloway returned and called Wild over to the doorway. "DI Marsh reckons Mr Causly isn't at home either. We're to gather evidence and see if Mrs Elleth knows anything."

Wild went through the formalities and then asked questions that Mrs Elleth couldn't answer, apart from the most important one: where was the gun and were any others kept on the farm? He had expected resistance when Olsen collected it to bag it up, but she saved that for when Ben Galloway removed the black cross from the wall. Wild sipped his tea as she berated Galloway for putting his job before his faith. On that basis alone, Wild figured he owed him a drink.

Mrs Elleth insisted she had no idea why her husband had gone out so early. Wild solved that mystery by checking their phone. Edwin Causly had rung them around six that morning.

Olsen carefully folded Gordon Elleth's coat and put it in a bag and then Wild sent Galloway upstairs on a fishing expedition. Mrs Elleth had a knack for making her feelings plain without raising her voice or blaspheming, but it cut no ice with Wild. His sympathy evaporated when he recalled the sight of Alexander Porter lying in a field, minus part of his cranium. Galloway completed his search and returned with a couple of bags of evidence, placing them to one side while he finished his tea and made a fuss of the dogs.

Wild stood up to marshal the troops. "It's really important that we speak to your husband, Mrs Elleth. When he comes back, can you please get in touch or ask him to ring us?" He proffered a card. "Or he can come directly to Mayberry police station."

She glanced at the card. "Mayberry? I thought that old place had already closed down."

Galloway looked up from the Labradors. "It's closing in the next few months and we're moving to Gable Cross." He said it with the wide-eyed enthusiasm that suggested she'd want to know. Her face told a different story.

She fussed with a teacup. "Well, just you make sure you bring our things back. And you take good care of that cross, Ben Galloway, or I'll be having words with your uncle. Like the good book says: 'And he who does not take his cross and follow after Me is not worthy of Me.' Never you mind this heathen." She looked directly at Wild.

"Thanks for your cooperation, Mrs Elleth. Marnie, Ben — we're done here."

CHAPTER 39

Galloway loaded up his car with the evidence. "What do you wanna do now, Skip?"

Wild shrugged. "They're hardly going on the run. Suggestions?"

Galloway's eyes shone, which told Wild something earnest but ridiculous was coming his way. "Maybe they've gone to seek sanctuary in a church."

Wild killed that theory with a hard stare. Like that would make a difference. "Marnie?"

She thought for a moment, staring out across the fields. "There'll be a purpose behind it. Could they know we've located Porter's shotgun, proving someone else had to be present at his death?"

Wild smiled at *we've* when they all knew finding the weapon was Olsen's doing. "You think perhaps they've returned to the scene of the crime? I can't see any purpose in that."

Olsen sighed heavily. "What links Elleth and Causly is their alibi." She stared up at Wild so suddenly that he flinched. "The weakest part of that alibi is anyone else who was also at the George that night and could contradict it, for example the landlady."

Wild scratched his chin. "It's good enough for me. Ben, get the evidence back to the police station. Marnie, you're with me. Call DI Marsh and tell her where we're going."

He didn't have a lot to say in the car. One thing still made no sense. Why now? Why choose that morning to up sticks and go wandering, the very day they were coming to pick them both up? For a fleeting moment he wondered if one of the team might have tipped Edwin Causly off. That didn't ring true somehow, or Gordon Elleth would have taken his shotgun and cross with him if he had any sense. Maybe not a tip-off exactly then but some inkling that they were moving against Causly at least and maybe Elleth too.

"You're awfully quiet, Wild." Olsen watched the road as carefully as if she were the one driving. "Cat got your tongue?"

He smiled and then a creeping dread passed through him. It left doubt in its wake.

Wild's car reached the George first. He recognised the two cars belonging to the suspects. It wasn't difficult — the only other car belonged to the landlady. A sallow light lit up one of the backroom windows in the pub. He wanted to go in and make the arrests but Marsh had laid down the law. They were to wait until she arrived. He took it as one more slight against his character and parked across the two vehicles for good measure. Causly's firearm had also been captured so he had no worries on that front. Now it was a waiting game.

He turned to Olsen, aware that an uncomfortable silence had settled on them. "You read any good books lately?"

She leant towards him. "Sorry?"

"Just making conversation."

"No need to on my account, Wild." She could see he was trying. "*Frankenstein* — by Mary Shelley."

He nodded. "The one with the monster in it. Robert De Niro, wasn't it? In the film, I mean."

She brushed imaginary dust from her sleeve. "We don't have to talk, you know."

Marsh arrived with Sergeant Galloway and DC Harris. Wild figured the PCSO would have drawn the short straw as delivery girl. The presence of the two suspects' cars did not seem to raise Marsh's spirits. She looked — and sounded — pissed off.

"I don't appreciate being given the runaround. Especially if I've had to get up early for the privilege. Sergeant Galloway and Marnie — side entrance. Wild, you're with me at the front. Harris, stay here in case anyone else appears. So we're all clear, two arrests and no messing about."

As they approached the main entrance to the pub, she buttonholed Wild. "I don't like this. It smacks of incompetence at best or something far worse. It's fortunate you located them here."

"Marnie's suggestion."

"Aye, she's a bright girl. Luckily for us."

The landlady didn't take long to respond. Causly and Elleth were seated inside, eating breakfast. They didn't look perturbed. Marsh read them their rights and led Elleth to the other bar, leaving Olsen and Sergeant Galloway to deal with Causly separately.

Wild managed to grab Marsh before she went on the offensive. "I'd like to talk to the landlady. Causly and Elleth meeting here gives us some leverage."

"As you wish. You'd better tell Harris to get another vehicle over and then come in."

Wild took the landlady behind the bar to a back room. He'd clocked her name, Faye Crawford, from the licence above the bar. The room looked homely — a plush green sofa in need of an upholsterer, with matching footstool, and a TV that had come out of the ark. All the room needed was flying ducks on the wall.

"I'd like to ask you some questions, Faye."

She blanched and sat down, hands tightly pressed against her knees. "I said I don't know anything."

He tried smiling. "Yeah, but that was before . . ." He didn't bother calling her a liar — he'd hold that in reserve.

"Before two suspects turned up unexpectedly at your door rather early in the morning."

She didn't bite at 'unexpected'. "Edwin Causly and Gordon Elleth are old friends. They sometimes supply the rabbit for our country pies."

Wild stayed on his feet, looming over her. "Yeah, not at night though, not with a shotgun." He reached for the footstool and drew it close, perching beside her, trying to ignore the button pushing into his buttock. "I'd like you to reconsider your previous statement — the one where you saw and heard nothing."

Her fingers twitched. "I've already told you—"

He raised two fingers, without the offer of benediction. "Faye, let me make this easy for you. I need a couple of things confirmed, that's all: who did Alexander Porter leave with and where did he go?"

Her face seemed implacable, weather-proof. Wild thought about appealing to her better nature but he could see this warranted a different approach. He asked himself, what would a psychology buff like Olsen pull out of the box for leverage? "Mrs Crawford," he lowered his voice, "I realise you don't have to help us. And maybe you genuinely know nothing. That'd be unfortunate, though, because I'd have to conclude that my next port of call would be your clientele, who must be holding out." He sighed for effect and clapped his hands together. "I'd have to come back later, and maybe the next day, to make sure I spoke with everyone. And the day after that as well, in case some of them needed their memories jogging and to build up their trust." He stood up. "And if I were coming here regularly, I might as well start checking tyres and MOTs and insurance, ask people to produce their documents at the station. It's a nice pub . . . before you know it this would become a coppers' pub and you won't see your regulars for dust."

She scowled. "This is harassment."

He looked her in the eyes calmly. "No, Faye, this is murder. Now, which is it to be? Two minutes of cooperation or this pub becomes my local." He saw the light fade in her eyes. He'd seen that happen many times — in interview rooms and at a heavy hand on the shoulder. Faye Crawford was smart. He never made idle threats, but he kept a lot of promises. "Okay, we'll start again."

"And this is off the record?"

He marvelled at the way film and television had encouraged the great British public to try and cover their arses. He tilted his head to one side, rolling a thought around. "Off the record unless it's used as evidence in court."

She wavered for an instant and he let her have that uninterrupted moment.

"Describe how Alexander Porter left the pub."

"Well, he got into an argument with Edwin Causly and Gordon Elleth. Don't ask me what about, I genuinely don't know. I heard raised voices and that's all. As I came through from the back bar, all three of them were leaving together."

"Very good. And they all went off together?"

"I believe so." Her face went still. "Come to think of it, Alexander Porter left his car. It was here come closing time, so he must have fetched it afterwards."

Or someone else did. "Thanks for your time."

She called after him as he left the room. "Is that it?"

"For now."

He couldn't be certain, but he thought she muttered 'Bastard'. When he rang the police station, he learned that DI Marsh had set up interviews with herself and Sergeant Galloway leading from the front. He left word for her that he was pursuing a loose thread.

* * *

The windows of the late Dr Walsh's house were shrouded with heavy curtains. Wild didn't remember them from his previous visit, but what did he know? Maybe it was tradition. He rang the bell and stepped back a couple of paces before the door opened.

Jeb Walsh appeared before him, grey as a lament. Wild knew the drill from his own father's death — food by necessity and sleep by the grace of God, or alcohol, or pills. Whatever worked best.

"I'm sorry to bother you, Jeb. I need a quick word."

"Am I in trouble? Only my nan really needs me here." He didn't elaborate. He didn't have to.

"Best to do this inside, don't you think?"

Jeb closed his eyes for a moment and then invited him in. "We can talk in my room."

Wild was surprised to see bookshelves stocked with history, philosophy, literature and the sciences. He'd expected a bohemian hideaway. What he saw was an intellectual's retreat. A collection of medical textbooks drew his attention and his mouth ran away with him.

"You studied medicine?"

A smile flickered across Jeb's face. "Well, I tried! It was Grandad's idea — family tradition and all that. Mum and Dad were both med students." He seemed lost in a memory and then snapped back to reality. "Yeah, I couldn't hack it. Too much like hard work."

Wild sat on a Lloyd Loom chair, facing a corner of the room where Jeb's guitar and top hat rested against a shelf like unwelcome guests. Jeb offered tea, which Wild declined in the hope that Jeb would settle. Instead, Jeb went off to make one for himself and check on his grandmother.

Left alone, Wild resisted the urge to search the room and instead tried to organise his thinking. Was he looking for lazy solutions rather than following the trail of evidence? He glanced at the ornate ceiling rose. "That's what we're here to discover," he said to no one at all. He scribbled a few lines in his notebook and awaited Jeb's return.

A few minutes later, at the very edge of Wild's patience, the door creaked inward.

"Sorry, Nan wanted one as well." Jeb's mug read: 'World's Greatest Grandson'.

From what Wild already knew, he'd have sued Jeb for false advertising. He let him speak first.

"Have you found whoever's responsible for attacking Grandad . . . ?"

Wild chose his words carefully. "We are questioning someone, but I can't reveal any details at this point."

Jeb sipped steaming tea. "I hope the bastard suffers."

Wild said nothing. He'd seen so often how grief turned to anger or hatred. When he judged that the moment had passed, he stretched back in the chair until he could feel the weave pressing against his spine.

"I came here to talk about the American visitor, Aaron Kravers. He said that you'd directed him to a 'find your family' website where you'd already uploaded a DNA sample, and that it proved to be a partial match for his DNA."

Jeb set his cup down on the carpet. "Did you tell her? Has she made a complaint? I never took advantage, if that's what she's saying." He blushed like a choirboy. "Well, okay, I did. But not, you know, like *that.* We got drunk and she passed out. I only needed saliva. They give you swabs."

"I know how sampling works." Wild checked his notebook for effect, until something came to mind. It usually did. "If you had the swabs then you must have already planned to get the samples." *Check*.

Jeb came over coy. "Please don't tell Pauline. She gets funny about me and other women."

"No shit — I wonder why."

"What *has* she said then?"

Wild remembered the golden rule: never lie to a suspect. Sadly, that narrowed down his options considerably. "Do you still have any samples here?"

Jeb paused for a moment, eyes looking inward. Then he folded like an end of season deckchair. "Yeah, I do. I kept one back to give to Aaron Kravers when he paid me. I thought he might want to double-check everything. He's backed right off though, probably because of you. You questioned him after Grandad died, right?"

"I'll take the sample now." Wild held out his hand in lieu of explaining himself.

Jeb got up. "It's in the freezer. I thought that'd be best — like on the telly. Wait here." He quickly returned with a see-through sandwich bag.

Wild took the bag. Inside, he saw a clear plastic tube containing a swab-stick, or possibly an earbud. "Under what circumstances did you . . . ?"

Jeb threw his hands up, as though he'd touched a live wire. "I told you. We're drinking buddies, and I might have sold her the odd bit of puff in the past. Fair enough, I did deliberately get her hammered that one time — although she didn't need much encouragement. I waited till she crashed out and then did some cheek swabs, like it said on the packet. It weren't difficult. Plus, she's a bit of a drooler when she's really pissed." He winked in that 'all blokes together' way that made Wild want to punch his face in.

Wild used every ounce of concentration to keep his brain focused and his face still. "For the record, Jeb," he lifted his pen, "what's her full name?"

"I was gonna tell her when the time was right. I thought maybe we could share the fee, sixty-forty."

Wild stared at him to get on with it. "Name?"

"Sorry, Caitlin Spenser — she kept her married name — used to be Caitlin Causly. Look, if she's made a complaint, I'd be willing to come to a financial settlement so long as Pauline doesn't have to hear about it."

Wild launched to his feet. He had to get out of there pronto. "Thanks for your time, Jeb. I'll be in touch." As soon as he got into his car he popped out a pill and glared at it, before hurling it against the windscreen. Then he screamed his rage through clenched teeth until his face hurt. Things started to make sense. The way Caitlin had given him, a stranger, her phone number. That weird date-or-mate no-man's land between them from the very beginning. And worst of all, the way he'd hinted at an early start for work, only to find Edwin Causly had done a runner when they came to arrest him. He glared at his own reflection. "Stupid, stupid bastard — always double-check the family connections." It was only later that he remembered Sergeant Galloway had interviewed Edwin Causly first.

Once he'd calmed down, he thought about calling Olsen to get her take on things. She'd be in an interview, though, so that would have to wait. And what insight could she offer anyway — poor you, you daft sod? He almost smiled at that as he drove off.

He talked to himself in the car, wondering what he could charge Caitlin with — nothing — and what advantage he'd gain in identifying her as Edwin Causly's apparently estranged daughter. He came up with nothing again, and then realised there was something important he had to do — corroborate the evidence.

A detour home and a quick examination of last night's dinnerware and cutlery gave him a second sample, albeit dried up and wrapped in clingfilm. When he got to his desk, he dug out his address book and rang the forensics team.

"Eloise Palmer?" She didn't sound sure.

"Hi, it's Craig Wild — DS Wild. How would you like to do me a massive favour?"

"Depends what you're after."

He played along, aware that his internal clock was ticking. "Nothing that would tax your abilities. I need two DNA samples checked . . . no, not against the database, only against one another. Yeah, you're right — confirmation of identity. Brilliant, I'll bring them over now."

CHAPTER 40

Marnie Olsen watched Edwin Causly studiously from the other side of the table. She'd interviewed suspects and witnesses before, although not in a murder case. DI Marsh did all the talking on their side and she was glad of it, it afforded her the opportunity to observe Causly's reactions to the DI's questioning at close quarters.

"Okay, Edwin, let's go back to the beginning. You rang Gordon Elleth early this morning and subsequently met him in a pub. What prompted your call and that meeting?"

Causly stared sullenly at Marsh. She repeated, for the recording, that Mr Causly had again declined to make a response, and then glanced at her watch.

"Let's take a comfort break. And when we return, we can talk about the events of the night Alexander Porter was murdered. Interview suspended." She hit the button and waited for the bleep. "PC Olsen will show you to another room and get you a hot drink and a biscuit if you'd like one."

Causly rolled his shoulders and waited for his solicitor to get up. Olsen stood by the door, watching the interaction between Causly and his brief. He might have been tight-lipped, but she could see it was a facade. After she'd shown them to a room, pointed out the toilets, and found a wandering PCSO to do guard duty, she went upstairs in search of the DI.

Marsh was in the briefing room, staring at the whiteboards. She nodded as Olsen entered the room. "What do you think?"

Olsen stooped a little. "Honestly, ma'am?"

"Of course." Marsh looked affronted that she might expect anything less.

"I think we've said nothing to surprise him yet." Olsen glanced down. "No disrespect."

"None taken. Tell me more."

"We know from Wild," she watched Marsh's face crinkle a little, "that Porter, Elleth and Causly left the George together, and they were arguing."

Marsh's mouth twisted cynically. "The three amigos."

Olsen bowed a little under the weight of expectation. "We know Elleth and Causly were both there when it happened. Maybe we need to apply more pressure on Mr Elleth?"

Marsh's phone rang. "DI — Where the bloody hell have you been?"

* * *

Wild put down his plastic coffee. "I'm at the lab — they're running a DNA comparison."

"A *what*? Explain to me why this takes precedence over a murder inquiry."

Wild stuck to the facts, hoping to fend off any criticism with science. Once he'd told Eloise the rationale for comparing the samples, given that they already had a first name match in a local area, she'd suggested scaling back on the DNA markers to reduce processing time. As it was, that still left over an hour.

Marsh listened quietly as he brought Caitlin Spenser into the picture and suggested he'd been played as an information source, although he took pains to point out he hadn't revealed anything. Except perhaps that he had been called in early, although he couldn't be sure.

"Craig, you should be smarter than that with your experience."

She winded him as surely as if she'd punched him in the guts. "Yes, ma'am. I'll come back right away." He offered a shy wave to Eloise and reminded her needlessly to send over the details tout suite.

* * *

Olsen wasn't surprised to follow DI Marsh into a micro-meeting with Sergeant Galloway and DC Harris. It seemed perfectly reasonable that they'd coordinate their breaks to compare progress. Marsh also had another trick up her sleeve.

"We'll speak with Elleth now and you can try Causly. You might have better luck."

Olsen wasn't entirely convinced, but Sergeant Galloway seemed happy to have a crack at Causly. DC Harris seemed happy to be taking part.

* * *

Wild did the thing he hated most, crashing someone else's interview. Causly spun round so fast that he nearly fell off his chair. Wild smiled for about half a second, suffered the ignominy of his intrusion being documented on the recording, and went off in search of Marsh.

Elleth seemed about as pleased to see him. Marsh didn't look thrilled either, but she announced him and pointed towards a spare chair pressed against the wall, having stymied Olsen's attempt to switch places with him. Before she could get a word out someone else knocked on the door.

"What now?"

Marsh got up to see to it and Olsen spoke up for the recording.

"PCSO Wishaw has entered the room, handed a piece of paper to DI Marsh and has now left the room."

Marsh looked a lot happier as she sat down. She waited for a couple of seconds, the way Wild liked to when he thought he had some new leverage.

"Mr Elleth, when we visited your home this morning — while you were absent — we recovered a black metal cross from a downstairs wall."

"You had no business taking that. Elizabeth likes to keep it near when she's reading her Bible."

"Here's the thing. Although you probably thought you'd wiped it clean, our lab found minute traces of blood on it." She waited again.

Wild couldn't help smiling. This was the best part of his day since leaving the pub.

Marsh continued. "Would you care to guess what the lab's analysis of the blood specks revealed?"

Elleth's solicitor bristled. "My client is not here for idle conjecture."

Marsh tilted forward. "No, he bloody well isn't. He is here as a murder suspect."

Wild brought his chair close and read aloud from the page. "Analysis confirms that the blood matches samples held for Alexander Porter." He thought Elleth looked confused. Confounded might have been a better word. "You see, when a weapon is discharged at close range, blood spatter is transferred. Your cross, you were there." He returned the page to Marsh and then folded his arms. Checkmate.

Marsh looked at the page again and shook her head. Pure theatre. "The blood spatter puts you — or perhaps your wife — at the scene of the crime, either as a perpetrator or a witness."

Elleth's solicitor turned towards him as if by magnetism, and then faced Marsh. "I must insist that I talk to my client immediately."

Marsh adjusted her blue-rimmed glasses. "I thought you might."

Fifteen minutes seemed more like an hour by the time Elleth returned. Meanwhile, Wild had found time for a piss and a phone call, both urgent. He'd requested that uniformed officers went to the Labyrinth café for Caitlin, and if she wasn't there to pick her up at her home address. And he wanted her phone as well.

* * *

Elleth came back into the interview room first, straight-backed, hands clasped together like one of the clergy. He had a far-off look in his eye, which Wild fancied was fixed on the time he'd be spending in prison if the 'Good Lord' didn't claim him first. The solicitor had the air of a troubled man. This, Wild attributed to whatever discussion had passed between him and his client. Having someone cough to a burglary or handling stolen goods — that was bread and butter to a firm of local solicitors. Murder was of another order entirely.

DI Marsh waited for Elleth and his brief to be seated and then set her glasses down. "Mr Elleth, you have now had the opportunity to consult your solicitor. Are you happy to continue with this interview?"

Elleth's face suggested that 'happy' would be a bit of a stretch. Hands still pressed together, he gave a single, affirmative nod.

"Thank you." She glanced at the solicitor and waited for the inevitable.

The brief moistened his lips and cued up his speech. "My client, Mr Gordon Elleth, has asked me to read out a statement . . ."

The way he held it, Wild could see the back of the page and make out that some words had been crossed out. He wondered what never made the cut.

"Mr Elleth admits to being in the field when Alexander Porter died as a result of a tragic accident. He is prepared to discuss this in more detail and cooperate fully on the clear understanding that his wife, Elizabeth Elleth, was not involved in any way."

Marsh's face relaxed. "Duly noted. Right, I'm listening."

It all sounded to Wild like a tragedy waiting to happen. Three men in a pub argue over money lent and money promised — because two of them know they are already stuck on the wrong side of the equation. Determined to discover who the new beneficiary is, Gordon Elleth brings along his cross as moral authority. Edwin Causly, however, takes the less traditional route and opts for a shotgun.

As Wild listened, his mind painted pictures and none of them were pretty. Somehow Elleth and Causly coerce Alexander Porter into one of the fields they are no longer going to receive and insist he swears the truth on the cross. The way Elleth tells it, Porter is drunk and belligerent, and pushes the cross away with a few choice words. Causly is outraged at his blasphemy and threatens Porter with his shotgun, since the wrath of God has failed to do the trick. Things escalate and Causly's gun goes off unexpectedly. Except, the thought that goes through Wild's mind, the one he will share with Marsh and Olsen later, is that Causly loading the gun beforehand smacks of premeditation.

Wild started to wonder how Edwin Causly would react when he heard that Gordon Elleth — *Uncle* Gordon — had ratted him out. Edwin didn't seem the forgiving kind. Oh to be a fly on the wall for that conversation. It wasn't the end, of course. Contrary to popular belief, a confession — or in this case an admission — wasn't the tumultuous end of a case, only a staging post. One old man's word against another's wouldn't be enough, even with the current forensic evidence. A jury would want a cogent narrative of how and why Alexander Porter came to die in one of his own fields. Now the job got harder because every get-out clause and alternative explanation had to be staunched.

As Elleth was being led to his cell, a call came down that Caitlin Spenser had been brought into the custody suite. Wild had barely put one foot in front of the other before Marsh touched his shoulder.

"Under the circumstances, I think it best you make yourself scarce for this one."

CHAPTER 41

As soon as Wild was beyond Marsh's line of sight he dashed upstairs and across to another staircase. Maturity, he decided as he clattered down the steps, holding the handrail for balance, was greatly overrated. He paused at the bottom to try and stop his legs shaking and then *casually* passed along the corridor and into the custody suite from the other side. His timing was perfect. Caitlin glanced over as the door swung in and locked eyes with him. He couldn't be certain but she might have mouthed the word *sorry*. It's what he told himself as he turned and let the door go behind him.

Surplus to requirements for one interview and unwilling to gatecrash another, he returned to his desk, called the technician and put in his order.

"Hi, it's Craig Wild. Before you put Caitlin Spenser's phone on the kiosk machine can you run a couple of checks first? Great. Do a historical web browser search for the day Alexander Porter died, and the day afterwards. Yeah, also check Google maps and Google directions. Call me back soon as."

Just a hunch, an idea that had begun to fester since Caitlin's family connection came to light. Someone had to have moved Porter's car, post-mortem, and gone looking for his shotgun. Edwin Causly wasn't exactly light on his feet so either someone else picked him up from Porter's house after he'd taken the car back, or they dropped off Porter's car and then did some interior redesign. And who better to trust than family?

He hoped he was wrong because otherwise he'd look like an even bigger idiot for not finding the Causly connection sooner. He was staring at a whiteboard in the briefing room when his mobile trilled into life.

"Really? No, she's busy. I'll come down."

Aaron Kravers looked like he'd been overpowered by a gentlemen's outfitters and forced to wear their stock. A cravat poked out from the neckline of a purple polo shirt, clashing somewhat with his tweed trousers. Kravers leapt up as soon as he laid eyes on Wild.

"Ah, Detective Wild. I was with Ms Spenser when she was arrested. I got here as fast as I could to offer my full support as a family member. Perhaps you can let her and her father know."

Wild didn't respond as he was momentarily dazzled by the ceiling light flickering off Kravers's gold watch.

"Can we talk somewhere, Detective?"

Wild found the smallest space possible, a former storage room that had never quite dried out. Even the chairs looked like rejects from a furniture sale. This would do nicely.

Kravers said what was on his mind. "I want to pay for the best legal team money can buy — and believe me, I have a lot of it."

Wild had heard that money was no arbiter of taste and looking at Aaron Kravers he believed it.

Kravers managed to swagger in his chair. "Just tell me what I need to do here."

Wild stuck to the tried and tested approach of 'small words, big font' and carefully walked Kravers through the process. Kravers already seemed acquainted with the facts of Edwin Causly's detention. That suggested Old Man Causly had rung his daughter from the police station — another mystery for another day, if it was worth the time.

Discussion over, Wild assured Kravers he'd pass on the message to Causly's brief. Then he escorted the visitor back to the waiting area and buzzed himself back into wonderland. He wanted to stretch his legs so why not pop up to the technical room on his way?

"Ah, DS Wild. I was going to ring you." She pointed to the mobile phone being electronically strip-searched for data.

Wild felt his hackles rising. "I thought I told you . . ."

"Excuse me, I know my job. We did your checks first but I wanted to get the main data extraction set up and running, especially with the phone's owner in custody."

He swallowed his pride. "Soz. What did you find?"

"Well, as you suggested, there was a location search on the night Mr Porter died."

Wild recited Porter's home address.

"Spot on. Searched for at," she checked her notes, "10.30 p.m."

Wild closed his eyes, imagining Causly ringing his daughter in a panic — or not — and asking her to come and take care of Porter's car. Or maybe she was already up at Causly's farmhouse, waiting. His eyes flashed open at the thought.

"Edwin Causly was lucky to get a call through on his mobile from the field." Luckier than Alexander Porter, anyway. "Makes perfect sense to search Porter's house for the shooter while you're there with the car. Saves risking a second visit."

She blinked. "I'm sorry?"

"Take no notice, I'm on a roll."

One more call, he decided. Eloise Palmer sounded a lot less breezy than before.

"Bad time, Eloise?"

"I owe you an apology. We're a bit short staffed and I hadn't got round to one of your black crosses. I've started the analysis but it will be a while before I can *confirm* . . ."

He felt his extremities tingling. "I'll settle for a preliminary finding for the time being."

"There's definitely polish of some kind on the second cross — from Edwin Causly's home."

"Brilliant, Text me when you have a chemical match or whatever you call it."

* * *

Wild knocked firmly on the door of Interview Room One. He heard Sergeant Galloway's garrulous tones as he got up and opened it.

"DS Wild has entered the room."

Wild introduced himself formally for the recording. In the absence of a spare chair he found a wall to lean against, still within Causly's scowling range.

"What's he doing here?"

"Come to tell you that Caitlin's been arrested."

Causly started hyperventilating, which drew a temporary close to the proceedings. He pushed his solicitor's hand away. "I just need some water, is all."

Wild offered to sit with them while Ben Galloway fetched the water. Sergeant Galloway followed him out. He looked glad of the break. As he turned by the open door, Wild held up two fingers — one for each minute.

Wild took a seat and drubbed his fingers on the table. "Aaron Kravers is downstairs."

"Excuse me, you can't talk to my client about the investigation."

"I'm not. I am just informing *your* client that Aaron Kravers said he will get Mr Causly the best legal team money can buy. He's gonna need it." He stopped tapping the table. "Do you think God forgives everything, Mr Causly?"

Causly rose to the bait like a hungry pike. "We can all be instruments of the Lord, Sergeant Wild. Even the likes of you. In the Book of Job there is a line . . ." Causly straightened in his chair. "He striketh them as wicked men in the open sight of others."

Wild bit at the skin around one of his fingernails. "I'm more of a *thou shalt not kill* man, myself."

Ben Galloway passed him on the way out, paper cup in hand like a grail maiden. Wild buttonholed Sergeant Galloway in the corridor and told him his theory about Caitlin's involvement. "Just something to consider." He decided not to question Sergeant Galloway's initial interviewing of Edwin Causly, while he was in London. No good would come of it now and they were, after all, on the same side. A text came in from Eloise Palmer at the lab and he checked it before letting the good sergeant read it for himself: *Chemical composition at Dr Walsh's fatal injury matches polish on Edwin Causly's cross. Report to follow.*

Wild went off to his desk to do some paperwork. The way he saw it, after Caitlin Spenser, there was a fifty-fifty chance of it being the last report he'd write from Mayberry police station.

PCSO Wishaw was the bearer of the good and somewhat surprising news that Causly had confessed to accidentally shooting Alexander Porter, taking his car home and then burgling the house in search of a shotgun. Causly also accepted responsibility for the accidental death of Dr James Walsh, who he insisted died as a result of an altercation over the contents of a missing diary.

If Wild were a gambling man, he would have put even money on manslaughter for both *accidents*. He wondered how Kravers would react when he realised that the distant relative he was loyally supporting was responsible for the death of the one person who might possibly have known where Melvin Kravers was buried — always assuming Dr Jacob Walsh had confessed to his son, the late Dr James Walsh. And then there was Jeb Walsh, whose appetite for easy money had indirectly cost his grandfather his life. Wild finished the final sheet and leaned back from the screen. Families, eh? Who'd 'ave 'em?

EPILOGUE

DI Marsh held two twenty-pound notes in the air as Wild squeezed past her chair. "As you're heading to the bar, whatever everyone wants."

He wasn't, but he knew his place. While he was waiting for the order, from possibly the world's most indifferent barman, Ben Galloway arrived late to the party.

"Alright, Skip?" A smile flickered across his face, as if he knew what an annoying bastard he could be.

Wild had given up on the whole 'use my name' thing. "Yeah, fine thanks. Can you give me a hand with the drinks?"

"I suppose you've heard," Ben sounded strangely adult, "about me putting in my transfer request? I think it's for the best, all things considered."

Wild changed the subject. "We never did find out who made the anonymous call about Alexander Porter. It would have been difficult to see from the lane . . . unless you were up at the ruins. Not *you* personally . . ." His face suggested otherwise.

Ben waved at the barman to add another beer to the order. "Maybe we'll never know, Skip. It's like that spate of car vandalism not long after you joined us. Some mysteries are never solved, eh?"

They carried the trays back to a resounding cheer and shared out the spoils. Marsh looked especially pleased when Wild handed back the change.

As she sipped her whisky her eyes closed momentarily, like an old religious painting. "Good stuff. Well, it looks like Aaron Kravers will be around for a while. He has a legal team coming over from London, which has not gone down well with the local solicitors. And the way I understand it, he is applying for permission to search Fortune's Field."

Marnie Olsen said what Wild was thinking. "How does that work if the land can't be disturbed as part of the bequest? I mean, the only evidence that Melvin Kravers is buried there is a diary from the forties."

Marsh took another sip. "They'll bring in ground penetrating radar, apparently. Like the archaeology programmes off the telly."

Sergeant Galloway gulped his bitter. "Come on then, Craig. Marnie tells me you're a dab hand at darts. We can always use a good player on the team, 'specially with Ben moving on to greener pastures. Let's see what you're made of."

Olsen raised her glass to send him on his way. Wild realised he still had a set of darts with him. Maybe it was a sign.

THE END

ALSO BY DEREK THOMPSON

THOMAS BLADEN SERIES

Book 1: STANDPOINT
Book 2: LINE OF SIGHT
Book 3: CAUSE & EFFECT
Book 4: SHADOW STATE
Book 5: FLASHPOINT

Don't miss the latest Derek Thompson release, join our mailing list:

www.joffebooks.com

FREE KINDLE BOOKS

Do you love mysteries, historical fiction and romance? Join 1000s of readers enjoying great books through our mailing list. You'll get new releases and great deals every week from one of the UK's leading independent publishers.

Join today, and you'll get your first bargain book this month!

Follow us on Facebook, Twitter and Instagram @joffebooks

Thank you for reading this book. If you enjoyed it please leave feedback on Amazon or Goodreads, and if there is anything we missed or you have a question about, then please get in touch. The author and publishing team appreciate your feedback and time reading this book.

We're very grateful to eagle-eyed readers who take the time to contact us. Please send any errors you find to corrections@joffebooks.com

Printed in Dunstable, United Kingdom

83466748R00139